Winter Across Worlds

A Holiday Collection

Melissa McShane

"Epiphany" © 2021 by Melissa McShane. Originally published in *Happy Holiday Historicals* (2021), edited by Lyn Worthen.

"Uncommon Gifts" © 2022 by Melissa McShane

"Midwinter Gala" © 2022 by Melissa McShane

"Joe Raven and the Christmas Job" © 2022 by Melissa McShane

"Wrapped Up with a Bow" © 2022 by Melissa McShane

"Stella Nova" © 2022 by Melissa McShane

"Charade in Three-Quarter Time" © 2022 by Melissa McShane

"Gift of the Oracle" © 2022 by Melissa McShane

Contents

Introduction

Some time ago, I had the opportunity to submit stories to a holiday anthology project. Though none of the three stories I wrote were accepted due to not being completely suited to the theme, I liked what I wrote and thought it would be fun to do something with them.

The problem is that I don't really write a lot of short fiction and didn't have the first idea where to submit something like that for publication. The longer I went without finding an outlet for the stories, the less inclined I was to make the effort. (I am sometimes embarrassingly lazy.) So I set them aside and did other projects.

Then, last Christmas, someone (my husband or my writing partner, I don't remember who) suggested I write a holiday story set in my world of Dalanine, setting for *The Smoke-Scented Girl* and *The God-Touched Man*. I did, and it was fun, but again I had no idea what to do with it.

It wasn't until I wrote some new fairytales for my collection *Warts and All,* which included two stories set at Christmastime, that I looked at all the holiday stories I'd written and realized I was close to having enough material for my own collection. I hadn't planned on a final book release in 2022, but this one was easy to put together.

And here it is. Four of the stories—"Uncommon Gifts," "Midwinter Gala," "Charade in Three-Quarter Time," and "Gift of the Oracle"—have some connection to my other writing. The remaining four are set in our world, at or near Christmas. I'm grateful to that anthology project for prompting stories where I had to learn about less-well-known holidays (literally holy days). This was a fun project and gave me a break between novels.

I hope readers will enjoy these stories as a little bit of holiday cheer. Thank you for reading.

—Melissa McShane

Epiphany

I wrote this story for an anthology project in which contributors were encouraged to write about other winter holidays than Christmas, to provide variety. Thanks to my having written eight historical fantasies set in the early nineteenth century, particularly the book Wondering Sight, *my mind immediately went to the English revels of Twelfth Night. While this story was ultimately not selected for the project, I enjoyed writing it and I think it turned out well.*

"Epiphany" *originally appeared in a different anthology than the one mentioned above,* Happy Holiday Historicals, *edited by Lyn Worthen.*

O n Christmas Eve they brought the woods indoors. Yew and hawthorn, holly and ivy, filling the air with rich, sharp scents and the promise of a distant spring. In Elizabeth's family, the women of the house wove the supple branches into wreaths and garlands to hang over the tall, narrow windows that looked out across the frozen Derbyshire fields. They draped them across fireplace mantels, where their scent mingled with the smoke of the fires, and twined them around bannisters so no one could descend without being prickled by their touch. Berries clung to the branches as long as they could before giving up their grip and dropping to the floor. Elizabeth had trodden many of them underfoot, leaving little dark smears on the wood and on her soft shoes.

Now, twelve days later, the beauty of the greenery had faded as the boughs dried and lost their scent. On Twelfth Night, this last day of the Christmas season, their condition seemed an ill omen for the coming year. Elizabeth had loved Twelfth Night as a child, spying on the adults enjoying their revels. Now that she was an adult herself, she could not believe she had ever been so ridiculously naïve.

She wandered the rooms of her father's house, counting the garlands and watching the servants prepare for that evening's gala. More greenery, this fresh and flowering: creamy clematis with its sweet, citrusy scent, white Christmas roses like tiny scallop-edged saucers, and lemon-yellow winter jasmine. They filled the tall vases on the floor and the little ones that sat on the mantels or side tables so everywhere one went one encountered something beautiful. Delicious smells arose from the kitchen for the midnight supper, contrasting wonderfully with the scents of the flowers. Despite Elizabeth's bad mood, the aroma of roasted meat and poached fish and the higher, sweeter notes of syllabub and rich puddings enticed her.

It was all she had to look forward to this evening. Less than an hour, and the first guests would arrive, and she would put on a false smile and pretend she did not hear the whispers:

...poor Miss Rennell, such a pity...

...and her sisters married so well, too...

...should not have been so choosy, she will never marry at her age...

She told herself not to listen to fools, but their assumptions that she was haughty and too proud hurt. As if the only reason a woman might remain unmarried at twenty-eight was a sense of self-importance that led her to reject any suitor who came calling.

Her gown rustled around her ankles as she brushed past two maids setting out the enormous white-iced Twelfth Night cake in the dining room. She had chosen to dress as Artemis for her parents' fancy dress ball, possibly in response to those anticipated whispers. Artemis, virgin huntress who did not feel the lack of a man. It was a good, hot, defiant gesture whose effects Elizabeth knew would not last the night.

The drawing rooms echoed with emptiness. All the furniture had been removed and the carpets rolled back to allow for dancing. The fires had been extinguished, chilling the rooms enough that Elizabeth in her thin muslin gown shivered. White walls covered with dark, brooding ancestral portraits gave an impression of greater space than there was, and if not for the elaborate moldings and carved rosettes in the upper corners, Elizabeth might have imagined the room carved of ice. Soon enough, the crush of guests would heat the room unbearably, and then she would be grateful for her costume. Now, she felt frozen to her core.

She stood staring into the empty fireplace, tracing the lines of the grate with her gaze, examining the iron poker in its stand until she became impatient with herself. So what if this evening would be no different from any other? So what if she were doomed to remain Miss Rennell, spinster daughter of Thomas and Anne Rennell, without a husband and without resources to support herself independently? She could still respect herself enough not to permit talk to wear her down. She could refuse to be defined by the whispers. And she could choose what she would make of this evening.

Distantly, she heard the front door bell ring. And so it began. Elizabeth straightened her gown and put on her pleasant smile. This would not be so terrible. She was foolish to dread something so simple as a gala. After all, there were people in England suffering far worse than a few hours of potential humiliation. She should not be so dramatic.

Two hours later, Elizabeth wished she had never been born.

As the house filled with guests dressed as historical figures or allegorical representations or animals, her defiant mood had ebbed. She had only danced twice, both times with friends of her father; she had drunk punch and found it distastefully sweet; she had smiled pleasantly at her neighbors and received nothing but false, awkward smiles in return. The music was too loud, and the room was, as expected, too hot. She could not understand how anyone could be happy in such circumstances.

Now she stood in a quiet corner and watched the revelry, all those brightly colored figures tossed about like autumn leaves in a breeze. Her heart ached with longing for something she could not identify. A home and family of her own, perhaps, or even just an appreciative smile from someone who saw her as something other than her parents' spinster daughter.

"It is a lovely gala, don't you think?"

Startled, Elizabeth turned to look at the woman who had addressed her. She was younger than Elizabeth, though not by much, and she was dressed in a gray silk gown of finer make than anything Elizabeth had ever seen. It was made up in the Grecian style, as was the woman's dark hair, and a golden owl pinned the silken folds at her left shoulder.

"Athena," Elizabeth blurted out.

The woman smiled, and her cheek dimpled. "As you are Artemis," she said. "But my name is Mel—that is, I am Miss Townsend." In her left hand, she held something small and rectangular that winked like a mirror in the light of the candles and the chandelier.

"I'm unfamiliar with your family," Elizabeth said.

"We are new to the neighborhood." Miss Townsend nodded toward the dancing crowd. "I came with my brother. Have you met him?"

Elizabeth could not see anyone unfamiliar. "Not as yet."

"You will." Miss Townsend said this with an odd, knowing smile, as if she had a secret she did not intend to share. It annoyed Elizabeth, this over-familiarity from a stranger, but she merely smiled and said nothing.

"This is your father's house, yes?" Miss Townsend continued. "I have wanted to see it for so long."

"You have?" Elizabeth could not imagine why. The house was comfortable, but not an architectural gem.

To her surprise, Miss Townsend blushed. "It is...I mean, it

reminds me of my own family's home." She glanced swiftly at the mirror, fast enough she could not possibly have made sense of anything she saw in it.

Elizabeth wanted to ask about the strange object, but such a direct question would be impolite. "I see," she said instead. She did not actually understand the woman's odd reaction, but again, politeness seemed called for.

"Elizabeth!"

Elizabeth closed her eyes briefly. Her sister Maria had arrived without her noticing. To Miss Townsend, she said, "Please excuse me, I must speak to my sister." Without waiting for a response, she stepped forward.

Maria walked arm-in-arm with her bosom friend, Charlotte Winters. Her lovely heart-shaped face bore an expression Elizabeth was intimately familiar with, her eyes narrowed, her mouth drawn up in a mocking smile. She had chosen to come as Queen Elizabeth, which next to Charlotte's feline-inspired costume looked ridiculous. But Maria had never permitted other people to define her. It was the only characteristic Elizabeth admired in her.

"Dear sister, why are you hiding away in this corner?" Maria said, widening her eyes in a look of astonishment Elizabeth knew could not be real. "You will never have a partner if you make yourself unavailable."

"I wished for a moment's peace," Elizabeth said. She would not be drawn by Maria, not again.

"From all your suitors?" Charlotte said, covering her mouth with one hand as if to hold back her tittering laugh.

A familiar numb despair spread across Elizabeth's face. She could not think of a response.

"Oh, don't be silly, Charlotte," Maria said, casting a malicious glance Elizabeth's way. "Elizabeth is too high in the instep to care about suitors. Isn't that true, sister?"

Weariness, and too many hours of deflecting words like those, caught up to Elizabeth all at once. "It's no wonder you believe that," she snapped, "given that you leaped at the first man who came sniffing around you. Was it desperation that led you to accept Mr. Carlyon, or the desire to be the first married of your friends?"

Maria's falsely pleasant expression disappeared. "*Shrew*," she hissed. "You will never be anything more than a hopeless, dried-up, priggish old maid who is a drain on Papa's income, and everyone knows it. It's past time you realized it yourself." Tugging on Charlotte's arm, she turned her back on Elizabeth and swept away into the crowd.

Elizabeth turned away, her eyes prickling with angry, humiliated tears. Maria's words struck her to the heart because they were what she feared was true: *hopeless, priggish, old maid.* She could not bear this overheated, noisy, terrible gathering another minute.

She took a few blind steps toward the nearest door and ran into someone. Blinking, she said, "Miss Townsend. I beg your pardon, but I must...I am leaving."

Miss Townsend put a restraining hand on her arm. "But you can't!" she exclaimed. "It will ruin everything!" She sounded unnaturally aghast, as if Elizabeth had proposed the most awful thing in the world, and once more glanced at her mirror.

Elizabeth could not bring herself to care about the young woman's odd behavior. "I cannot remain here any longer," she said. "Please excuse me. I hope you will enjoy the ball."

"No, wait," Miss Townsend said, her grip on Elizabeth's arm tightening. "This is an important night, isn't it? Twelfth Night. The eve of Epiphany. It's a night when anything can happen."

"I have never known Twelfth Night to be anything but a misery." Elizabeth tried to pull away, but Miss Townsend held her fast. "Release me."

"Just...stay for the course of one more dance," Miss Townsend pleaded. "Then you may do whatever you like. One dance."

Her pleading face made Elizabeth hesitate. All around them, the music and the noise of conversation filled the air, but where they stood seemed a pocket of clear air, where the noise and confusion were all happening at a distance. Well, what was one dance? Not even fifteen minutes. She could give this strange young woman fifteen minutes.

"One dance," she agreed.

Miss Townsend released her. "Good," she said. "I must leave you, but remember, you promised." Without waiting for a reply, she darted away, slipping between two guests dressed as Father Time and Miss Muffet and disappearing into the crowd.

Elizabeth shook her head in wonder. This was, if nothing else, the strangest Twelfth Night she had ever experienced. With a sigh, she moved away from her quiet nook. She might at least look for a friendly face, though all her close friends had long since married and moved away.

She came up against a knot of guests she could not pass, all of them laughing over a joke she had not heard, and backed away. Immediately, she bumped into someone who did not move at the impact. Her first mad thought was that she had struck a wall, but as she turned around, she discovered it was a man, dressed head to toe in black velvet. "I beg your pardon," she said. "I was not looking where I was going."

"You need not apologize," the man said. "This is a sad crush. I am surprised more people have not bumped into me, nor I into others."

He was a stranger, not precisely handsome, but with a charming smile that warmed his dark eyes and made Elizabeth feel flustered. "It is quite the crowd," she said, her tongue speaking independently of her brain as she tried to recall the man's name.

Surely she knew all her father's acquaintances? "You are...Hamlet, yes?" It was an unconventional costume, especially since the man's demeanor had little in common with that of the melancholy Dane.

The man made her a little bow. "Do I have the pleasure of addressing the immortal Artemis?"

"Indeed," Elizabeth said, returning the bow with a curtsey. "I don't believe we have been introduced."

"Ah, but at a private ball, we assume everyone has been introduced to everyone else, and therefore no formalities are needed." The man's smile broadened. "And I hear a new dance beginning— may I ask the pleasure of your company?"

Stunned, Elizabeth could think of nothing to say. She extended her hand and permitted him to offer her his arm.

They joined the line of dancers in silence, and for the first few passes Elizabeth cast about frantically for some topic of conversation. When they came together a third time, she blurted out, "Why Hamlet?"

Her partner laughed heartily, making Elizabeth blush. "I like that you do not mince words. I fear I waited too long to choose my role, and this and Harlequin were all that remained available." He dusted an invisible speck from his doublet front. "And I prefer to be thought too serious than a fool. I hope I maintain a happy medium between those extremes."

"I despise assumptions," Elizabeth said, more hotly than she had intended, but his mention of being judged by his appearance struck a nerve. "I hope I will never treat another person poorly because of what he appears to be."

The man's eyebrows rose sharply. "That sounds as if you have personal experience on the matter."

Elizabeth fell silent. Why she had let him draw her out, she did not know, except that he was a stranger, he apparently did not know who she was, and he was the only person aside from Miss Townsend who had not spoken to her with pity or dismissive anger. The man said nothing else as they turned and clasped hands in the steps of the dance, but she could feel him waiting for an answer. Finally, she said, "I know what it is to be the subject of gossip on the subject of things beyond my control, that is all."

"That is not a small thing," her partner said. He smiled, giving him a mischievous look. "And what sins have you committed? Murder? Larceny? The hideous sin of wearing a bonnet that does not match your gown?"

He sounded amused rather than dismissive, and despite herself, Elizabeth laughed. "No, merely the sin of being Mr. Rennell's oldest daughter, unmarried and with no prospects." It seemed less dire when she said it to him, as if he transmuted her pain into something bearable.

The man jerked in surprise and nearly missed his step. "*You* are Miss Rennell?"

Elizabeth's pleased feeling vanished. She stiffened. "I am," she said, her tone of voice commanding him to say nothing more. She continued in the figures of the dance, refusing to meet his eyes even when she faced him again. Suddenly fifteen minutes seemed an eternity.

To her astonishment, his smile returned. "I had no idea," he said. "You are correct; you are the subject of much gossip. Does it help if I tell you I believe none of it?"

"It is of no concern to me what you believe, sir." This was not the first time she had resorted to over-formality as a defense. It *was* the first time she had ever felt even a trace of guilt at doing so. The man did not seem dismissive of her, or cruel, but she did not need his pity.

"Very well." His smile remained, but now he looked thoughtful. "Forgive my astonishment. Now you will detest me, and I will not be able to convince you to give me another dance."

"I do not detest you." It was even true. She liked what little she knew of him, and he had not mocked or secretly laughed at her.

"Then dance with me again," the man said. "I wish to know you better. You are unexpected."

"Am I?" Elizabeth shot back. "What about me did you not expect, from everything you have no doubt heard?"

The music came to an end, and all around them, couples bowed and curtseyed to one another. The man swept her a graceful bow. "I did not expect," he said, "that you would be beautiful."

Elizabeth, halfway to making her curtsey, nearly lost her balance. She knew she must look ridiculous, mouth hanging open in astonishment, eyes the size of Christmas roses. The man continued to regard her with those dark eyes, waiting for a response. Elizabeth straightened. "Tell me your name," she demanded.

His lips quirked slightly. "It is Townsend," he said.

"Oh!" Elizabeth felt grateful that the general hubbub drowned out her exclamation. "Oh," she said, more quietly, "then I have met your sister."

Mr. Townsend's eyebrows furrowed. "My sister?"

"We spoke earlier. She said you came here together. I wonder now that she did not introduce us."

But Mr. Townsend was shaking his head. "You must be mistaken. I have no sister."

Elizabeth blinked. "You mean...your sister is not here?"

"I mean I have no sister. Not here, not anywhere. My parents had three sons, of which I am the middle child." Mr. Townsend glanced around as if expecting to see this sister whose existence he denied. Then he extended his hand to Elizabeth. "Now, I intend to collect on the dance I'm certain you meant to promise me."

Elizabeth, too, surveyed the room. At the far end, she caught a glimpse of grey silk. "I would like nothing better than to dance with you," she said, "but there is someone I must speak to. Will you...you will wait for me, yes?"

She was coming to enjoy his smile, humorous and warm as a spring sunrise. "For you, I will wait all evening," he said.

Elizabeth quickly squeezed his hand and hurried away before she could be conscious of the impropriety. She shoved past costumed guests, nearly knocking over a tall vase of winter flowers that stood against the wall, and pushed the door open.

This door led, not to the well-lighted entrance, but to a darkened passage that smelled of the supper that would be served soon. Elizabeth had been born in this house, had lived here her whole life, and although she knew where this passage went, that night it felt alien, as if it were part of some other house entirely.

Light spilled from beneath two doors farther on. On the right, the light was warm and bright like fire, the door to the kitchens. On the left, where a little-used storeroom lay, a paler, pearly glow shone, the light of a full moon. But the moon was dark that night, and Elizabeth could think of no other source that would provide that kind of light. Slowly, feeling her way along the newly strange hall, she groped toward the silvery light. Her hand fell on the latch, and with an inexplicable shudder, she thrust the door open.

The light instantly grew bright enough that she blinked away tears. When she could see again, she realized Miss Townsend stood there, her hand pressing her strange mirror flat against the far wall. And in the wall, something glowed. It was a patch of silver-blue light half the size of a grown man, oval-shaped and quivering like a pool touched by a summer breeze.

Elizabeth gasped. Immediately, Miss Townsend turned to face

her. Backlit by the silvery glow, her expression was not immediately visible. "Go back to the party," she said. Her voice had changed, her accent become less precise.

"You cannot expect me to simply walk away!" Elizabeth took a step forward. "What *is* this? Who are you?"

Miss Townsend, or whatever her name was, lowered her head with a sigh. "I shouldn't have spoken to you. And then I couldn't find William Townsend. But then you met on your own—I should have had more faith that it would all work out. History is what it is."

"You make no sense," Elizabeth said.

"I'm sorry—I mean, I beg your pardon. 'Sorry' means 'wretched' in this time, doesn't it?" The oval had grown until it was nearly big enough for Miss Townsend to step through.

Elizabeth heard a high, ringing sound, like the tiniest silver bells. It came from the oval. "I don't understand," she said, pleading for an explanation. "I don't—*who are you?*"

The woman cast a glance over her shoulder at the oval, then returned her gaze to Elizabeth. "I can't bear this," she said. "Look. Don't despair, please? You will marry, and have five children, and they will have children, on and on, until...I can only tell you this because no one will believe you if you spread it around, and you looked so sad, but that won't last forever. I promise."

Elizabeth's chest ached because she had forgotten to breathe. She drew in breath and let it out, willing it to carry her confusion away with it. "How can you know?" she whispered.

Straightening, the woman withdrew her hand from the wall, bringing the rectangular thing—it could not possibly be only a mirror—with her. "Because my name really is Townsend, and when I had the chance to meet my family, I took it. Have a wonderful life."

The oval was now bigger than a man. With a single backwards

glance, Miss Townsend stepped through the oval as if passing through a waterfall, and vanished.

Elizabeth started forward, reaching out. Before she could touch the oval, it shrank in on itself with another chime of bells, dwindling to a pinpoint of light that emitted a bright flash. Elizabeth threw up her hands to shield her eyes. When she lowered her hands, the light was gone. All that remained in the dimly-lit pantry was a grimy wall and several laden shelves. No light, no silvery oval. No Miss Townsend.

Elizabeth let out another deep breath. Then she felt her way out of the pantry and down the hall.

No one seemed to have noticed her absence. Laughter, and conversation, and music filled the drawing rooms until Elizabeth thought she might explode from the noise. She stood in her corner and watched the dancers execute a complicated quadrille. From within the figures, one would see only one's own path. It wasn't until one stood on the outside that the pattern became clear.

When the music ended, she went in search of Mr. Townsend. He stood near the empty fireplace, resplendent in his black velvet, and smiled when she approached. "I was afraid you had found someone more to your liking," he said.

Elizabeth remembered Miss Townsend's strange but compelling words. "Do you know," she said, slowly, feeling her way as she had in the darkened passage, "I cannot imagine anyone who meets that description."

Mr. Townsend raised both eyebrows nearly to his hairline. "You realize supper is served after this. It is tradition to take one's dance partner in for that meal."

"That tradition charms me," Elizabeth said, smiling back at him.

He led her to where the couples were forming up for the next dance and took her hand in his. Elizabeth did not have to hear the whispers over the general noise to know their content. None of it mattered.

She made her curtsey and took her first steps as the music began. Over the sound of viol and harp, she thought she heard the sound of tiny, tinkling silver bells.

Uncommon Gifts

I wrote a collection of fairytales entitled Warts and All *featuring the kitchen witch Chloe and her family, caught up in adventures that take them through several favorite tales. In planning an upcoming expanded, illustrated edition, I wrote three new fairytale adaptations, among them this one based on "The Elves and the Shoemaker," one of my childhood favorites.*

Motherhood means facing tragedies great and small, but I'd never seen anything so heartbreaking as a six-year-old child trying so hard not to cry his whole body shook. Darius had a tendency to run sobbing from any difficulty, so for him to make such a valiant effort, I guessed something was really wrong.

I knelt and took my son in my arms, not too tightly because of the spiky plastic dragon he held. "What happened?"

"Daddy stepped on it," Darius said, his voice trembling and hoarse. "It's smashed. Can you fix it?"

I glanced up at Ethan, who stood behind Darius. His lips were pressed together in a tight, frustrated line that told me he was holding back chastisement. I already knew what must have happened, so I refrained from asking if his father had stepped on it because Darius had once again left his precious toy in the hall. Darius no doubt knew whose fault the calamity ultimately was.

"I'm really sorry, Darius," Ethan said with remarkable calm. "I know you love that dragon." He crouched beside us and put his arms around both of us. "Your mom will take a look, all right?"

Darius nodded and disentangled himself from our embrace. He held the dragon out to me. "It's really broken."

I gingerly lifted a wing that was only barely still connected to the flame-red body. The filmy membranes were torn and fluttered limply as I moved the wing. The tail had come off entirely, and the connecting pegs had sheared off at their bases. Both arms were cracked, and the left leg moved too loosely in its socket. I pressed each of the three spikes at the base of the skull, one at a time. They were supposed to make the dragon roar, growl, and blow smoke. Now the roar was a strangled moan, the growl didn't sound at all, and something inside the dragon's body made a grinding sound without producing the cloud of water mist meant to look like smoke.

I suppressed a joke about whether Ethan had stepped on it more than once; this wasn't the time for levity. My parents had given Darius this expensive toy for his birthday, and he loved it more than anything else he owned. "You're right, it's really broken," I agreed. "Honey, I don't want to lie to you. I'm not sure I can fix this. Magic has limits. But I'll do my best."

Darius nodded. "I'm sorry I left it out," he said, and tears spilled over his cheeks.

Ethan and I hugged him again while he cried. When his sobs wound down, Ethan said, "Let's have cookies and milk. Mommy baked them fresh today, and we should make sure they are good enough for Santa, right?"

Darius wiped his eyes. "Okay."

I left them to their feast and carried the poor broken toy into the living room. Belinda sprawled on the floor near the Christmas tree, reading by the light of the fire and the tiny twinkle lights. My familiar, Farnsworth, snored on the hearth nearby, his pointed collie ears twitching. "Do you want me to turn on the overhead light?" I asked.

"I'm fine," Belinda said. "I like how warm and cozy it is with the light off."

I thought about saying she'd ruin her eyesight reading in the dimness, but decided she had young, resilient eyes and wasn't likely to go blind from one night's reading. Instead, I turned on the lamp over the desk and set the dragon down. The antique desk had a back with dozens of cubbies for holding pens or paperclips or rolled-up papers, and I withdrew my wand from its customary storage space and ran my fingers up and down its length, warming it up.

Some things were easy to mend—doll arms that had slipped their joints, ceramic mugs whose handles had broken off, basketballs with a slow leak. But something broken this badly...it would take time, if it could be fixed at all, and while I could repair the cracked arms and loose leg socket, I wasn't at all sure how the internal mechanisms worked, and without knowing that, I would have trouble putting them back together.

I waved the tip of my wand, the smallest back and forth motion, and one of the arms contracted, sealing the crack. I examined the mend, and my heart sank. The crack was gone, true, but the arm was thicker along the place where it had been and looked visibly mended. Darius wouldn't mind, probably, so long as he got his precious toy back, but the shoddy work bothered me.

I sighed and laid my wand down. I'd spent most of the day baking in anticipation of Christmas, four days from now, and I was exhausted, which probably accounted for the poor mending job. The dragon could wait until tomorrow. I left it on the desk and said, "Belinda, bedtime in twenty minutes. If you get in your pajamas now, you can read in bed for a bit longer than that."

Belinda rolled to her feet and dashed for the stairs. We'd given her the tower bedroom in our rambling, eccentrically-designed house for her eighth birthday, and she'd embraced her new free-dom, as she saw it, with enthusiasm. I hoped she would stay enthusiastic through the heat of summer; the tower didn't have good air conditioning.

I walked back to the kitchen and stood in the doorway watching father and son share cookies. They looked so much alike, heads bent over glasses of milk, dipping cookies just enough to keep from dunking their fingers, that the sight filled me with love for both of them. Darius shared his father's gentle spirit and sense of humor along with his dark hair and tall frame. Belinda looked more like me, blonde and somewhat on the plump side. I hoped she didn't share my personality, because if she did, her teenage years would be unbearable.

Ethan looked up and smiled. "We pronounce the cookies Santa-ready," he said, waving half a cookie in my direction. "Now, finish up, Darius, and I'll read you a story after you put on your pajamas."

Darius stuffed the rest of his cookie into his mouth and scam-pered away, cheeks bulging like a black-haired chipmunk. Ethan rose and cleared the dishes away. "He'll be all right," he said. "I don't suppose you fixed it?"

"I'm not sure I can." I took a cookie from the plate and bit into it. It was only basic chocolate chip, what Belinda and Darius insisted was Santa Claus's favorite, but it tasted good and was just the right kind of chewy. I swallowed and added, "I'll see what I can do tomorrow. I'm too tired tonight."

"Understandable. It amazes me how much food you produce for the holidays." Ethan put his arms around my waist and pulled me close. "How about we make it an early night? You do look weary."

"You have excellent ideas," I said, and kissed him.

I woke to the bluish light that said snow had fallen while we slept and the patter of small feet in the hall outside my bedroom. Darius flung the door open and leaped onto the bed. "You fixed it! It's fixed now!"

"What—" I said blearily. Beside me, Ethan stirred and sat up.

Something angular and flame red filled my vision. Darius waved the dragon in my face. "Thank you, Mommy," he said, and wrapped his arms around my neck. The hard plastic dug into my spine.

"I didn't do anything," I said. "Darius, what are you talking about?"

"Let's see it," Ethan said, removing the dragon from where it pressed against my back. I stretched, yawned, and hugged Darius for a moment before turning to look at what Ethan held.

The dragon was in perfect shape. It didn't look as if it had ever been broken. Astonished, I held out my hand and Ethan gave it to me. I ran my fingers over the dragon's spiky spine, then pushed the third spike at the base of its neck. A roar, deep and loud, startled me so much I dropped the dragon on the bed.

Darius snatched it up and hugged it to his chest. "I'm so glad," he said.

"Wait a minute, Darius," I said when he moved to slide to the floor. I took the dragon and examined its arms. Neither were broken, but one was still thicker than the other in a line where the crack had been. The other looked perfect. I worked the tail and the wings, testing the joints, then handed it back. "Go have some cereal, if you haven't eaten yet," I told him. Darius ran off, holding the dragon high like it was flying.

"That was excellent work, honey," Ethan said.

"It was," I said. "But it's not my work. I didn't look at the thing until just now."

Ethan's brow furrowed. "That's impossible. It couldn't fix itself."

"Of course not. But I have no explanation. Unless I've started doing magic in my sleep—but even then...Ethan, I was serious about how broken it was. Even Farnsworth wouldn't be able to fix it."

"Well, I didn't buy a replacement. Do you know how much those dragons cost?"

"Yes, and even if it was cheap, we wouldn't set the example that carelessness with your toys is rewarded. Besides, it's definitely the same toy, not a replacement." I flopped back onto my pillow and stared at the ceiling.

"It's a mystery," Ethan said. "And since it's a mystery with a happy ending, I'm not inclined to pursue it. Come on. I'll make breakfast, and we'll all go sledding this morning."

Ethan might have been able to set the mystery aside, but it nagged at me all through breakfast and into the sledding expedition. I hadn't fixed it. My familiar Farnsworth hadn't fixed it. It hadn't spontaneously regenerated. That meant someone or something else had done the repairs. Someone or something had come into our house last night.

The idea chilled me more than the frosty weather. We lived in a good neighborhood, without a lot of crime, but thefts still occurred. But they were mostly crimes of opportunity, some kid not locking her bike or someone leaving their toolbox in the open bed of a truck. There'd never been any cases of home invasion robbery.

On the other hand, this wasn't a robbery—quite the opposite. I'd never heard of anyone reporting a break-in where the intruders had *improved* the house. The insane notion of rogue interior decorators entering by night and repainting a bathroom or replacing someone's ratty old couch crossed my mind briefly. Even so, it didn't matter if the intruder's purpose was benign; it was still an invasion of privacy, and it still made me nervous and angry.

By dinnertime, I'd worked myself into an irritable, grouchy state in which I snapped at everyone over ridiculous things until Ethan took me into the living room, away from the children's hearing, and said, "Chloe, what's wrong? You've been in a terrible mood all day."

I squeezed my eyes shut briefly. "I'm sorry, Ethan. I can't stop thinking about what happened with the dragon. Someone must have come into our house last night—doesn't that frighten you?"

"I'm not convinced that's what happened. We have good locks on the doors, and they were all locked from the inside when I checked them this morning." Ethan put his arms around me and stroked my hair. "It's more likely either you or Farnsworth mended it and forgot."

"You mean, in our sleep? Ethan, that's impossible."

"Well, what do you propose we do about it?"

I stepped away from him and surveyed the living room. The hutch near the tower stairs was filled with knickknacks, small souvenir plates and bells from places I'd visited when I was young, a couple of china figurines I wasn't fond of but kept out of sentimentality, a glass bowl filled with potpourri on a brass wirework stand. I picked up one of the figurines, a statuette of a young woman in a flowered dress gazing sappily at a black cat on a wall, and dropped it. It hit the floor with a crash and cracked neatly into five pieces and a shower of china slivers.

I picked up the pieces, careful of the sharp edges, and set them in the center of the desk. "I'm going to hide and watch," I said. "Whatever did this doesn't wait for an invitation. I want to find out what's going on."

"Chloe," Ethan said, then fell silent.

"I don't think this is crazy, Ethan. Something happened last night. I want to know what."

He sighed. "You're right. But where are you going to hide?"

I pointed at our Christmas tree, full and bushy and backed into a corner. "We'll pull this away from the wall a bit more, and there will be plenty of room."

"For one person."

"I wasn't going to make you join in my insanity, sweetheart." I worked my way behind the tree and crouched as best I could, taking hold of the trunk near where it was screwed into the Christmas tree stand. "Help me with this."

Ethan grasped the trunk just above my hands, and together we lifted the tree in a jangle of ornaments and swishing of tinsel and moved it two feet away from the corner. "Now I'm worried," he said when we'd set it down. "If you're right, and someone is entering our house at night, it's not safe for you to confront them alone."

"I won't confront them. I'll just observe. Besides, it's still a tight fit back here, and I'd knock the tree over if I tried to jump out at an intruder." I squeezed myself through the still-small gap and brushed fir needles off my sweater. "You could sit at the top of the stairs if you want," I added.

"I'm certainly not going to be able to sleep," Ethan said.

With the children settled in their beds, Ethan and I did the dishes and tidied the living room. The broken china figurine sat at the center of the desk top, in a clear space that looked like I'd pushed everything else on the desk away, mainly because that's what I'd done. I cast glances at it the whole time we were cleaning, superstitiously afraid if I took my eyes off it for more than a minute, it would repair itself and I'd never know what happened. But it remained still and unmoving.

Finally, Ethan kissed me and went upstairs. I'd opted not to change into my nightclothes, just in case I did have to leap out and subdue an intruder. With my wand securely gripped in my off hand, I fit myself into the space behind the tree and settled in to watch.

Ethan returned, wearing his pajamas, and paced back and forth in front of the tree. "You're completely hidden," he said. "I'll sit at the top of the stairs, out of sight. And I don't care what you see, if something enters the house, blast it and yell for me, understand?"

"I do. I'm glad you'll be nearby."

When Ethan's footsteps on the stairs died away, I switched my wand to my other hand and wiped my sweaty left palm on my jeans. Now that the house was quiet, my anxieties rose, not in fear, but in anticipation. My imagination supplied me with all sorts of bizarre possibilities, the least strange of which was rogue interior decorators. Whoever or whatever it was, the intruder could work magic, which meant I would have to be especially careful and alert. I wasn't a novice witch by any definition, but I didn't kid myself that that meant I was superior in skill to every witch and warlock and sorcerer in the world. This might be a dangerous encounter.

My back and thighs ached from kneeling up, and I sat back on my heels and stretched out my lower back, making the tree jingle and rustle again. From where I sat, the edge of the wall clock was visible. Not quite ten-thirty. Still a long way to go before midnight.

I wasn't sure why I'd decided midnight was important. There was no reason to expect a magical burglar to have a schedule, let alone one to whom midnight mattered. But the idea wouldn't leave me alone. Finally, I decided that at least anticipating midnight would give me something to focus on. I wished I had a book.

The minutes crept past, ticking away loudly in the silence. I stopped looking at the clock every few minutes, even though it didn't ring the hour and I'd have no notice if midnight came and I wasn't paying attention. I entertained myself by going over the Christmas dinner menu in my head. I was cooking for my entire family, not just Ethan and the kids but my parents and siblings and their spouses and children, so it was a complicated affair. Then I reviewed the list of gifts I'd bought. Then I daydreamed about what Ethan might give me. I told myself I could look at the clock when I'd finished all that.

When I finally did check the time, I was startled to see my mental distractions had carried me all the way to seven minutes to midnight. I shifted position so I could see the desk and the shattered figurine clearly and switched my wand to my other hand again.

Nothing happened. I kept my eyes fixed on the figurine. If midnight passed with no changes...well, I couldn't just give up and go to bed, but I might take a moment to sneak away for a book.

Then the air shifted, bringing with it the scent of yew leaves and snow. Tiny bells, not the ones on our tree, jingled a merry little chorus, the sound of a shop door opening. The air near the desk thickened, like heat haze on a summer pavement. I watched, fascinated, as the air thickened further in five places, growing dark and solid.

And just like that, five small winged figures came into focus. They were no bigger than Belinda's favorite doll, slim and with womanly shapes I could see clearly because they wore pastel-colored dresses of some filmy material, and gossamer butterfly wings fluttered at their backs. Fairies. They swooped in erratic flight paths down to the hearth and crowded close to the banked fire, which still gave off plenty of heat. I watched them jostle and elbow each other for the best position, all in perfect silence.

After a few minutes, the fairies retreated from the fire, flying more confidently now, as if the warmth had revived them. They landed on the desk and surrounded the broken china figurine, walking around it with their heads tilted as if considering its condition. Then the dark-haired one in the pale blue dress picked up one of the pieces and rotated it. Sparkling dust drifted from her idly flapping wings, falling like sifting sugar onto the desktop and disappearing into it.

Another of the tiny women, this one in light peach, lifted a different piece, and then each of them was holding one of the fragments. They walked around each other, occasionally holding pieces together, until two of them made theirs fit. The other three lifted off the desk, still holding their own fragments, and flew in a complicated pattern over the other two. Magical dust flew in great shimmering clouds all over the mated pieces.

And then they were whole.

I covered my mouth to hold back a surprised gasp. The last thing I wanted now was to startle the fairies. The mending had happened so quickly I hadn't perceived the magic at all, though I suspected the fairy dust was responsible for most of it. The only thing I knew about fairy magic was that it was more powerful than anything a witch could manage. That, and how rarely fairies used it on humans' behalf. Why these fairies were here, I had no idea, but scaring them away was unthinkable.

The flying ballet continued until the figurine was whole again. No sign of cracks remained, though I knew I hadn't picked up all the tiny slivers of china. The fairies set the figurine down again. I expected them to vanish, but once more they flew to huddle before the fire, rubbing tiny hands down tiny arms. It made me feel cold just looking at their clothes, so inadequate for the winter.

After a few minutes, they joined hands and flew in a circle, slowly at first, then faster and faster until the air once more thickened—and then they were gone.

I crouched behind the tree, unable to look away from where they'd been, until my back insisted it was going to cramp up if I didn't stand. Then I sidled out from my hiding place and walked over to the desk. As I'd thought, it was a perfect repair. I set the mended figurine down and crossed the living room to the stairs. "Ethan," I said. "Ethan. You're never going to believe this."

"Fairies?" Belinda said. "Actual real live *fairies*?" Her eyes gleamed with excitement, and she jigged in her seat as if she wanted to dance around the room.

"Real live fairies," I said. I'd told my family the story twice now, the second time in more detail as I recalled things I hadn't noticed at the time. How carefully they'd handled the china. How they gestured with their hands as if that was how they communicated rather than speech. How their dresses, pretty as they were, were tattered and had holes in places. "They were so beautiful.

Like if your Kaytee dolls came to life, only even more delicate. And with wings."

"But why did they help us?" Darius said. He still held his dragon, which he'd become even more attached to than before, but for once he didn't seem aware of it.

"I don't know," Ethan said. "Maybe they were in the area and saw we needed it. Or maybe they visit all the houses, mending things."

"I'm sure at least some of it was needing to get warm," I said. "Those dresses are all wrong for winter."

"Maybe we could give them clothes," Darius said. "To thank them."

"I don't—" I stopped, caught by another thought. "You know, I'm not sure fairies get thanked very often. All the stories talk about what they do for humans, not what humans do for them."

"Mom, Mom, I know!" Belinda burst out. "We can give them my Kaytee doll clothes! I have lots." Her face fell. "Except they wouldn't fit over the wings."

"But you could fix that, right?" Darius insisted. "You could cut holes for the wings."

"Maybe," I said, still thinking.

"I don't want the fairies to be cold," Darius said. "We have to help."

Ethan and I exchanged glances. "He's right," Ethan said.

"I know. I'm not disagreeing. Just thinking about accommodating wings," I said.

I t took most of the afternoon, between Darius and Belinda picking out a fairy wardrobe and Ethan, with his artist's eye, experimenting with the clothes they hadn't chosen to find the best way to alter them. My job was implementing the changes. With Farnsworth's help, I snipped and magically stitched new seams and fastened tiny hooks while the others admired my work.

Finally, we had five beautiful dresses, all fancy enough to satisfy Belinda and Darius and warm enough for Ethan's and my approval. They fastened across the back of the neck and above the waist, leaving a large oval gap that wouldn't pinch those butterfly wings. We'd talked about including shoes, but the Kaytee wardrobe didn't extend to well-made footwear, just blobs of plastic we couldn't guarantee would fit. In the end, we compromised with adding accessories instead, tiny pearl beads in a rainbow array of color strung on elastic thread so they could fit over a head or wrap around an arm.

Then Ethan helped Belinda and Darius build a blanket fort in the living room, one with a good view of the desk, while I hunted for something I didn't mind breaking. I was just superstitious enough about our plan—suppose they realized we were there, watching?—to not want to break something I couldn't mend myself. I ended up taking apart a picture frame and piling the pieces on the desk, which took some doing as they insisted on sliding off. Eventually I found a way to make them all fit atop the glass that covered the family portrait the frame usually held. Then I carefully laid out the dresses and beads where they would be clearly visible to someone hovering above.

It was nearly ten o'clock when Ethan and I dragged the Christmas tree farther into the room and positioned ourselves behind it. Farnsworth had gone upstairs, since there wasn't anywhere he could be concealed, but he'd said, "You can tell me all about it later." After we'd hushed Belinda and Darius for the seventh time, the room was quiet and still.

Ethan and I sat with our backs to the wall. I could see only half of the desk, but Ethan had a good view of the other half and I was sure we would know if the fairies returned. Belinda and Darius were now so quiet I hoped they hadn't fallen asleep. This wasn't something I wanted them to miss, and we could all sleep late Christmas Eve day.

My mind drifted back to last night and my memories of watching the fairies. I didn't know why they, of all the magical creatures in the world, were so reclusive as to be almost mythical, but it still felt like a tremendous honor to have seen them, regardless of anything they did for us. I wished I was an artist like Ethan to capture what I'd seen in oils—no, watercolors suited their ethereal nature better. Watercolors, and gold dust to capture that beautiful fairy shimmer. I hoped I was right, and the fairies would return so Ethan and the children could see them. They were too remarkable for me not to want to share the experience.

I shifted to look at the clock, and froze. "Almost midnight," I whispered, and moved back to where I would be concealed. Ethan's hands twitched where they rested on his knees, but otherwise he remained still. Something rustled inside the blanket fort, and I heard Belinda hush Darius.

Then the air thickened, and once more, the fairies appeared. They rushed immediately to the hearth, jostling one another as they had the previous night, but this time I realized the jostling wasn't selfish; they were huddling together to warm one another as well as be warmed by the banked fire. I watched, breathless, as their restless movements gradually calmed, until by silent accord they all five flew to the desk.

I knew the moment they saw the clothes, because they all stopped at once and hovered, wings beating frantically, over the pile of frame pieces. Then the dark-haired fairy slowly descended. Her tiny hand ran over the smooth, heavy satin, light blue that gradually grew darker until the hem was the color of midnight. It was my favorite of the dresses. I held my breath as she touched the fabric again and glittering fairy dust rained down on it. Then she picked it up and held it against herself, measuring.

In the next moment, all the fairies dove on the dresses, snatching them up, stroking their fabric or rubbing it against their faces. They started removing their clothes without losing hold of the new dresses, and for a flash of a moment I considered Darius's possible reaction, but the little fairies were no more explicitly shaped than the Kaytee doll, and it was impossible to think of them as naked women.

I realized Ethan had taken my hand, though all his attention was on the fairies. I squeezed his hand lightly, thrilled to share this experience with him. The fairies were now fully clothed, with bead strands draped around necks and waists and arms, and had dropped their old dresses on the floor to lie like bits of translucent wrapping paper on the carpet. They darted and flew in every direction, performing aerial acrobatics that made their long skirts flutter without dragging at their bodies. Fairy dust flew everywhere until the air was a mass of glittering golden clouds. I breathed some of it in, and instead of coughing, I felt warm and light enough to fly myself.

I didn't know how long this went on, but after what felt like an hour, the fairies congregated around the desk once more. Just like the previous night, they each took pieces of the disassembled frame and circled one another until they made them fit together around the photo. Then they laid the picture on its back on the desk. I expected them to join hands again and vanish, but instead they hovered over the picture, studying it.

Then, one by one, each fairy flew low and shook dust across

my family's smiling images. The dust didn't disappear or sink into the picture the way it had on the desk, but drifted with the breeze from fairy wings until the surface shone. Not until all five fairies had performed this little ritual did they finally form a circle and disappear into the thickened air.

None of us moved at first. Then the blanket fort shifted, and Darius rushed to the desk. "Mommy, look!" he exclaimed. "They left us a picture."

I squeezed out from behind the tree and dodged the fort to look at what he was pointing at. The framed photo was of our family in the woods last summer, when we'd gone camping for a few days. Golden fairy dust clung to the ridges of the mended wooden frame, making it look, not gilded, but as if golden light glowed from within.

But I saw immediately that the frame was not what had caught Darius's eye. Around our posed group was a ring of tiny figures clasping hands to encircle us. The golden figures were more like impressions of figures than realistic images, but they had butterfly wings and dresses that fluttered around their ankles.

"No, don't!" I exclaimed as Ethan reached past me to touch one golden figure. "You'll wreck it!"

"I don't think so." Ethan displayed his finger, which had no trace of gold. "Look. It passed through the glass to cling to the picture. And it's cohered the way embossing powder does when you heat it. It's astonishing."

Sure enough, Ethan's touch hadn't shifted the dust at all. I hesitated, then picked up the picture and held it upright. No dust fell. From that angle, with the lights of the Christmas tree falling on the glass, it seemed as if the dust had always been part of the photo.

"Do you think they'll come back?" Belinda asked.

"We can't take advantage of their generosity by breaking

things on purpose," Ethan said.

"You know what, though?" I said. "I don't know that they'd come back even if we had something that broke accidentally. What more can we do for each other than we've already done?"

"That's what I think," Darius said. "I bet they fixed things because they were grateful for our fire. They're warm now, so they don't need it anymore."

I exchanged glances with Ethan. "That makes sense, Darius," I said. "Very smart."

"Can we sleep in the fort?" Belinda asked, yawning.

"Absolutely you can sleep in the fort," Ethan said, "both of you. And tomorrow is Christmas Eve, and Gran and Gramps will be here, so sleep well."

Ethan turned off the Christmas tree lights, and he and I walked upstairs. I felt physically exhausted, more than I thought was justified, but my mind kept returning to that beautiful fairy dance. "So unexpected," I said with a yawn of my own.

"I already know how I want to paint them," Ethan said. He took my hand and brought me to a halt at the foot of our bed, near where Farnsworth slept. "Though I'm not sure I can top what they did to that photo."

"It will be beautiful," I said, putting my arms around his shoulders. "And no one will believe you painted it from life."

"*I* almost don't believe it. It feels like a dream." Ethan hugged me and let me go. "I'm not sure I'll be able to sleep after that."

"Neither am I."

We settled into bed, and my gaze drifted to the window, where the full moon shone on the snow piled on the sill. It glittered like fairy dust, and for a moment, I thought I saw winged figures darting in intricate patterns across the sky. It was just my imagination, I knew, but as I drifted off to sleep, I was sure I heard the sound of tiny, tinkling bells and the flutter of gossamer wings.

Midwinter Gala

My novel The God-Touched Man, *sequel to* The Smoke-Scented Girl, *is possibly the least well-known of my books due to a confluence of terrible events, but it happens to be my son's favorite. He loves the main character, Piercy Faranter, who appears to be a fop and a man about town and is secretly a government agent. At the end of the novel, Piercy marries his true love and goes to live in her country with her. (The book came out in 2016. I think the statute of limitations on spoilers has run out.)*

And that's where it ended until in late 2021 I started thinking about putting together a holiday short story collection. I only had three or four stories, and someone, either my husband or my writing partner, suggested I write a story about Piercy. That got me thinking about celebrating winter holidays in places where winter isn't cold and snowy, and this story arose from that. Coming back to the world of Dalanine was unexpectedly satisfying, and I'm sure it's because Piercy is one of my favorites, too.

T here was something deeply wrong, Piercy reflected, with a snowless Midwinter.

He had been born far north of Santerre, in Rainoth, had lived his entire adult life even farther north, in Dalanine's capital city of Matra, and Midwinter had always been a time of ice and snow and freezing winds. The weather had made the holiday perfect, because one appreciated the warmth of friends' houses, hot drinks by the fire, and candles driving back the dark.

But here in Bellema, Santerre's capital city, ice and snow and freezing winds were a thing of myth. The city lay nestled into the curve of the great bay overlooking the warm southern ocean, where even the fiercest winds blew hot and damp, tempering the sun's blistering rays to an all-pervading wet heat. Midwinter in Bellema meant the winds shifted to the west, shaking the palm trees and picking up grit to blow into unwary eyes. The temperature did drop, true, but only from "hot" to "slightly less so." Midwinter, Piercy had learned, meant nothing more to today's Santerrans than a reason to leave Bellema for their upland estates, assuming they were wealthy enough to own estates. Which most of his Santerran colleagues and acquaintances were.

And now, seven days before Midwinter, Piercy had only memories of snowfall blanketing Matra to remind him of the turning of the year.

With a grunt of exasperation, he loosened his neckcloth and then removed it entirely. He had argued about the neckcloth— about his entire official wardrobe, in fact—with the Dalanese ambassador, Teria Olonter, upon his arrival in Santerre six months before. He had pointed out that the ambassadorial party dressing as the Santerrans did showed Dalanine's respect for Santerran traditions. He had reminded Miss Olonter that he was married to a prominent Santerran noblewoman, had taken her surname, even, and that his continuing to dress in Dalanese fashion might be considered an insult. He had even said something—possibly something ill-judged, he couldn't now remember except that it had come out in a moment of frustration—about how ridiculous all the layers of Dalanese clothing were in a tropical climate. He had achieved new heights of eloquence.

And Miss Olonter, smiling pleasantly, had deflected every one of his arguments with variations on the same theme: "We must maintain our national integrity, Mr. Faranter."

"Sethemba," Piercy had said through gritted teeth. "It's Sethemba. Piercy Sethemba."

"Of course," Miss Olonter had said with an even more pleasant smile that Piercy knew concealed her annoyance that Piercy had, in her eyes, gone completely native and therefore was unsuited to the role of junior Dalanese ambassador.

Now Piercy tossed the ridiculous neckcloth on the well-polished surface of his desk and unbuttoned the top three buttons of his linen shirt. At least linen was more comfortable than fine wool in this heat. He had already removed his frock coat and hung it neatly on the rack by the door, below his Dalanese hat that was only slightly less ridiculous than the neckcloth. He leaned on the window sill and breathed in the sea air.

The sun hung low on the horizon, setting the sea ablaze and turning the sails of the ships going in and out of the harbor from brilliant white to golden cream. In the distance, sea birds cawed, a sound somewhere between a croak and a shriek. As far as he could tell, these were the same kind of birds that swooped and screamed above the Dalanese city Inveros, also a coastal town, and yet the cries were completely different.

He breathed in again and let his mind wander. Most of this

assignment was what he'd expected. He had known the Santerrans, victims of an invasion and occupation by men whose skin was the same color as Piercy's, would not be welcoming and might be actively hostile. He had guessed his marriage to a Santerran noblewoman who was also a hero of the resistance would not win him friends, given that most Santerran nobles believed a Dalanese had no right marrying any woman of their people. He had even been certain that many Santerrans would believe they had the right to express their hostility overtly, which they had, from shunning him socially to calling him by the deeply derogatory term "pale" to his face.

What he had not anticipated was how his own countrymen would treat him. He had believed their shared heritage would bring them together, all of them strangers in a foreign country. But the Dalanese of the embassy staff and ambassadorial party treated him with a formality that kept him at a distance and whispered about him behind his back, not even where he could not hear. None of them used the word "traitor," but they all believed Piercy had gone over to the other side by marrying Ayane Sethemba, and they all believed he was no longer a true son of Dalanine.

He eyed the shadows cast by the setting sun. This far south, the shadows didn't vary with the season as much as they did in Dalanine, and when the shadow of the embassy's clock tower—another Dalanese import, and one the Santerrans made fun of where the Dalanese couldn't hear—touched the embassy gate, Piercy could go home. Home, at least, was a refuge.

Someone knocked lightly on his office door.

Piercy made an involuntary lunge for his discarded neckcloth, then stopped himself. He could dress any way he wanted in his own office. He skirted the desk and opened the door, squaring his shoulders as if in anticipation of a blow.

One of the embassy staff stood there, a short young woman dressed properly in a chintz gown with full skirt and fitted bodice, just the way Dalanese fashion demanded. She took in Piercy's state of undress without comment. "Mr. Sethemba, sir. Miss Olonter's compliments, and she requests you join her in her office at your earliest convenience." She spoke in Dalanese, though every member of the embassy staff was required to be passably fluent in Santerran. It was the only thing on which Piercy and Miss Olonter agreed.

Piercy noted the young woman's reddish complexion, how beads of sweat clung to her hairline, and thought of his over-warm frock coat with distaste. "Thank you, I will go immediately," he said.

The young woman didn't stay to watch him don neckcloth and frock coat, for which Piercy was grateful. He needed time alone to achieve the inner peace necessary to keep his conversation with the ambassador civil. Not for the first time, he wished there was a graceful way to tell the government in Matra that Miss Olonter's behavior did not reflect well on Dalanine. But even if he were the kind of sneak who went behind his superior's back, Miss Olonter had risen high in the Foreign Office because she was intelligent and canny and devoted to promoting Dalanine's interests abroad. As far as the Foreign Office was concerned, her performance was perfect. No one in Matra, not even the Foreign Office chief Miss Tedoratis, who respected Piercy's abilities, would be willing to act on a junior ambassador's untested assumptions about international relations.

He walked through the halls of the embassy, nodding at his fellows without really seeing them. Most of them acknowledged his nod; they were all too well bred to shun him overtly. Fortunately, the embassy was Santerran-built and therefore well suited to the environment as Dalanese dress was not. Palm-frond fans hanging from the ceiling, impelled by magic, wafted the heavy air into cooling currents, and many of the windows were open to catch the sea breezes of evening. In the morning, when the winds blew strongest, they remained shut, and the smells of tea and coffee and sweat were overpowering.

Piercy's office was on the other side of the embassy from Miss Olonter's, not because she disliked him but because that was where the previous junior ambassador's office had been. The route to her office took Piercy to the main entrance of the embassy, from which visitors could access the public offices and the vast reception hall.

Piercy paused briefly to admire the reception hall. Santerrans knew to build high ceilings to trap the heat, and the arches supporting the tall roof, some thirty feet high, were all carved to look like palm tree trunks. The light-colored wood paneling from a tropical tree Piercy didn't know the name of smelled sweet beneath the tang of lacquer. Other doors leading out of the reception hall were barely visible as thin black lines crossing the pale walls. The hall looked nothing like its Dalanese counterparts, and yet here Piercy always felt as if his two worlds had a chance of coming together.

He knocked on Miss Olonter's door, once more squaring his shoulders. He wished he had his old walking stick, a hawk-headed length of weighted oak that looked like a gentleman's cane and could strike an assailant unconscious with a single blow. It wasn't so much that he felt he needed to defend against Miss Olonter's attack as that he liked the security of knowing such a defense was possible.

At the muffled "come in," Piercy pushed the door open and walked forward six paces, which put him directly in front of Miss Olonter's desk. "Ma'am?"

"Mr. Sethemba," Miss Olonter said, with the barest hesitation before his surname that Piercy could not take offense at. "Thank you for coming. Won't you sit?"

Piercy sat in one of the chairs facing the desk. It was too low, bringing his knees nearly to his chest and making him feel like an errant schoolboy, which was probably intended. He pretended he felt no discomfort and waited for Miss Olonter to speak again. Experience told him small talk was not a good idea.

Miss Olonter waited a few seconds after Piercy settled himself. "I asked you here to discuss the Midwinter gala."

Startled by this mention of the subject he'd been dwelling on just minutes before, Piercy blurted out, "What Midwinter gala?"

Miss Olonter smiled. It even looked genuine. "The embassy hosts a Midwinter celebration every year, Mr. Sethemba. We honor the new year by inviting many prominent Santerrans to join in our traditions. One of those traditions is that the junior ambassador plans the gala."

"That's seven days from now," Piercy said, again caught off guard. "You want me to plan a gala in seven days?"

"No one expects anything dramatic, Mr. Sethemba," Miss Olonter said. "Decorate the reception hall, arrange for drinks and a few refreshments. In truth, very few Santerrans ever accept our invitation. Typical, given that they show little respect for us—but then, you'd know that better than I, wouldn't you?"

Piercy ground his teeth together, holding back the retort *If we showed respect to them, maybe they would reciprocate.* When he gained control of himself, he said, "Décor, and drink, and food. Is that all?"

"Well, I suppose music, if you can manage it. I'm not sure there are enough Dalanese musicians in Bellema for a traditional double octet." Miss Olonter's attention was drifting to some papers on her desk. "Really, Mr. Sethemba, I hope I can leave it to you. It's not beyond your abilities, is it?"

"Of course not, Miss Olonter." Piercy unfolded himself from the chair with some difficulty and bowed politely. He let himself out without slamming the door. He stood for a moment, eyes closed, reaching for calm. Then he strode through the halls of the embassy and out the great front doors. The shadow had not quite reached the embassy gate, but he didn't care. He was done for the day.

Bellema was a younger city than Matra, but its roads were paved more smoothly, with curbs that separated the road from the sidewalks and gutters that were cleaned every few days. There were no public carriages; even the nobles walked unless they intended to travel outside Bellema or wanted to make a point. Piercy didn't mind walking, though he wished he was dressed like the Santerran men who shared the sidewalk with him, in knee-length, wide-legged trousers, long-sleeved white linen or cotton shirts to protect against the sun, and vests in vivid colors and patterns that, unlike his own waistcoat, were not made to button. Even wearing sandals instead of sturdy boots would be more comfortable.

His home was only a five-minute walk from the embassy. He and Ayane lived in one of the many large mansions surrounding the queen's palace—though even that wasn't a palace like the one in Matra, but instead was itself a mansion, proof against invasion as Bellema's last palace had not been. Ayane's family home had burned when that palace did, and when she and Piercy had settled in Bellema, they had purchased this mansion, which had belonged to a family mostly destroyed in the Despot's invasion. Ayane assured Piercy the remaining members of that family were glad to sell, but Piercy had felt slightly ghoulish about it for a few weeks.

Now, however, it was home in a way he had never experienced. Nothing had prepared him for coming home to a house he shared with the love of his life. He could leave his uncertainties and frustration and anger at the door. It was a typically Santerran mansion, fronted by a large screened porch that served the same purpose as a Dalanese sitting room, though no Dalanese home would be as exposed to the elements. But it did not matter that the architecture was nothing like he'd been raised to; what mattered was who he became when he entered.

"Ayane?" he called out as he pushed open the door.

Silence greeted him. He tried not to feel disappointed. Ayane was even busier than he was, ostensibly the brightest socialite in Bellema, secretly Queen Cyrah Hathakuni's spymaster. It made for an interesting tension between them, neither of them able to talk about every detail of their work, and six months ago he'd feared the tension would become a wall. But it had proved remarkably easy to compartmentalize his life, given that most of what he did at the embassy was either inconsequential or non-confidential. He hoped that didn't mean something dire about his career prospects.

At any rate, Ayane's absence meant nothing awful. He was early, that was all, and she would return soon enough.

He strolled through the house, nodding to the servants who bustled about tidying and dusting, breathing in the aroma of supper. Piercy was used to maintaining a staff, even when he'd lived alone in his Matra townhouse, but Ayane insisted on twice the number of servants he was accustomed to. She'd explained it was Santerran tradition that those who had money were expected to use it to better the lives of others, and a popular way of doing this was to hire as many servants as one could afford. A side effect of this was that because the relationship was seen as one of people helping each other, their Santerran servants were not as servile or humble as Dalanese servants were, something Piercy discovered he liked.

The servants were also among the few Santerrans who treated Piercy with respect, though he wasn't sure if that was because he was their employer, or because they were more sensible than the average Santerran, or because their respect and admiration for Ayane spilled over onto him. He didn't care. It was refreshing, and he would take what he could get.

He entered the bedroom he shared with Ayane and began undressing. This was a Santerran custom he fully supported, this notion of married couples sharing a room rather than having separate bedrooms as the wealthy and noble of Dalanine did. Piercy wasn't sure he could have endured traveling back and forth between his bedroom and Ayane's, knowing the servants watched and were aware of their master and mistress's intimacies. Plus, he loved sleeping beside his wife, who denied that she snored.

When he was down to his undershirt and drawers, he flopped face first onto the bed, spread-eagled, and sighed. The fan hanging from their ceiling had a funny little hum that was almost a buzz, and he hadn't gotten around to investigating it because the soft noise soothed him. He wasn't sleepy, but the soft warmth of the bedclothes and the cool breeze and the buzz relaxed all his muscles enough to let his annoyance over Miss Olonter's demand slip away.

He wasn't sure how long he lay there, his mind fuzzy with contentment, before the door opened and Ayane said, "Well. A nearly-naked man in my bed. Whatever shall I do?"

"Nothing, I hope," Piercy said, his voice muffled by the bedclothes, "as I feel completely incapable of exertion, even the pleasant kind."

Ayane sank onto the bed beside him and ran a hand over his shoulder. "I would say I'm disappointed, but I'm too tired for any exertion, either. It might surprise you to know how exhausting trivial conversation is."

"I am well aware." Piercy rolled onto his side. Ayane did look tired, her golden eyes shadowed and her mouth drawn down at the corners with weariness. She, at least, was dressed for the weather in Santerran semiformal garb, an ankle-length sheath gown with no sleeves, to which a gauzy half-cape was pinned at the shoulders. The creamy linen made her dark skin glow. He touched her dozens of thin braids, which had been pinned high on her head that morning and had started to come down on one side. "You are heartbreakingly beautiful, my dear."

Ayane smiled and leaned over to kiss him. "And you look over-burdened, love. Did something happen at the embassy?"

Piercy groaned and sat up fully. "I have been assigned to plan and execute the embassy's Midwinter gala. In seven days. I cannot tell whether Miss Olonter invented this task solely to punish me."

"Well, she didn't invent the gala. They've had one every year since Dalanine established an ambassadorial presence in Bellema." Ayane vainly pushed her braids higher, only to make them sag more deeply. She gave up and added, "Cyrah says it's dull, but she never goes, so I don't know how she knows. Or maybe she went once, and that's the source of her knowledge. I'm so sorry, Piercy. What will you do?"

Piercy buried his face in his hands briefly. "What I must," he said, raising his head. "But..."

When he didn't immediately continue, Ayane said, "But?"

An idea tugged at Piercy's consciousness, not even a fully-fleshed idea, more a hint of a thought. "Miss Olonter said no one ever gave the gala much attention. She said I wasn't responsible to do much. Suppose I prove her wrong?"

"Piercy, you have that mad genius look in your eyes," Ayane said. "Why would you want to give this...this joke of an assign-ment any effort?"

"Because it is a joke of an assignment," Piercy said. "Because Miss Olonter cares nothing for how Dalanine might reach out to Santerre in respect. Because I am caught between two worlds, not fully Santerran and no longer fully Dalanese. Ayane, I intend to make this gala something Santerre will talk about for years to come."

Ayane bit her lip, but her eyes were laughing. "You realize," she said, "if it's a colossal failure, they'll talk about that for years, too."

"I believe I will take that as a challenge," Piercy said.

Seven days later, Piercy stood in the center of the reception hall with his hands on his hips and his head flung back, surveying the results of his labors. It had taken some doing to find a Santerran antiquities dealer, as most of Bellema had burned with their king's palace, and even more work to convince that man Piercy was sincere and meant no disrespect. But Nyogo Kathuni had proved to be an excellent ally, one willing to rent items from his stock rather than selling them outright. Piercy didn't think he could get away with drawing on the embassy's funds to that extent.

Now he cast his gaze over the enormous paper lanterns, vivid red and deep green and a glowing gold that looked like a handful of tiny suns hovering beneath the high ceiling. They hung at different heights, creating an illusion of depth that made Piercy feel he was in danger of falling up and into their embrace.

Flexible paper screens lined the walls between the tree-trunk columns, each painted with a scene from Santerran history—a past distant enough that some of those events were legend rather than fact, but Piercy was sure they would evoke responses from his guests. The screens themselves were not antiques, but the work of a contemporary artist Ayane had introduced Piercy to. The artist, who went by the single name Kyotha, had not been immune to the Faranter charm, hence the loan of a dozen screens. Piercy had promised to ensure the woman's name reached the ears of the guests as well.

He had been unable to hire a Santerran cook to produce the specialty dishes he'd had in mind, but a conversation with the embassy servants, all of whom appreciated Piercy's respectful treatment of them, revealed that the Dalanese cook, Haralt Serentis, loved Santerran cuisine and was eager to practice his skills on Piercy's and the gala's behalf.

Piercy remembered Serentis's enthusiasm and considered whether he ought not lure the cook away from the embassy to work for him and Ayane. A problem for another time. He decided not to observe Serentis's work now. Trust had to start somewhere, and he was nervous enough he would just transmit that nervousness to the staff. And at this point, there was nothing he could do if Serentis failed.

He closed his eyes and inhaled deeply, breathing in the scents of cinnamon and cloves. They reminded him of his childhood, of Midwinter celebrations and spiced cider—but cinnamon and cloves ultimately came from Santerre, and he liked the combined meaning, bringing two worlds together. As he hoped to tonight.

The sound of many people entering the hall brought him back to the present. Santerran men and women carrying drums and pipes and the deep-bellied string instruments that were cousin to the Dalanese viol were filing in. None of them stopped to speak to Piercy, instead making their way to the three-tiered platform in the far corner from the main door and arranging themselves and their instruments. Piercy had hired the musicians three days ago on the recommendation of one of Ayane's friends, and their leader, whose name was either Bengwe or Benthi, had not been friendly to a Dalanese, even one who paid in advance. But Piercy had had years of experience turning enemies into allies, if not friends, and he judged Bengwe/Benthi turned his rudeness on everyone impartially. Again, it was too late to worry about it now.

He left the musicians to their tuning up and hurried down the narrow passage that led to the servants' quarters. There, he found the eight young men and women he'd collared into dressing in the archaic versions of their typical Dalanese garb. "You all look splendid," he said, though in truth they looked very odd, a mix of modern and old-fashioned Piercy hoped no one would criticize. "Remember, when you serve a Santerran, you say, 'A joyful year to you.' In Santerran, obviously."

The youths nodded. They all looked eager, as if they were about to step onto a stage for the greatest performance of their young lives. That was probably better than if they thought of this as a typical serving event.

He surveyed them one last time, then returned to the hall. The musicians were still tuning, though one of the drummers beat a quiet rhythm Piercy found soothing. He'd done everything he could. Now it was just a matter of waiting for the guests to arrive. He had no doubt Ayane had done as she promised.

He pushed open both halves of the main door and secured them so they would stay that way, hooking fat velvet ropes fastened to the walls over the knobs. Thanks to the many lanterns, the entry chamber was cooler than the reception hall, but Piercy didn't think the difference would be terribly uncomfortable. The entry was completely empty; by this hour, all the staff would have gone home, most of them to prepare for the gala. From what Piercy had heard whispered all week, they considered the gala a boring, necessary evil. Piercy had laughed silently at the surprise he had planned, but now that the moment had come, he wondered if he'd been too quick to mock.

He adjusted the fit of his old-fashioned sleeveless doublet, an item of clothing he'd brought with him from Matra on a whim that had inspired his plans for the night. He didn't have a full set of clothing in the style of two hundred years previous, but he had enough to make his point. Beneath the doublet, he wore a bell-sleeved linen shirt that lay open at the neck, product of a friendly seamstress's lightning efforts. Baggy trousers that bloused over his usual boots completed the ensemble. It didn't matter if anyone thought he looked foolish; he felt comfortably cool in Dalanese clothes for the first time in six months.

Behind him, footsteps on the shining wooden floor told him the embassy servants were arriving. One of them approached and asked, "Did you want someone to wait at the front door, sir?"

Piercy hadn't considered that. "Oh—yes. Yes, one of you—we should open that door, as well."

He crossed the entry to pull the embassy's front door open just as someone else pushed on it from outside. Ayane stood framed in the gap, and Piercy was caught breathless at her beauty, her hair loosed from its braids to make a soft black cloud around her face, her silvery-blue silk gown that left one shoulder bare fitting her body perfectly and contrasting beautifully with her dark skin. She smiled, and he forgot what he'd planned to say.

"Don't stand there gaping, Piercy, there are more people coming," she said, extending a hand to take his. Piercy jerked himself back to the present and led Ayane inside. Behind him, the young servant hauled both doors open, letting in a warm wind that stirred the scents of cinnamon and cloves.

Ayane stopped short at the reception hall door, staring. "Piercy, it's *extraordinary*," she said. "Truly breathtaking. I've only seen this sort of thing in paintings."

At that moment, the musicians began playing, a light, lilting tune punctuated by silver chiming taps on tubes of metal that dangled from a frame. Ayane let out a gasp. "'How Sweet the

Chimes Ring'—my mother used to sing it to me. Piercy, how did you know?"

"About your mother? That is coincidence, sadly. But this group is known for their performances of old Santerran music, both in its original form and in contemporary arrangements." Piercy put his arms around Ayane and kissed her. "I hired them sight unseen, so to speak, so it is a relief that they are as good as they professed."

"I want to look at the screens. Kyotha has done more work since I last saw her gallery." Ayane drifted forward, and Piercy followed her, his heart light. It no longer mattered whether he impressed the Santerrans, or the Dalanese, or Miss Olonter. He had made Ayane happy.

"Mr. Far—Mr. Sethemba."

Piercy turned. Miss Olonter's voice had been quiet, but backed with steel. Piercy composed himself to display a placid expression. "Yes, Miss Olonter?"

"I believe I gave you specific instructions. Why have you disobeyed?"

Piercy looked around, wide-eyed and innocent. "You said, specifically, décor, drinks, food, and music. I realize the drinks and food have not yet appeared, but then neither have our Santerran guests. Time enough for that, don't you agree?"

Miss Olonter walked forward until the hem of her full-skirted gown, spread out over her crinoline, brushed Piercy's legs. "You know very well what I intended. How dare you waste embassy funds on this...this ridiculous show? And what is that *thing* you are wearing?"

Piercy brushed the front of his doublet as if sweeping away lint. "This ridiculous show, as you call it, reflects Santerran Midwinter traditions from some two hundred years ago. A time, you may recall, when Santerre and Dalanine were on friendlier terms."

"Nonsense. You're making it all up." Miss Olonter's face grew redder by the moment.

"I am not. My degree from the University of Matra is in history, and I am quite familiar with Santerre's past, almost as familiar as I am with Dalanine's." Piercy smiled pleasantly, pretending not to notice Miss Olonter's wrath. "You will note that I and the embassy staff assisting me tonight are dressed...well, not authentically, but we did make an effort to find Dalanese garb from the same era."

"This embassy has a duty to maintain Dalanine's national integrity, Mr. Sethemba," Miss Olonter spat. "We are not interested in sacrificing our traditions to suit our southern neighbor's sensibilities. You—"

"I beg your pardon, Miss Olonter, but our guests are arriving," Piercy said smoothly. "Unless you feel this is a conversation we should have in front of them?"

Miss Olonter cast a glance over her shoulder. Several Santerrans dressed in formal clothes, the men in knee-length silk robes, the women garbed like Ayane, had entered the reception hall and stood staring up at the lanterns, whispering to one another. Piercy noted the approach of the first servers, bearing trays with tall glasses of sparkling wine and followed by more servers with trays that smelled deliciously of seafood and tangy sauces. Serentis had come through.

Miss Olonter returned her gaze to Piercy. "We are not finished," she said in a low voice. "Once this travesty of a gala is over, you and I will have words."

"I look forward to it," Piercy lied.

Miss Olonter stalked away, ignoring the server who offered his tray of drinks to her. Piercy accepted a glass and sipped, though he wanted badly to drink it down in one gulp and wanted even more badly for it to contain hard liquor. He had hoped Miss Olonter would appreciate his solution. Well, there was nothing for it but to move forward.

He wandered through the growing crowd. Many of the guests were friends of Ayane, or at least nodding acquaintances, which told him Ayane had succeeded in enticing the cream of Santerran society to attend what they had to believe would be a waste of their valuable time. Most of them ignored him, which left him feeling very downcast, given that they all seemed pleased or surprised at the display. He had gone to great lengths to recreate an old-fashioned Santerran Midwinter, and apparently he'd been successful, but nobody knew to thank him. Not that he'd done it to be thanked, but...no, what he'd wanted was some acknowledgement that he, at least, cared about reaching out to Santerre to heal some of the bad blood between the country of his birth and the country of his adopted home.

The sound of a horn blowing six notes in succession drew his attention from where he had been staring at but not seeing one of the painted screens. It wasn't until he became aware the music had stopped that he realized the horn was not one he'd hired, but belonged to someone dressed in royal livery standing just inside the main door. Then the entire crowd of Santerrans—he had no idea when the room had become packed full of people—bowed or curtsied low, and over their heads, Piercy saw Queen Cyrah Hathakuni silhouetted in the doorway.

She caught his eye, and belatedly Piercy bowed in the official gesture of respect from someone not the queen's subject. Queen Cyrah surveyed the crowd, then gestured for them to rise. She was not a tall woman, but she held herself as if she overtopped everyone in the room. She wore her hair shaved close to her scalp, an attractive style that highlighted the elegant bones of her face and the smoothness of her brown skin, not as dark as Ayane's. Even had he not recognized her, Piercy would have known she was royalty.

Piercy felt someone at his elbow. "I told you she would come if I asked," Ayane murmured.

"I believed you, but—is there a word for believing and being dumbfounded at the same time?"

"If you don't know it, probably not." Ayane hooked her hand around his elbow. "Piercy, it's a wonderful success. Everyone is talking about what a perfect replica of an old-time Midwinter celebration it is."

Piercy watched the queen cross the room, flanked by her attendants in their necklaces of broad hammered gold plaques, to where Miss Olonter stood. "Ambassador Olonter," Queen Cyrah said. "What a remarkable display."

Miss Olonter hesitated only a moment. "Thank you for accepting our invitation, your majesty."

"I am amazed at your fidelity to our traditions," the queen went on. "I believed Dalanine chose to celebrate only its own culture at this time of year. This is a gesture of respect I will not forget. Tell me, was this your idea?"

Piercy held his breath.

Miss Olonter inclined her head. "Of course, your majesty. I have long felt that Dalanine and Santerre should seek to celebrate their common heritage, and I chose to draw on our shared past."

Dizziness struck Piercy, and he realized he'd been holding his breath too long. But when he inhaled again, the dizziness didn't fade. Beside him, Ayane's grip on his elbow became painfully tight. "Piercy, she—"

"Please do not make a scene, Ayane," Piercy whispered.

"But—" Ayane's voice dropped. "This was *your* idea, and that harpy is taking all the credit!"

"It does not matter whom the queen honors," Piercy said. His chest ached, and once more he made himself draw breath. "The important thing is that Miss Olonter knows at whose door she can lay the credit. I still won."

"You can't believe that. Piercy, Miss Olonter lied! What kind of ambassador would sacrifice her subordinate like that?"

"A successful one, I fear." Piercy closed his eyes briefly. "I wish we might simply leave, but I am still responsible—for the lanterns and the screens, if nothing else."

Ayane made him look at her. "I know the truth," she said fiercely. "And I have never been prouder of you than at this moment."

They walked the circuit of the hall once, then separated. Piercy made sure to mention Kyotha's name whenever he heard someone commenting on the screens, and told two people where they might obtain paper lanterns of their own. At least *he* had kept his word. *He* had behaved honorably.

The longer the night dragged on, the angrier Piercy became at Miss Olonter's hypocrisy. For her to chastise him over the gala, and then to take credit for his work—it was a level of treachery that could not be excused by their mutual dislike. He found himself arguing with her in his head, playing out dozens of possible confrontations. Finally, weary of the internal shouting, he made himself eat something delicious—yes, Serentis needed to come to work for him and Ayane—and paced the room until the last guests left. He had sent Ayane home an hour earlier, not liking how tired she looked. Miss Olonter had disappeared sometime after Queen Cyrah made her departure. Finally, he and the musicians were the only ones who remained.

He waited outside the back door for the antiquities dealer Kathuni's men to collect the lanterns and collapse them for storage. While they were disassembling everything, Kyotha herself came to supervise the removal of eleven of the paper screens. To Piercy's surprise, she presented him with the twelfth. "Lady Sethemba has been so gracious, and honestly, you will both appreciate it better than some jumped-up minor noble," she said in her decisive way. Piercy didn't feel like arguing.

When everyone, including the musicians and the servants, had left, Piercy tucked the rolled-up screen under his arm and trod the long, long halls to Miss Olonter's office. He knew she would be there, waiting, but the line of light beneath her door when every other door in that hall was dark made his heart beat faster anyway.

He pushed open her door. Miss Olonter sat at her desk with her fingers steepled in front of her. She regarded him dispassionately. Piercy, for his part, felt nothing but emptiness. Now that the moment was here, all the arguments he had imagined seemed irrelevant.

Miss Olonter cleared her throat. "I will not apologize," she said. "You acted in the embassy's name, and I accepted Queen Cyrah's accolades in the same spirit. It should never matter which of us takes credit."

A dozen responses ran through Piercy's mind. He considered arguing the point. He considered shouting at his superior. He considered bowing himself out with good grace.

But what came out of his mouth were the words, "I resign."

Miss Olonter straightened, her eyes widening. "I beg your pardon?"

"I believe you heard me the first time," Piercy said. "I might have accepted your arrogance in accepting praise for something you not only did not do, but actively derided as ridiculous and foolish. I might have considered your words to Queen Cyrah in the light you represented them to me just now, as praise accruing to the embassy irrespective of personalities. But, Miss Olonter, I will not continue to act as the subordinate to someone who can lie to the queen of an allied country and tell herself she is justified in doing so."

Miss Olonter shot to her feet. "If you think you can carry that story to anyone who will care, I promise I will see you buried, Faranter."

"You misunderstand me," Piercy said. "I am not interested in sabotaging your career, even though you have done your best to sabotage mine. This is entirely a matter of principle. You have no interest in building amity between Dalanine and Santerre, and as that is something I care very much about, I do not see that you and I will be well served by continuing to work together."

The paper screen roll slipped, and Piercy hitched it higher. "I will remove my things from that office tonight, and tomorrow I will sign the papers releasing me from diplomatic service. Until then, good night, Miss Olonter."

He turned his back on his former superior. Miss Olonter spat a profanity, then said, "Don't think this impresses me, Faranter, this show of moral superiority. I am the ambassador, and you are *nothing*, a jumped-up nobody who thinks so little of his own country he chose to abandon it for a lot of foreigners who mock and belittle him. You think Santerre will welcome anyone who reminds them of the Despot's invasion? Think again!"

Piercy ignored her and let the door shut behind him without slamming it.

He gathered what few things he cared about from his office. The Dalanese hat, he left on the rack. Then he walked home in the darkness. Part of his mind warned him that burdened as he was, he made an excellent target for thieves and assailants; the rest of him was too weary and angry to care. In fact, he would welcome an assault that gave him an excuse to beat someone, with or without his walking stick. But no one attacked, and he trod the steps to his house and managed to open the door without dropping anything.

Most of the lights were out. Piercy deposited everything in the screened front porch, taking care to prop the paper screen in a corner where it could not be damaged. He pulled off his boots and stockings and trod barefoot through the house to his bedroom. Light outlined the door, and for a moment he recalled Miss Olonter's light-limned door and felt a flash of anger. Then he let it go. He was home, and Miss Olonter could not trouble him further that night.

Ayane was sitting up in bed reading when he entered. She set the book aside and said, "Piercy, you look awful. What happened?"

Piercy untied the doublet and removed it and the shirt beneath. "I am no longer employed by the Dalanese government."

Ayane gasped. "Miss Olonter let you go?"

"I let myself go. I realized I could no longer maintain that position and keep my self-respect." Piercy tackled the laces of his trousers. They had become knotted, and he had to pick at the knots until they loosened. "Do you mind being married to an unemployed wastrel?"

"You're not a wastrel." Ayane stood and walked to face him, putting her hands on his waist. "You did the best you could. I'm sure Miss Tedoratis doesn't know what Miss Olonter is like, or she would never have given you a position subordinate to her."

Piercy sighed and put his arms around Ayane. "And we will no longer have to conceal the facts of our employment efforts from one another. I find I am relieved. I want nothing more than to share everything with you, my dear."

"I feel the same." Ayane hesitated, then said, "In fact, I had something I intended to tell you tonight, but now I'm not sure it's the right time."

"If it is something good, I assure you I wish for nothing more than to hear it."

Ayane nodded. "I suppose I should first ask if you're willing to recreate what you did tonight. For us, I mean, next year."

Puzzled, Piercy said, "Not on such a grand scale, but of course, if you wish. I didn't realize it meant so much to you."

"It did, but it's more than that." Ayane looked him full in the face, her golden eyes glowing in the lamplight. "I want our child to experience her heritage. Both her heritages."

For a moment, Piercy didn't understand. Then the import of her words struck him full in the chest. "Our child?"

Ayane nodded. "It's why I've been so tired, or so the midwife tells me. You're happy, right?"

"Happy?" Piercy drew her into his arms and held her close. "Ayane, I know no words to describe how I feel. You are well, though?"

"Very well, just tired." Ayane hugged him more tightly than he was hugging her. "I won't break, you know. And the women of my family always have easy pregnancies. You needn't worry."

Piercy heard her words coming from a far distance. A child. He was going to be a father. "You know it is a girl?"

"No, but I would like a daughter. Or do you want a son?"

"Since I doubt my wishes have any influence on the outcome of that question, I can say with some surety that I care only that it is a healthy child." Piercy kissed her, and joy rose up in his heart when she returned his kiss passionately. "A child we will raise to appreciate both her mother's and her father's cultures."

"I look forward to it," Ayane said.

Piercy slept late the next morning. Ayane was gone when he finally rose, but she left a note on the pillow telling him she would return mid-afternoon. He took his time dressing and shaving and eating, not fearing his morning's responsibilities but not thrilled about them, either.

He did not see Miss Olonter, merely her secretary. Miss Olonter had prepared the documents releasing Piercy from government service, and all Piercy needed do was sign in three places. He spoke to no one in the embassy, and everyone he passed averted their eyes. Clearly Miss Olonter had not been guarded about what she told others regarding Piercy's leaving. Or maybe she'd lied, and blackened his name. He didn't care.

When he returned to his house, he was startled to find a number of men and women in royal livery standing in a line outside it, a line that ran from the royal carriage all the way to Piercy's front door. Brow furrowed in confusion, he walked past the retinue. They all ignored him, staring at something in the middle distance as if meeting other people's eyes was ill-bred.

Before he reached the front door, he saw people waiting in the screened porch. He knew some member of the royal family was paying him a visit, but it still startled him when he entered the porch and discovered Queen Cyrah seated in a large armchair as if enthroned. She had disdained the footstool pulled up before the chair, and both her hands rested on the wooden armrests, not fidgeting even the smallest amount.

Two armed men stood to either side of the chair and regarded Piercy closely. He sized them up, automatically plotting how to disable them if they attacked. Then he mentally shook himself and bowed. "Your majesty."

"Mr. Sethemba," Cyrah said. "Have a seat."

Piercy reflected briefly on the ridiculousness of someone

telling him to take a seat in his own home, even the queen, but he sat on the sofa that faced Cyrah's chair and rested one hand on the armrest and the other on his lap. "Your majesty, may I ask to what do I owe the honor of your presence?"

The queen smiled, a little sideways smile that might have been directed at herself rather than at Piercy. "Ayane was right about how formal your speech is. Is that how you were taught to speak Santerran?"

"Ah, no, it was not. In fact, I speak my own language as formally. I am fond of history, and I respect an earlier era when men and women used words with greater caution and delicacy than they often do now."

"I see. You should know most Santerrans will assume you are less fluent in our language than you are." Cyrah's smile vanished.

Piercy shrugged. "A side benefit, as far as I am concerned. I spent many years being taken for other than I am, and I found that misapprehension useful in my former career."

"Former career." It was not a question.

Piercy's curiosity about why the queen was here grew the longer this bizarrely inane conversation went on. "I gave notice at the embassy last night, and formally penned my resignation just half an hour ago."

Queen Cyrah nodded slowly. "I assume your decision had something to do with how Ambassador Olonter usurped credit for your work on the gala."

Stunned, Piercy said, "She—how did you know?"

"When Ayane asked me to attend, she told me of everything you'd done to make the gala something more than a token or an insult," Cyrah said. "I knew the truth when I spoke to the ambassador, and I offered her the opportunity to give credit where it was due. Though I admit I was mostly certain she would claim responsibility. The ambassador is rather transparent in her attitudes."

Piercy swallowed. "It doesn't matter who—"

"Of course it matters," Cyrah said sharply. "The man who went out of his way to show how Santerre and Dalanine were once friends and might be so again is someone who deserves to be honored. For his integrity, if not for his vision. I am extremely disappointed in Ambassador Olonter, and I have already sent a strongly worded letter to the Dalanese government, asking for her recall."

"You have?" Piercy's astonishment silenced any other response. Cyrah watched him closely. When he realized she was not going to continue, he said, "It—that is, I quite understand your decision, but it makes no difference to me. It will not restore me to the diplomatic corps."

"I certainly hope not," Cyrah said. "You're wasted in Dalanine's Foreign Office. Wilfreya Tedoratis is a stellar individual, but her loyalties, quite rightly, lie with Dalanine. What our countries need is someone who cares deeply about *both* Santerre and Dalanine and is even-handed and honorable enough to do what it takes to bring them into harmony. Someone like you."

"I fail to understand your meaning."

Cyrah's smile was more natural this time. "I am offering you a position. Official Santerran liaison to Dalanine's government, reporting directly to me. You will work with the Dalanese ambassador's office on my behalf, and you will serve as a...I suppose 'cultural attaché' is an appropriate title. I would like our countries to understand one another better. You didn't have to research any of what you displayed at that gala, did you?"

"No, your majesty, my degree is in history—"

"And your experience is in the present. I believe you will suit admirably. Do you accept, Mr. Sethemba?"

Piercy let out a deep breath. "I am honored to accept, your majesty."

"Good. I didn't want to make Ayane lean on you to change your mind, not in her condition. Congratulations, by the way." Cyrah rose from her seat, prompting Piercy to leap to his feet. "Don't feel you must see me out. I'm sure you need some time alone."

Piercy watched through the screen as the queen descended the stairs and stepped into her carriage. When it and the royal retinue were gone, he sank back onto the sofa. Cultural attaché? It felt... right. Good. For the first time in six months, Piercy felt he was where he needed to be.

After a few minutes, he left the porch and walked through the house, speaking briefly with the servants. He ended up in the bedroom, where he stared at his wardrobe for a moment. It was full of Dalanese clothes, most of them inappropriate to the climate. And yet getting rid of all of them felt wrong.

He ran his fingers down a fine wool sleeve. Then he undressed and hung his Dalanese suit in the wardrobe. With careful deliberation, he dressed in Santerran clothes, wide-legged short trousers, long-sleeved linen shirt, brightly colored vest. He examined himself in the full-length mirror. At first, he looked odd, like someone playing dress-up, but the longer he looked, the more comfortable he became. He was never going to be Santerran, and he was no longer fully Dalanese. With luck, he would end up being a little of both.

Joe Raven and the Christmas Job

*This story was written for the same project as "Epiphany,"
but ended up not being sufficiently gritty for the anthology. Despite this, I feel I should warn readers that if you
are looking for a sweet, heartwarming, somewhat romantic experience from this collection, you should probably skip this story. It's a
noir detective story, and while it's no darker than anything I ever
write, it is quite a bit different from the rest of the collection. I had
fun writing it.*

Believe it or not, I've always loved Christmas.

I know how it looks. I've got a fifth-story walkup on
the wrong side of downtown, crammed with a heavy old
desk and bookcase that nobody's ever taking out of here without
taking home a hernia too and a Murphy bed that spends most of
its time in the wall so it don't scare the clients. The window's

never fully clean, which is fine because it looks out on the fire escape and an alley the neighbors are competing to fill with trash first. And you can't see any of it because the light in the ceiling buzzes and flickers on good days and flat refuses to light all the rest of the year.

But the sink behind the hanging sheet in the corner is always clean—can't stand the smell of rotting food—and there's my name on the door, JOE RAVEN INVESTIGATIONS, just like any gumshoe hanging out his shingle uptown, and I ain't beholden to no one. You got to have self-respect, my pop always said, and everything else will come in time. I don't know if he was right, but as a motto, it ain't bad. And my self-respect says I don't got to be ashamed for liking Christmas.

So that afternoon, when she knocked on my door, that's why I opened it with a fistful of tinsel from trimming my little tree. "Come in, sweetheart," I said, then felt like I'd been socked in the gut, because the girl was gorgeous. The kind of girl I'd dream about if I could afford that sort of dream. She was tall, with curves in all the right places and legs a million girls would kill for. Peroxide blonde, but on her it looked good, like she was correcting whatever wrong color Nature had given her. A second glance brought home the brilliant scarlet of her dress, with a bodice that crossed in front to show off her assets, and a matching hat with a dainty little net veil that couldn't hide the blue of her eyes.

She gave my tinsel strands a dismayed look and said, "I'm sorry, is this the right place? Raven Investigations?"

The way she said it, like she'd expected something else, made me want to stand in front of my little tree to hide it from those disapproving blue eyes. "It is," I said. I tossed the tinsel at the tree, where it hit in a clump and rebounded to lie on the floor like some cat had horked up a festive ball. "Come in. Have a seat." I held the chair in front of my desk for her, then sidled around to sit opposite. "How can I help you?"

The girl twisted her red-gloved hands on her pocketbook. "You're Mr. Raven?"

"Since the day I was born. And you are...?"

Her blue-eyed gaze flicked to a spot behind my shoulder, where I knew my framed investigator's license was. I kept it there to reassure the more timid folks who didn't believe anyone who lived like I did was any good. "My name is Greville. Miss Greville."

I cocked an eyebrow at her. "*Miss* Greville?"

She blushed as pretty as a flower in first bloom. "How did you know?"

"There's a ring on your left hand under the glove. Is there some reason you want to be 'miss'?" I leaned back in my chair in a way that usually put clients at ease.

"I, well, it's just that I..." She wetted her lips with the tip of a delicate pink tongue. "I didn't want to be identified. And who I am doesn't really matter for what I want done."

I thought about challenging her, but decided to hear the rest of whatever else she invented first. "And what's that?"

Miss Greville leaned forward. "I want someone found, Mr. Raven. Someone horrible."

That interested me. I got no quarrel with the things people want me to do, because their problems are their own. But I'd never had anyone who looked this good walk into my office sounding so determined. I leaned forward to match her. "Someone who done you wrong?"

She blushed again. "You're making fun of me."

"I'm dead serious. You got to tell me more if you want my help."

Miss Greville nodded. "About a year ago, we lost our life savings. The bank failed—well, you probably know a lot of banks failed in 1930. Only I'm certain it didn't just fail. The bank president, Carl Wheaton, stole everything. He pinned the blame for the failure on his partner and faked his own death."

"That's quite the story," I said. "How do you know all that? If he's dead—"

"He is *not* dead," Miss Greville insisted. "I'm certain of it. He left a note saying how sorry he was for failing the bank's customers, but I know Mr. Wheaton well enough to know he is never sorry for anything. He's out there somewhere, Mr. Raven. And I want you to find him. I want my money back."

She opened her pocketbook and dipped a hand inside. "I don't know what the usual retainer is for a private investigator. Is one hundred dollars enough?"

I kept my face still and accepted the wad of twenties she held out to me. "It's enough," I said. It was a whole lot more than enough, and it set all my hairs to warning me off. But she was beautiful, and Christmas was a week away, and I could use the cash. "But I got to warn you, that's not a lot to go on, just a name and a phony suicide note."

"That's not all." Miss Greville's color was returning to normal, but her eyes still blazed with fervor. "There's a man who might know the truth. Bruce Bannatyne. He was chief clerk at the bank. He was on holiday when everything happened, and he swore to the police he didn't know anything, but he lived in Mr. Wheaton's pockets. And he came into a lot of money a few months later that he claimed was an inheritance, but don't you think that's strange? It makes more sense that Mr. Wheaton paid him for his silence."

"That sounds like a good story I ain't got a way to prove," I said. "But I'll look into it. You don't know his address, do you?"

She reached into her pocketbook a second time and withdrew a folded sheet of paper. Now I was really suspicious. Usually clients don't tell me everything up front, mostly because they're afraid of looking bad or because they think they can put one over on me. So I was used to that. But this was more like the girl had already decided how things were going to go and was stringing me along. I should have given back the money and the note and referred her to a colleague I hated.

But it was Christmas. And I'm a sucker for a hard luck story.

I'll deny I ever said that.

"Give me your number, and I'll call you when I have news," I said. I unfolded the paper and pushed it toward her along with a pencil.

Miss Greville jerked her hands away like I'd offered her a dead rat. "You can't call me at home. You just can't. I'll be in touch with you in a week—is that enough time?"

"That's Christmas Eve," I said.

She gave me a look that said I was a couple of nickels shy of a dollar. "This is more important than any holiday, Mr. Raven."

Now I knew she was desperate. But I didn't know why. If her story was true, she'd waited a year to go after the guy, and that didn't add up to desperate. I tilted back in my chair again and let my eyes rest on the currently not-working ceiling light. Turning her down made sense. But she'd fired my curiosity. And, I admit, she was easy on the eyes. And, well, Christmas.

"All right," I said, sitting up. "Meet me here in a week, same time."

I rose when she did and took the hand she offered me. It was small and looked delicate in the red kid gloves, but her grip was firm and determined, just like the rest of her. "One week, Mr. Raven," she said, and she was gone.

I blew out a breath, staring at the space where she'd been. Then I picked up the tinsel and went back to draping it over the tree. What I'd bought at the nearest tree lot wasn't much, about chest-high and a little bent, but its branches were full and green and it made the room smell like a pine forest.

Beyond it, out the window, snow had started falling, big fat white puffs of tangled snowflakes that drifted to cover the boxes and piles of trash clogging the alley. By morning, the city would look like a winter wonderland—right up until the trucks got busy churning all that white into a mucky brownish-gray. But all of that was invisible from where I stood, so long as I didn't look down.

I settled the carved wooden angel atop the tree. So maybe its paint was chipped in places, and there were cracks in the wings. I liked it anyway. Probably Miss Greville, or whoever she was, went home to a perfect tree with a perfect angel. And yet she needed my help, me who wasn't perfect at all. That was some kind of Christmas thing, what's it called. A metaphor. This might be my strangest Christmas ever.

It took me a day or two to hunt down Bruce Bannatyne, what with the few other clients I had. Mostly people let their problems simmer around Christmastime, put up with Aunt Marge's kleptomania or Cousin Floyd's infidelity or whatever so they can have peace on earth for a few days. But there was always someone whose anger or pain was too much for them to ignore. So, like I said, I didn't get to Bruce Bannatyne right away. When I did, I got a shock—he was in the phone book. By what Miss Greville had said, I'd thought he was more likely to be on Mars. But no, he was in the regular old phone book.

I decided to try the nice way first and called his house rather than showing up on his doorstep. I got his wife, who took my word that I had business with Bannatyne and helpfully gave me his business address. I thanked her and wished her a Merry Christmas. I like doing that. Most people say it back to you, and then no matter who the person is, whether they're a naïve housewife or a hardened criminal with a set of brass knuckles and a gap-toothed snarl, it's like you have something in common for those couple of seconds.

Bannatyne hadn't gone far from his roots after his last job went sour—he was an assistant manager at a place downtown, First Federal Savings & Loan. I dropped by one afternoon three days before Christmas. It hadn't snowed again since the day Miss Greville brightened my life, and the slush was as gray and full of dog turds as I expected. People thronged the streets, some of them carrying brightly-wrapped gifts, all of them with their heads ducked against the cold and the possibility of meeting someone's eyes.

I held the door to the S&L open for a careworn woman whose coat was three seasons out of date, and smiled when she glanced my way. She had a face Time hadn't been good to, but a spark of pleasure lit deep within her eyes when I gave her that Merry Christmas. I probably wasn't the sort of person she'd give the time of day to normally, me in my elderly suit with the knees a little shiny with wear and my pop's overcoat that was a size or two too large for me, but that's what the season does to you.

The lobby of the S&L was a lot warmer than outside, or maybe it only felt overly warm because of the many lights casting a golden glow over the white walls and brass cages where the clerks sat. The carpet was soaked and muddy right by the door, which was a shame because it was a nice carpet, green and purple with yellow curlicues around the edges. The room smelled of the oranges that decorated the Christmas tree in one corner, and more faintly of cigarette smoke. I put out my own cigarette in the tall brass ashtray just inside the door. Sometimes giving people the chance to offer you a gasper puts them at ease, which always works in my favor.

A pretty girl in a navy skirt and white blouse directed me without question to Bannatyne's office. I wasn't sure what to make of that, whether it meant Bannatyne was a low-level schlub whose time wasn't valuable, or whether I looked like I had legitimate business despite my appearance. Either way, I walked confidently—a confident walk will take you far, even if you're a little shabby, like me—across the lobby to a little door with a brass plaque reading BRUCE BANNATYNE and let the girl open the door for me.

Bannatyne's office looked like a smaller version of the lobby, though the carpet was red and gold with black curlicues and didn't look as if anyone had ever walked on it. Bannatyne himself was a short, round little man who looked like he'd bounce if you dropped him from somewhere high. He had one of those thick, bristly little mustaches like someone broke a toothbrush off under his nose, and the hair on his head wasn't so much receding as making a break for sunnier lands. I didn't like the look of him, though it took a minute to figure out why. When he stood to greet me, I realized how small and close-set his eyes were, and how empty of emotion. You couldn't imagine this guy doing anything so normal as taking a bath or kissing his wife.

"What can I do for you, Mr., ah...?" Bannatyne said when we were both seated.

"I'm investigating the death of Carl Wheaton," I said, ignoring his unspoken request. "I have some questions for you."

Instantly, Bannatyne's small, piggish eyes got smaller as he stared me down. "And you are here on behalf of...?"

"My client insists on confidentiality," I said. "Did you have any clue that Mr. Wheaton intended to kill himself?"

"I don't have to answer any questions. You're not the police." Bannatyne half-rose from his chair. I stayed put.

"You don't," I said, settling into a relaxed pose with my ankle crossed over my knee. "But you might not want them prying into that 'inheritance' you received. Just a thought."

Bannatyne sat back down, slowly. His hands gripped the chair's armrests. "Are you threatening me?"

"Just pointing out the facts. I'm sure the police were satisfied with what they learned. Mr. Wheaton's bank fails, he commits suicide out of remorse. All very straightforward, until you come into a sizable inheritance only a few months later."

"I don't know what you're talking about." Bannatyne's dead, remorseless eyes looked frightened now.

I stayed relaxed, which was good not only for relaxing a suspect but also gave them the impression that I was in control of the conversation. "Let's play a game, okay? It's called 'What If.' What if all that money didn't get lost in the bank's collapse? It had to go *somewhere*, right? And what if Mr. Wheaton took advantage of the collapse?"

"He's dead." Bannatyne's voice shook. He took a silver cigarette case from inside his suit jacket and removed a slim cigarette he then tapped absently against his other fingers. He didn't offer me one. With a hand that trembled as much as his voice, he fumbled out a lighter that matched the case and lit the cigarette. The pungent scent of freshly-burning tobacco made me wish I hadn't gotten rid of mine.

Bannatyne took a long drag on his cigarette and let out smoke in a thin stream that drifted in an air current I hadn't been aware of. Visibly calmer, he said, "Mr. Wheaton is dead. So is his partner. There's nothing more to say."

"If that's the case, you won't mind if I look into that inheritance." I rested my hand on my knee. "It's public record, of course, so it's not like you can stop me. And then I can investigate whatever kind relative left you that money. And *then* I can discover whether you paid taxes on that inheritance. I'm sure the feds will be interested in the answer to that question, too."

Bannatyne stared at me with those horrible piggy eyes. I stared back, calm as ever. Well, it wasn't me I was threatening to destroy. Bannatyne's pasty skin had gone a pale red, and sweat glistened along what was left of his hairline. He raised his cigarette to his lips, but didn't inhale. I waited. I'd been guessing, but I was a good guesser, and I was sure I'd hit Bannatyne where he lived.

Finally, Bannatyne said, "I'm not admitting anything."

"Of course not," I said.

"Because I'm not guilty."

"Of course not."

"And I know nothing about any malfeasance Mr. Wheaton might have committed. I was out of town when he killed himself." Bannatyne tapped ash off the tip of his cigarette into a ceramic ashtray with a picture of a couple of palm trees in its center. The ash made the trees look like they'd contracted some terrible disease.

"Naturally you wouldn't know," I said, in a friendly but not too cheerful tone. I didn't want to risk him shutting up.

Bannatyne glanced at his window, which was high and narrow and full of that pebbly glass it's impossible to see out of. "But if you spoke to Martin Lennox," he said, drawling out the words like they were cut with honey, "you might learn something more." Either the cigarette or the conversation had put him to rights, because he wasn't shaking anymore.

"Martin Lennox," I said. I took my small leatherbound notebook out of my jacket and made a note. I didn't actually need the notebook, but it gave people the impression that I was serious about their problems. "And he lives where?"

Bannatyne smiled for the first time. It made him look even more like a pig, but one that had trampled the farmer and eaten one of his limbs. "I don't remember."

I felt like I was losing control of the situation. I might have frightened Bannatyne before, but that fear was gone. "That's all right," I said, rising from my chair. "I'll find him. Merry Christmas."

Bannatyne continued to look at me with those awful eyes. "I'm sure it will be for some," he said.

I let myself out and headed for the door, walking slowly so it wouldn't look like I was running away.

I cleaned my place on Christmas Eve day like I always did.

That's a lie. I never cleaned more or less on that day than I did on all the others. But I told myself I was making things nice for Christmas Day and didn't listen to the jeering voice in my skull. The one that taunted me with how Miss Greville, who was married and almost certainly unavailable, was coming over soon and probably wouldn't even notice the state of my apartment. Which was more a room than an apartment, like I needed any more reminders of how successful I wasn't.

I drew water at the sink with its one cold-water tap and wiped down the antique desk and bookcases. I dusted the books. Then I had to wipe down the bookcase again to get rid of the flecks of gray dust that stuck to the wet boards. I washed the window for the first time in months, even digging into the corners with my thumbnail to get all the gunk. I swept the floor and scrubbed the spots where I'd dropped food and been too lazy to wipe it up right away. I moved the bottle of Jack Daniel's from the deep bottom drawer of the desk to the corner "kitchen" cupboard and pulled the sheet on its hooks to hide everything back there.

Then I stood in front of the Christmas tree, not really looking at it, just thinking about years past. How mom and pop always made Christmas special, even when we didn't have nothing but a pine branch in a corner. We hung up our stockings every year, and every year they had something in them. Sometimes it wasn't more than a Christmas orange, but it was something. I guess maybe that ought to make Christmas a bad memory, now mom and pop are gone and it's just me in this tiny room, but it never has.

A knock on the door startled me out of the past. I checked my breath, smoothed my hair back, and took my time ambling over to the door. Today, Miss Greville wore a blue dress three shades darker than her eyes, along with a black hat with an iridescent raven's feather in it and black shoes with a neat little bow over each toe. She was as much a knockout as ever. I kept myself from drooling like an ape and invited her in.

If she noticed my cleaning, she didn't say nothing. She took the seat in front of the desk and held her pocketbook, blue to match her dress, on her knees like a girl carrying a lunch pail to school. "Mr. Raven," she said.

"Miss Greville," I replied. "Merry Christmas."

She blinked as if she didn't understand the words. "Did you find anything?"

Much as I liked having that greeting returned, usually it don't bother me if someone don't say 'Merry Christmas' back. This time, it felt like a slap to the face, and I wasn't sure why. "I did," I said, hiding my disappointment. "I'm not sure it will satisfy you."

Miss Greville just nodded. "I'll be the judge of that."

I leaned back in my chair the way I do when I'm delivering good news to a client. I hoped it was good news, anyway. "Mr. Bannatyne definitely had something to do with the con. He confirmed that Mr. Wheaton faked his death and ran off with the money."

Miss Greville closed her eyes and let out a breath like I'd saved her from falling. "I can't believe it. I felt I was right, but that's not the same as having the truth confirmed. Where did he go?"

I hesitated. I had expected Miss Greville to be glad, of course, but she had sounded satisfied the way a predator is when it runs its prey down. It made me uncomfortable, and I never let clients get to me that way. "He's going by the name Martin Lennox now. I found out Mr. Lennox don't have much of a history before last year, and he's wealthy enough to be Mr. Wheaton if Wheaton stole all that dough. I also got a picture of Mr. Wheaton out of the newspaper archives, and it's definitely the same guy."

Miss Greville's eyes flew open. "You make it sound like this Mr. Lennox lives in the city."

"Outside the city a few miles, but yeah. Close enough."

Her lips pressed together in a hard, white line, a contrast to the pink that crept over her face. "Curse him," she whispered. "Steals everything from me, and has the nerve to stay where his crime was committed. Curse him." Her black gloves twisted her pocketbook out of shape, though she didn't look like she knew she was doing it.

"I think we have enough to go to the police," I said. Then I cursed myself for how helpful I'd sounded. This wasn't my job. My job was to find out whatever the client asked for, not hand people over to the cops. But this girl had me thinking crazy.

Miss Greville's gaze came back into focus. "The police?"

"Isn't that what you wanted? To bring Mr. Wheaton to justice?" She'd spoken with such astonishment I doubted my own memory for a minute. What *had* Miss Greville asked for?

"And what will the police do?" She now sounded scathing, like I'd suggested something so stupid she couldn't believe she had to tell me it was idiotic. "They won't believe me. Or Mr. Wheaton will buy them off." She wiped her eyes with one gloved hand. "It doesn't matter. All I wanted was to know I wasn't delusional."

"You said you wanted your money back." I didn't know why I was still pushing, except that none of this made no sense.

"He's spent it all by now. And how would I get the money back, anyway?" Miss Greville stood. "Thank you for your time, Mr. Raven. What more do I owe you?"

I hadn't kept track of what I'd put into finding Wheaton/Lennox. "I, uh, another twenty."

Miss Greville pulled out a thin wad of cash and peeled off a twenty. "Are you sure?"

"It wasn't hard work. And it's Christmas." I knew I was babbling, but I couldn't shut myself up.

"Then...because it's Christmas," Miss Greville said, and handed me a second twenty. "Please, take it. With my thanks." And then she was gone, out the door and out of my life for good.

I stared at the back of the door for a bit before coming to myself and putting the cash away in the desk. Then I sat in my chair and pulled open the bottom drawer before I remembered I'd stashed the whiskey in the kitchen corner. It felt like too much effort to go all the way across the room just for a slug. So instead I leaned back until my chair's front legs left the floor, and I stared at the ceiling and tried to make things make sense.

Miss Greville had been clear the first time, now that she was gone and I could think straight. She had wanted me to find Wheaton so she could get her money back. And now, after I'd found Wheaton in his new identity, she'd given up. Worse, she'd lied to me about what she wanted. Maybe she'd counted on me being so fuddled by her beauty that I wouldn't question her. And maybe it had almost worked. But I hadn't survived in this business for a dozen years by letting a pretty face and great gams sucker me.

I got up and threw on my overcoat. There was one other person who knew the truth about what Miss Greville wanted. And I had a hunch he'd be home on Christmas Eve.

Martin Lennox's house was set way back from the road between some low hills, surrounded by forest that in summer would hide the place completely. Even in winter, the trees' branches made for good cover. I guessed they were oaks, mainly because that's the only kind of tree I know. Probably they were something fancier only rich people could afford to plant.

I nearly drove past the side road leading to Lennox's estate and had to back up, skidding some, to make the turn. Once I was inside the trees, the snow didn't fall so heavy, and it was easier going. The trees caked in snow leaned in over me like some kind of guardians, watching my old Studebaker and judging it. I'd got it at a police auction three years ago, and it wasn't anything special, but it got me where I needed to go and it sometimes fooled people into thinking I was better off than I was.

Ahead, one of the trees dumped a load of snow on the road in front of me, and I braked too hard and skidded again. I laughed at myself. Nervous because of a bunch of trees. I wasn't ever nervous of anything. It was the snow, and the silence, and the not knowing what lay ahead that did it.

Eventually the road opened up, and the house appeared. Martin Lennox's home wasn't so much a house as an estate, a big old stone and glass thing that reminded me of that one place where the king of England lives, Something Castle. The one with all the windows. It was three stories tall and most of a city block wide, with a sloping roof the snow frosted like the biggest ginger-bread house ever made. The snow made it look brighter than it was, all that dark stone and the unlit windows that said Lennox wasn't entertaining for Christmas Eve. Lights burned at the covered doorway and in a couple of windows on the third floor, but other than that, it might have been deserted. I was pretty sure old King George's castle never looked this abandoned.

The road turned into a curved driveway, barely visible under the thick snow, that made a big circle in front of the covered door-way. Tire tracks slowly filling with white flakes showed where someone else had driven up recently, though I didn't see a car. Those tracks veered off to the right side of the house and vanished. I guessed there was a garage on that side. Since I was a guest—an uninvited guest, even—I parked in front of the house a few feet away from the door.

The snow was heavy enough now it fell into my shoes, freezing my feet as I hurried to the door and rang the bell. There was a little covered patio over the two massive front doors that looked even more like they belonged on a castle. Even the bell was fancy, a pull rope rather than a buzzer. I yanked on the rope harder than I probably had to and stuck my hands under my arms to warm them. Even my gloves weren't enough to keep the chill away.

No one answered. After a minute, I pulled the bell rope again. This time, I heard it ring in the distance, the faintest jingle like frozen Christmas bells. Still no one came to the door. I stamped my feet to get some feeling back into them and knocked on the right-hand door. I didn't think I'd knocked all that hard, but the door swung open, spilling golden light over the doorstep. It was too cold to hesitate. I pushed the door open the rest of the way and walked in.

The room beyond wasn't an ordinary hall, it was as big as a theater lobby and had the same smell, warmed-over cleanser mixed with flowers. The light came from a chandelier covered in crystals that glittered like sun on snow. It was bright enough to show clearly all the paintings hanging on the walls between wide, empty doorways on either side and the rooms beyond. One of them was a dining room, its glossy chestnut-colored table bare of tablecloth or place settings. The other had a bunch of chairs and couches that all matched, and more paintings hung on those walls. I don't know anything about art, but I guessed those were all originals, because what would be the point of living somewhere this fancy and not having the most expensive stuff you could buy?

I wiped my feet on the rug, hoping it wasn't one of those expensive Persian carpets, and stuck my hands in my coat pockets so I wouldn't touch things just because they probably shouldn't be touched. "Hello?" I called out. "Hey, the door was open, and..." That made me sound weak. I walked toward the stairs, remembering that the lights I'd seen from the outside were on the third floor. "Mr. Lennox? I want to talk to you about Carl Wheaton."

My voice echoed a bit in that huge space, but I still heard no one but me. I came to a stop at the stairs. Someone had walked up them recently, someone with small feet whose shoes had left wet marks on the first three or four steps. Warning bells went off in my head, though I didn't know why. The house was too quiet, and why wasn't there some butler or something to open the door?

I was most of the way to the third floor when I heard voices, one male, one female. The man's voice was low and rumbling, not at all excited. The woman's voice was a lot higher, of course, but it also sounded agitated, sometimes hitting a shrill, angry note. I knew that voice. I sprinted the rest of the way up the stairs and ran for the only open door I could see, one where a pale wedge of light lit up the carpet beside it.

I flung that door open, not thinking it might be a stupid idea.

The room beyond was hotter than asphalt on a summer day thanks to a blazing fire in a fireplace big enough to sleep in. It was the only light in the room, too, making as many shadows as it did lights. The shadows flickered over the giant executive's desk and leather upholstered chairs and the bookcase filled with books all the same color and height. Beyond the three tall, narrow windows, the snow blew in great gusts that rattled the glass.

The firelight cast shadows over the other two people in the room. The man was tall and slim in a suit that cost more than my car had when it was new, with well-cut dark hair going silver and a narrow face all the girls probably went crazy for. He had his back to the windows and stood with his hands well away from his sides, like he was trying to calm the situation.

Miss Greville stood facing the man, which put her back to me. She wore a black coat trimmed with mink and the same black hat she'd worn that afternoon at my place. In both hands she held a Browning 1911 aimed at the man's heart. She didn't flinch or turn when I entered.

"It's over," the man said. "Put down the gun, and you can walk away. I won't call the police."

"It won't be over until you're dead," Miss Greville said. Her voice shook the way her hands didn't.

"You want a witness? Someone to swear to how you murdered me?" The man didn't sound at all worried, which told me he wasn't as smart as he thought he was. He probably thought one woman was no danger no matter how big her gun. But I've known plenty of women capable of killing, and I figured this guy should maybe shut his mouth. I didn't say anything, though, just sidled around slowly to where I could see Miss Greville's face.

She still didn't look at me. Tears made long silver streaks down her face, but her jaw was rigid. "I don't care what happens to me.

They can hang me if that's what it takes to finally bring you to justice."

"Mrs. Norland," the man, Carl Wheaton or Martin Lennox or whatever, said. He took a step forward, still with his hands outstretched. Miss Greville's gun twitched, and Wheaton stopped. "We can work something out."

That name was familiar. "Norland," I said. "That was Wheaton's partner. The one who..." Things were falling into place.

"My husband," Miss Greville—Mrs. Norland—said. "He worked hard and did his best to keep the bank solvent, and then *you*—" The gun twitched again. "You stole everything and left him facing criminal prosecution. He killed himself because he couldn't live with the shame. Killed himself *on Christmas Eve*, you fiend. And now I'm going to balance the scales."

Wheaton glanced at me. "Stop her," he said through gritted teeth. "You're not going to watch her shoot me in cold blood, are you?"

I stayed put. "Mrs. Norland," I said, keeping my voice calm. "This guy is the one who should go to prison, not you. If you shoot him, the courts won't care that it was justice."

"Justice?" Wheaton exclaimed. "How is this justice?"

"You shut up," I said. "Listen to me, Mrs. Norland. Is this really what you want?"

For the first time, Mrs. Norland looked at me, just the briefest glance, then back at Wheaton. "Yes," she said, and pulled the trigger.

The gunshot sounded like cannon fire in the low-ceilinged room. Wheaton staggered backward into one of the windows, which cracked, but didn't break. Bright crimson blossomed on his white shirt, spreading fast like oil on water. He blinked at me, once, twice, and then he slid down the window to sprawl on the floor beneath it.

Mrs. Norland stood with the heavy gun gripped in one hand, staring at the body. Her chest heaved with her breathing, deep gasps like she'd just run ten miles. Then she let the gun fall to the floor and turned to me. "So that's it," she said. Her voice sounded dull, almost numb. "I'll go without fighting you. If you don't mind taking me in. I'm not sure I have the nerve to drive up to a police station and confess on my own."

I took a good, long look at her. She was as beautiful as the day she'd walked through my door. Tears still ran down her face, and I was pretty sure she didn't know she was crying. She was looking at my chest, not my eyes, the image of someone who'd made it to the finish line and didn't know what to do next.

I took her hand and examined it. "Gloves," I said. "Good. No fingerprints."

Her head came up fast, and those amazing blue eyes met mine. "Fingerprints?"

"On the gun. And it's too big a gun for a woman. That's good, too. Did anyone let you in?"

She shook her head. "He said the staff have the night off. For Christmas."

"Even better." I snugged my own gloves tighter over my hands. "Now, get out of here."

Mrs. Norland looked more confused than ever. "Get out? But I killed him."

"I never saw you. You and I were never here. By morning, the way the snow is falling, no one can prove otherwise." I turned my back on her in a deliberate, this-conversation-is-over way.

I heard her let out a deep sigh. Then the door creaked open wider, and footsteps sounded in the hall, gradually fading to silence.

I gave her a few minutes to get her car out and on the road. I was right about the snow, and it wasn't likely anyone was coming out here before morning, but it's smart not to take chances. Then I nudged the gun with my toe before deciding it could stay where it was. Better keep things simple.

After I'd counted to one hundred, staring down the body like I was daring it to stand up and challenge me, I left the room and shut the door behind me. The house still smelled like a theater. The smell of blood was just my imagination.

There were fresh tire tracks on the driveway when I got to my car. I started the Studebaker up and drove slowly away, keeping my eyes on the road. My headlights lit up the snow that now gusted and blew in the wind, making it look like white streaks rather than individual flakes. I'd never seen anything so beautiful.

When I got back to the city, I parked my car and strolled up the five flights of stairs to my room. I didn't bother turning on the light, which probably wouldn't have worked anyway. Instead, I got the bottle of whiskey and the last of my glass tumblers and sat behind my desk, tilting the chair back until the front legs left the ground. I poured myself a splash of amber liquor and sipped it rather than tossing it back like I usually did.

The odds weren't great. People who committed crimes usually confessed eventually, either out of guilt or out of a need for others to know what they'd almost gotten away with. But I had a hunch Mrs. Norland would beat the odds. And maybe now this holiday wouldn't be a nightmare memory for her. Maybe I'd given her that.

What can I say? I've always loved Christmas.

Wrapped Up With a Bow

And now for something lighthearted to follow that last story…

I don't generally write straight-up romances, being interested in fantasy stories with a strong romantic element, but when I was challenged to come up with a romance centered on a Christmas-adjacent holiday, this one sprang into being fully formed.

St. Stephen's Day, or Boxing Day as it is in modern times, is surrounded by a lot of tradition no one can prove true or false. The accepted story is that December 26 is a day when rich people give charity to their servants or other of the poor in the form of boxes of food or used clothing. In the course of planning this story, I skimmed the internet looking for any evidence for the origins of this tradition and came up blank. I decided this gave me leeway to assume pretty much anything I liked about the tradition, and thus this story was born.

Alexander, Duke of Sherburne, cast his gaze around the drawing room, decorated in an outdated, baroque style by his mother twenty years ago and never changed since. Gilding decorated the moldings and doors and every chair and sofa and round-topped table crowding the room, complemented by the shining brass chandelier dripping with crystals that winked tiny rainbows across every surface. Family portraits occupied every inch of wall space, their frames gilt. It was his least favorite room in the house, and he wished he had not been lured here. It represented his dissatisfaction with his current lot.

The Christmas season should have been a time of unalloyed happiness. He was wealthy, titled, and had an estate that made him the envy of his peers. He was even considered handsome, though in his more cynical moments he thought being wealthy, titled, and landed might improve his appearance substantially as far as young, unmarried ladies' opinions went. He should have had the many events of the season to look forward to—the balls, the pantomimes, the evening parties.

Instead, what he had was the Countess of Brightwell nattering on at him about his Duties to the Name, a subject she could speak on endlessly. How she managed to insert capital letters into her speech was a mystery of the ages.

"...and, Alexander—are you listening?"

"Yes, Sarah," Alexander said, not listening. Sarah, Lady Brightwell, was his younger sister and had been a nag even as a child. He had perfected the art of hearing her without listening years before.

"I *said*," Sarah said in some irritation, "you really should choose a young lady to open the ball tonight. You have a Duty that should not be Neglected. Why you will not settle down and produce an Heir to the Name, I cannot comprehend. Now, the younger Dane girl is not acceptable, she is rather Eccentric, but the Honorable Eugenia Dane is eminently suitable as a partner—"

"It's your dance, Sarah, not mine. Yours is the responsibility to open the ball." Alexander immediately regretted being drawn into the conversation. Sarah was even better at goading him into a response than she was at nagging.

"I'm afraid I have business to attend to," he added before she could respond. "Pray, excuse me." He strode off down the hall and through a door, not concealing the fact that he was fleeing. Sarah would not stoop to running after him the way she had when they were children, but it was better not to take the risk.

He passed the door to his study without pausing and pushed through the green baize door to the servants' quarters. The kitchen smelled deliciously of roast goose and pork, Christmas pudding and sweet syllabub, all in preparation for supper. With Christmas falling on a Sunday this year, Sarah had not wished to host a gala until the day after, St. Stephen's Day. Alexander never minded her co-opting his home for her lavish parties, as her own estate was deep in the country and her husband, Lord Brightwell, detested entertaining. But Alexander had made it clear from the start that he would not be involved. He had other concerns on St. Stephen's Day today.

He made his way to what his manservant Lassiter referred to as the "mud room," though Alexander had never seen it other than perfectly clean. Here was where the gardeners stowed their overalls and other accoutrements of the trade, where boots were taken for cleaning and where, in a cubby, the boot-boy slept. He was not there now, but Lassiter was, holding a pile of folded clothes. "Here you are, your Grace," he said.

"I am indeed, Lassiter," Alexander said. "And not before time, too."

"They do not mind waiting on you, your Grace." Lassiter set his armload aside and assisted his master in removing his coat, pantaloons, and shirt, carefully folding each item and topping the pile with Alexander's starched cravat. Alexander quickly donned the clothing Lassiter provided: a roughly woven shirt, workman's trousers, and a coat stained at the cuffs with something dark Alexander chose not to inquire about.

"Boots, your Grace," Lassiter said, handing the items over. Alexander shoved his feet into them without assistance and accepted the wide-brimmed hat Lassiter extended to him.

"How do I look?" he said.

Lassiter shuddered. "The very picture of a common laborer, your Grace. The hat alone—"

"Perfect," Alexander said. "Is everything loaded up?"

"To my knowledge, yes, your Grace. Are you certain you don't wish me to join you?"

Lassiter asked this question every year, and every year Alexander took pity on him. "No, that will be all, Lassiter. Thank you for your assistance."

Lassiter bowed, but Alexander caught a glimpse of his face; he looked ruefully amused at his lordly master's idiosyncrasies. "Then good luck to you, your Grace."

Alexander pushed open the back door and emerged into the kitchen garden. It was mostly dead at this time of year, the frozen stalks all that remained of last autumn's harvest. Grey overcast concealed the sun, and without even its feeble wintry rays to melt it, frost still clung to the earth and the dead plants like sugar crystals dusting a cake. Alexander drew in a deep, chilly breath and let it out in a great plume of condensation. He liked winter, how it invigorated him. He liked the winter holidays. But he liked St. Stephen's Day best of all.

He strode through the garden and around the corner to where

the estate wagon waited, the horses already harnessed. Boxes, bags, and a largish barrel were packed neatly in its bed. A servant shivered nearby, the reins in his hands. "Your Grace," he said, "everything's ready for you."

"Thank you," Alexander said. It embarrassed him that he did not know the man's name. He did make an effort, but the estate required so many servants to keep it running, and Tarleton, his steward, continually hired new ones, not to mention the men and women Sarah had brought in to help with the gala. He compensated by smiling warmly at the man, who shivered again. "Go and have some tea," he told the servant, who immediately handed over the reins and hurried for the kitchen door.

Alexander climbed up and snapped the reins. The horses, big stolid beasts who looked capable of pulling the wagon for days, stepped out promptly, their own breath steaming in the cold air. In minutes, they were well away from the house and headed up the long driveway leading to the gate.

Alexander consulted his mental map of the area. He could not, of course, take his bounty to his own parish church, where he would be recognized. The point of this was to give anonymously, after all. And he had recently been to St. Anne's over Buxton way, so that would not work either. But the church at Arringford...he did not know the name, but it was sizable and would be perfect for his needs. He flicked the reins again, and the horses sped up.

He never felt so close to the memory of his father as on St. Stephen's Day. The tradition of putting together boxes of food or clothing or small household items for the poor was, well, traditional among his social class, but Alexander's father had taken it a step further by delivering the goods himself. "It is easy for those of us who have plenty to give," he had told a young Alexander the first year the boy had been allowed to come along, "but we should never make it so easy that we have nothing at all to do with the giving." And Alexander, wide-eyed and thrilled at his father's attention, had helped carry boxes to the parish church and fallen asleep on the wagon seat afterward.

Now Alexander considered whether he should not make a serious effort to find a wife, so he could have a son to pass the tradition on to. It was just that all the young ladies he met—women Sarah flung at his head, to be honest—were pretty and vapid and self-absorbed. None of them were the kind of ladies who would understand why St. Stephen's Day mattered. He sighed and pushed the awkward hat back on his head. Someday, maybe, but likely not tonight, not if the very suitable Miss Dane waited in his future.

The journey to Arringford took nearly an hour. Alexander met very few travelers during that time, and none of them looked up to acknowledge him. The lack of friendliness lowered his spirits, and when he reached the church at Arringford, he almost wished he had not bothered. He reminded himself that charity was not about being thanked and drove the wagon into the churchyard.

His was not the only wagon there. Three others laden with boxes were in varying stages of being unloaded, and men dressed as Alexander was carried their burdens around the rear of the church. Alexander climbed down, looking for direction. No one seemed to be in charge. He shrugged and walked to the wagon's rear to unload.

He came around the wagon's corner and ran into someone who let out an exclamation of surprise before hitting the ground. "I beg your pardon, this is all my fault," he said, and bent to offer the young lady a hand up. Then he stopped, arrested by a pair of large, black-fringed eyes that were the bluest he had ever seen. He realized he was staring with his mouth open and shut it firmly. "Let me give you a hand up," he added, this time remembering to mimic Abel the dairyman's lower-class accent. It wasn't a good imitation, but he rarely needed it to be.

"Oh, that is—of course, I—really, I should have been watching my step," the young lady said. She sounded as flustered as he felt, and as soon as she was on her feet she ducked her head, concealing her remarkable eyes. Dark blonde hair tied tightly back from her face peeped from beneath her plain brown bonnet.

"No, not at all," Alexander said. Then, out of nowhere, he said, "My name is, er, Comstock. Mr. Comstock." It was actually the name of his factor in London, but it was the first that came to mind. He certainly could not give her his real name.

"Thank you, Mr. Comstock." She raised her head, and although the air was chilly, Alexander was certain her cheeks were red with embarrassment and not with cold. Then she smiled. She had the most beautiful smile Alexander had ever seen.

"Now that I've embarrassed us both, can I ask your name?" he asked.

Her smile deepened. "Miss Overton. I help with our church's St. Stephen's Day collection every year."

"That is—that be right generous of you."

Miss Overton blushed again. "Oh, no, it is—really, it is the least I can do. Have you a contribution? Oh, how silly of me, of course you do. Let me show you..." Her voice trailed off, and she waved a hand vaguely in the direction of the church. She spoke like someone whose rural accents had been polished at a dame school. Alexander found it unexpectedly charming.

He hefted a box from the wagon and was alarmed to see Miss Overton take a small bag as well. "You shouldn't feel obligated," he said.

"I have two good hands, and I don't see why I shouldn't put them to use. Follow me, Mr. Comstock." She marched away, and Alexander followed, more charmed than ever.

Alexander was not an expert on church buildings, but he thought this one might be older even than Protestantism, and might perhaps have once been a monastery based on its odd construction. The ancient stones radiated cold, even indoors, and Alexander was grateful for his gloves and the heavy coat.

Inside, tables had been set to collect the gifts. They were already overflowing with boxes and bags. "It's a lovely display, isn't it?" Miss Overton said. "So much given in charity. My old—that is, an old friend said it might as well be all wrapped up with a bow to make it festive, but I think the spirit of giving is what makes it beautiful, don't you?"

"That were my father's belief, too." Alexander maneuvered past another man, awkwardly because he did not wish to lose sight of the young lady. Perhaps she would return to the wagon with him. Speaking to her again was suddenly his main preoccupation.

A curate directed those unloading to set items down in groups according to type. Alexander put his box with the rest of the food-stuffs and turned to ask Miss Overton a question, any question, anything that would allow him to continue their conversation. But when he turned around, she was gone.

Disappointed, he went back for another load only to find more men busy taking boxes from his wagon into the church. All that remained was the barrel, which Alexander knew to contain good fresh cider, not hard yet. He put his arms around it and tried to lift it. The barrel rocked slightly, but otherwise remained where it was. He squatted, took a lower grip, and heaved with his legs.

Pain shot through his thighs, a great tearing sound came from behind, but the barrel lifted. Alexander heard a giggle behind him. He turned, bringing the barrel with him, and saw Miss Overton standing there, a hand held over her mouth to capture any more giggles. "It's my trousers, isn't it," Alexander said. "I'm afeared that were all the dignity I had to hand."

"I apologize for laughing, Mr. Comstock," Miss Overton said. Her marvelous blue eyes did not look as if they regretted their mirth.

"Not at all. I would laugh meself if I had breath to spare." Alexander managed to set the barrel down and climb out of the wagon. "At any rate, they'll keep until I get home."

"Pray, permit me to mend them," Miss Overton said. "There are so many gently-worn clothes in the donation boxes, and you can wear something from them while I stitch yours."

Alexander opened his mouth to protest that she need not put herself out, but the thought that this would give him more time with her stopped his words. "That be right kind of you, if you're sure you can be spared."

"It is no trouble. Come with me."

She led him to a small room opening off the nave and left him to change into the trousers he'd selected from the piles of clothing. The room was as cold as the rest of the church, with walls unadorned by anything except a single lamp that cast strange shadows over the walls and ceiling. Alexander wondered what it was normally used for. Surely nothing that required changing clothes, as he was nearly frozen from the short time he stood there in his drawers and stocking feet.

Eventually, he emerged and handed the torn trousers to Miss Overton, who had a needle and thread ready. He watched her stitch the seam with tiny, neat stitches that surely were the result of many years' practice. It occurred to him that likely none of Sarah's eligible young ladies had such experience. Then he wondered why it mattered. Miss Overton was beautiful, and charming, and skilled, and generous, but she was almost certainly some farmer's daughter, no one of his social class and no one he should entertain such thoughts about.

"How did you get to have such skill, Miss Overton?" he asked to distract himself from dwelling on her lovely small hands working so deftly with the needle.

Miss Overton laughed. "I sew my own clothing, Mr. Comstock. Many women do."

"I suppose." Sarah had three seamstresses in her employ and had never to his knowledge threaded a needle. Again, the difference in their stations struck him, this time with a pang of sadness. It was all very well in novels for noblemen to wed poor girls and elevate them, but that never worked in real life. Then he wondered why he was thinking about marriage in connection with a young lady he had met scarcely half an hour ago.

He realized Miss Overton was addressing him. "You do not live in this neighborhood, do you?"

"No, I...live in the next parish over." That did not make sense; why would he have driven all the way here if he had a parish church near to hand? "They...had a right surplus this year, and suggested I come here with my collection."

"That's very generous." Miss Overton did not sound suspicious, and Alexander relaxed. "And generous of you to give up your time."

"It means I met you, so I hardly regret it." The words left Alexander's mouth without engaging his brain. Miss Overton blushed again and ducked her head, but she was smiling. Her smile struck him to the heart.

"Tell me where you live," he demanded. It was foolishness, but he could not bear the thought of letting her go. He would court her as Mr. Comstock, and hang the consequences.

Miss Overton's smile vanished. She knotted her thread and bit it off, completely unselfconsciously, then handed him the mended trousers. "I live ten miles from here," she said. "Near Buxton. This is my affianced husband's parish."

Alexander once more felt as if he had been struck, but this

time it hurt like shards of ice piercing his flesh. "I see," he said, his face numb. "You intend to marry."

"After Epiphany." Miss Overton's blue eyes met his. "I should —that is, I regret—"

"Say no more," Alexander said, managing a smile through frozen lips. "I have enjoyed our meeting, Miss Overton. Thank you for your assistance." He bowed and went back into the tiny frozen box of a room, where he stood motionless. Affianced husband. Of course. That was fortunate; her engagement had saved him making an utter fool of himself. They could not be happy together even if she was free.

He slowly changed into the mended trousers and pulled his boots back on. It was not as if they had known each other for more than an hour. He was a fool to make more of their connection than that. Tonight, he would make an effort to get to know Sarah's eligible young ladies, and eventually...

He drove home huddled into himself against the cold. How astonishing that he had ever embraced it.

Despite his reservations about his sister's gala, Alexander had to admit she had outdone herself in the décor. In previous years, she had brought in elaborate swaths of silk and toile to drape the walls, or set up lattices woven with gold ribbon, but this year, she had chosen simplicity. Green pine boughs draped every window and door, brightened by the glossy red apples wired to them. More fruits, oranges and apples of many hues, filled glass vases that stood on the mantel and on tables by the doors. The show of nature's bounty drove the cold wind that blew around the house a little farther away.

He stood in the doorway to the drawing room where the card tables were set and observed the scene. Candles filled the three chandeliers to bursting, shedding a brilliant warm light over the parquet floor and the many guests thronging the ballroom. The room smelled deliciously of pine and sweet apple and hot wax, smells that relieved some of the tension Alexander felt. For once, he was not crowded about by guests, though that would last only as long as Sarah did not realize he was present.

He had not been able to stop thinking of Miss Overton all afternoon and cursed his weakness. She was completely unavailable, and dwelling on what he couldn't have was not only foolish, it was counterproductive, if what he wished was a wife. He should be grateful to her for making him see his own desires clearly. But the memory of her eyes and her wonderful smile would not leave him.

Snarling at himself, he strode through the crowd, which bode well to become a sad crush, but at the moment was thin enough he didn't need to worry about bumping into people. Where was Sarah? Greeting her guests, no doubt, but she would make time to introduce him to her many young ladies. The eligible Miss Dane, who was probably stick-thin with a face like a horse, the way his luck was running.

He heard Sarah over the din of people talking and laughing. She was using her hostess voice, with rich, round tones and an aristocratic accent even plummier than the one she used for everyday. For a moment, he paused, feeling his usual reluctance to be drawn into Sarah's plans. But there was nothing for it, if he wished to find a wife. Sarah might tease him, but he could endure that.

Sarah spotted him across the entrance hall and indicated he should join her with a small nod. Alexander smiled and shook hands and nodded at the guests, most of whom he did not know, until he reached his sister's side. "A great success," he told her, pitching his voice above the noise.

"Of course it is," Sarah said. "Oh, Lady Hakesworth, what a pleasure. May I introduce to you my brother, the Duke of Sherburne?"

Alexander bowed to the elderly lady whose puce dress would have better suited a much younger woman. "Will you open the dancing soon?" he asked Sarah when the old lady was gone.

Sarah's eyes widened. "I did not believe you cared."

"You may have a point about my, er, duties to the title." Alexander suppressed his annoyance at being effectively his sister's supplicant. "I should at least make an effort to be polite."

Sarah gripped his forearm. "Of course you should. And I know just the young lady."

"The estimable Miss Dane?" Alexander reminded himself not to roll his eyes.

"Indeed, and you will find her most engaging, Alexander." Sarah converted her grip on his forearm into hooking her arm through his so it probably appeared he was guiding her instead of her tugging him inexorably forward. "So charming, so accomplished, and possessed of quite the fortune, not that that matters to you, of course..."

"Yes, Sarah." Alexander had once more stopped listening. She would introduce him, and he would ask the young lady to dance, and then he would repeat the process, over and over until the evening ended. And he would tell himself he enjoyed it.

Sarah led him to where two ladies were conversing. The one facing him was an older woman, still quite handsome, her blonde hair showing only a trace of silver. The other had her back to him, and at the sight of her dark blonde hair gathered loosely at the back of her head, his heart skipped a beat. Surely it could not be she. That was impossible. Miss Overton—but the height was right, the hair the correct color, even the slope of her shoulders was familiar.

Alexander's steps quickened with eagerness until Sarah jerked on his arm and said, "Really, Alexander, must you be so uncouth? It is not as if Miss Dane is going anywhere." She brought them to a halt beside the women and said, "Lady de Winter, Miss Dane, may I make known to you my brother, the Duke of Sherburne? Your Grace, Lady de Winter and the Honorable Eugenia Dane."

Miss Dane turned to face Alexander, and he braced himself for an outburst of surprise as she realized who he was. Then he saw her face. She was not Miss Overton, after all. She did not even resemble Miss Overton except in her coloring. Even her eyes, while blue, were a washed-out shade that did not come close to the brilliance of Miss Overton's.

Alexander bowed low so as to hide his irrational disappointment. "Lady de Winter, Miss Dane, it is a pleasure. You are new to our neighborhood, are you not?"

"Yes, my lord, and we have received *such* a welcome as I never expected!" Lady de Winter's voice was high-pitched like a canary's, tweeting high on every word she emphasized. "I do declare it is a *pity* Lord de Winter did not join us tonight, as I'm certain he would positively *dote* on an acquaintance with you, my lord."

"I shall look forward to meeting the viscount one day," Alexander said politely but without warmth. Miss Dane was smiling at him, but in a coquettish way that did not suit her rather narrow features and faded eyes. Now he regretted the impulse that had put him in Sarah's power, and by extension this young woman's. But he was here, and there were Things expected of him. He groaned inwardly. Sarah's capital letters were contagious.

"Miss Dane," he said, "I—"

"Oh, Clarissa!" Lady de Winter said, beckoning to someone

behind Alexander. "Do join me, child, and pray do not stumble so."

At that moment, someone bumped into Alexander and exclaimed, "Oh, I beg your pardon, sir! I fear I missed my step."

Alexander whipped around, his mouth open in astonishment. "You," he said, then could think of nothing else to say.

It was Miss Overton.

She let out a little shriek, then covered her mouth exactly as she had that morning. "You," she said. "But—"

Without looking away from those brilliant blue eyes, Alexander grabbed Sarah's hand. "Introduce us," he demanded.

"Why—good heavens, Alexander, release me," Sarah said, wrenching away. "Miss Dane, this is my brother, Lord Sherburne. Lord Sherburne, the Honorable Clarissa Dane."

"Miss Clarissa Dane," Alexander said.

"Lord Sherburne," Miss Overton—Miss Clarissa Dane—said.

"Yes, my lord, this is my younger daughter," Lady de Winter said.

"The eccentric one," Alexander said without thinking.

Sarah gasped; Lady de Winter said, "I *beg* your pardon, my lord!"; and Miss Dane let out a disdainful sniff. But the younger Miss Dane laughed. Her smile enchanted him all over again. It *was* she!

Excitement and joy and a trace of relief bubbled up inside Alexander. He extended his arm. "Miss Dane," he said, "might I have the pleasure of this dance?"

She took his arm, and he thrilled at how her whole face shone with pleasure at his touch. "It would be an honor, your Grace," she said.

The elder Miss Dane let out a squeak of dismay. Alexander ignored her.

He escorted Miss Dane away and suddenly realized the

dancing had not started yet. He gracefully steered her into a quiet corner beneath an enormous swag of pine studded with rosy apples. "I beg your pardon," he said. "I seem to have abducted you."

"That is as well, for it saves me the trouble of abducting *you*," Miss Dane said. "How—you deceived me!" Her accent was more patrician than it had been before, but it still sounded like music.

"And you deceived me. I believe that makes us even." Alexander could not stop staring. She was the same woman he had met that morning, but her hair was arranged prettily rather than being caught back tightly from her face, she wore diamond eardrops that caught the light and flung it in sparkles across her cheeks, and her white muslin gown figured with pink roses flattered her figure in a way her plain stuff gown had not.

Miss Dane blushed, and Alexander's heart beat faster, because with that, she finally looked exactly as he remembered. "Then why did you pretend to be a poor man?" she demanded.

"I prefer to be anonymous on St. Stephen's Day. So much better to give without receiving undue praise. And you?" Alexander hardly knew what he was saying. Miss Overton, here, and... "Is there truly an affianced husband waiting for you in Arringford?"

Miss Dane bit her lip. Her eyes danced with silent laughter. "I could not...oh, it is too embarrassing. I believed you to be interested in me, and I couldn't think of any other way to dissuade you that didn't involve me revealing my identity. Of course, I could not permit a farmer to, well, to feel an interest, however attractive he was."

Alexander knew he was smiling like a fool and did not care. "And Lord Sherburne?" he asked. "Is he permitted to feel an interest?"

Miss Dane ducked her head shyly. "If he is the man I met this afternoon, I welcome it."

The musicians struck up the first dance. Alexander released his companion. "I must regretfully rescind my earlier invitation."

Miss Dane's eyes widened. "But why?"

"Because," Alexander said, leaning close, "I intend to wait for a dance that will permit me to take you in to supper, as I selfishly wish to monopolize your time in a socially acceptable manner. If you don't mind waiting, that is."

She smiled again. Alexander was sure he could never get enough of her smile. "I suppose I can bear waiting," she said. "If you will promise to tell me why you celebrate St. Stephen's Day the way I do."

Alexander saw, for the briefest moment, the two of them celebrating the holiday together, next year and every year to come. "I believe you already know," he said.

Stella Nova

I needed one more story to fill out this collection, and I had an idea based on the folk tale "Stone Soup," where a man claims to make the most delicious soup with just a stone—and then idly mentions that stone soup tastes great with a little potato, and some carrots, and an onion... So my idea was to make my story snowball as one by one, the characters bring just one thing: a tree, decorations, etc., until they have a Christmas to remember.

This is not that story.

I don't know how creativity works or how an idea can turn on itself and become something completely different. What I know is that I wanted to set a story in one of those lonely old motels that are gradually vanishing from the American landscape, and in searching online for pictures of vintage motel signs as inspiration, I came across one that had a shooting star, yellow neon and red bulbs for a tail. It wasn't until I was halfway through writing the story that the significance of Stella Nova, "new star," in a Christmas story struck me. It's not what I intended, but it satisfies me.

The neon NO VACANCY sign was acting up again. It never just stopped working, because that would be too easy to fix. No, random letters would darken for a few hours or days and then light up again with no one touching them. Right now it was the V and the second C that had gone out, and since the NO wasn't lit, the Stella Nova Motel's sign was garishly lit from below with the letters ACAN Y.

Fran leaned with both elbows on the front counter and gazed through the lobby window at the sign. Snow had been falling all day, first lightly, then with a growing intensity until at 6:37 this evening, all Fran could see of the sign aside from the glow at its base was the shooting star outlined in yellow neon, trailing its tail of red bulbs, a third of which were burned out. In this mess, the sign wouldn't be visible for more than half a mile away. Not much chance of anyone stopping tonight, not unless they were desperate. Not on Christmas Eve.

She let her gaze drift from the window to the front door, where Scott, the motel's manager, had hung a Christmas wreath. Scott's connection to holidays was a little askew, like he'd learned about them through reading a textbook missing half its pages. So the wreath was just a circle of pine branches, with a couple of pinecones, too few for its size, wired haphazardly to it. Fran liked Scott, who was easy to work for, but the wreath depressed her.

The tree had been worse. Scott had brought in a five-foot Douglas fir that looked like it had been cut off a much larger tree, hammered a couple of planks to the bottom of the trunk, and draped colored lights around it. But when he wormed his way behind the tree to the outlet and plugged the strand in, half of the lights stayed dark.

Scott's dismay had secretly amused Fran, though it was amusement mixed with sympathy. She didn't know why she'd volunteered to lay out the lights on the scratchy old Berber carpet and test each bulb, one at a time. True, the alternative was having a Christmas tree with a dark gash across its middle like it had been eviscerated, but it wasn't like Fran cared all that much about Christmas. Call it a temporary loss of sanity. Now the tree glowed with tiny colored lights that reflected off the window panes, defying the cold.

This was exactly what she expected from the holidays, she reflected, her gaze moving from motel sign to wreath to Christmas tree. It was a sad, pathetic Christmas, a Christmas for those stuck working the holiday, but it beat being home where nothing had been decorated and Mom and Dad either yelled at each other over whose turn it was to pay the electric bill or sat in matching La-Z-Boy recliners watching *Wheel of Fortune* until one or both fell asleep. At least here Fran had the illusion of peace.

She slid off her stool and made the rounds of the lobby. Four chairs upholstered in fake blue leather clustered near the tree, their chrome legs and armrests shiny enough to catch the twinkle lights and turn them into colored smears. Fran shifted one chair so they faced one another in pairs, then adjusted the out-of-date magazines spread on the table between them. Travel magazines, fashion magazines, one entertainment magazine with Hollywood's hottest couple gracing the cover, except Fran had heard about their divorce last week, so maybe it was time to get rid of that one.

She checked the coffeemaker in case it had spontaneously started working again. Right now, all it produced was hot water. Scott had promised to fix it three days ago, but then the roofs of numbers 10 and 11 had started leaking, and he'd been too busy trying to get repairmen out here the week before Christmas to worry about it. Fran didn't blame him, and anyway she brought her own coffee from Brew It Up every day, so it wasn't like it affected her.

Idly, she straightened the framed photo that hung behind the counter, the picture of a ruddy sunset over red and orange mesas somewhere in the Southwestern United States. It should have coordinated perfectly with the light tan walls, but the frame was an awful cheap aluminum that made both walls and photo seem garish. Fortunately, the thing hung at her back and she almost never looked at it.

She paused by the window, which radiated cold like the snow and wind were trying to get inside, and was startled to see a huddled shape hurrying across the corner of the parking lot from the left-hand row of rooms. Reflexively, she opened the door for the person, who turned out to be Scott. Snow caked the shoulders of his leather jacket and his dark hair, and his cheeks and nose were rosy. "Thanks," he said, brushing snow away. "Oh, sorry, I shouldn't—"

"It's fine." Fran grabbed the broom and swept the fallen snow out the door before it could melt into the carpet.

Scott kicked his boots against the door frame, then wiped them on the COME ON IN! mat Fran personally thought was the most enthusiastic employee of the Stella Nova. He stripped off his gloves and tucked them into his back pocket. "The leak has spread to numbers 9 and 12," he said, swiping an arm across his red nose and sniffing. "Nobody's come in this evening?"

Fran shook her head. "There's just room 3's usual occupant, and Mr. Gregory in room 6."

"Room 3," Scott said, frowning. He was thin and tall, not graceless enough to be called gangly, but he walked with a slight limp that made him seem older than the twenty-six Fran knew he actually was. "On Christmas Eve?"

Fran shrugged. "Maybe she doesn't have anywhere else to go."

Lily Sinclair checked into room 3 once a month, three to four days at a time. She always told Fran not to bother with housekeeping and hung up the Do Not Disturb sign for good measure. And every month she had visitors, all of them male, all of them furtive. Fran had asked Scott in a sideways, uncomfortable way if she ought to do something about room 3's activities, and Scott had told her not to worry about it. So Fran didn't.

"Not a good time of year to be alone," Scott said now, and limped into the employee break room, where Fran heard him open the refrigerator. She returned to her stool behind the front desk, idly kicking the lower rungs. She didn't think being alone was any worse this time of year than any other time. Maybe she'd learned about the holidays from the same textbook Scott had, if she couldn't summon up any Christmas spirit.

The door swung open again, letting in a gust of snowy air and a heavyset man with graying hair and glasses that fogged over the instant he stepped inside. He removed the glasses and squinted myopically at Fran. "There's a smell coming from my bathroom," he said.

"What kind of smell, Mr. Gregory?" Fran asked. Emmett Gregory was another regular, a sales rep who traveled the country by car because he hated airplanes. Fran thought he looked more like a university professor than a pharmaceutical salesman.

Mr. Gregory's squint turned into a frown. "Ripe. Pungent. The kind of smell I'd expect from a much-used Port-a-Potty in mid-July."

Scott emerged from the break room holding a bottle of Diet Dr. Pepper he set on the counter. "I'll get right on that," he told Mr. Gregory. "I apologize for the inconvenience."

"Inconvenience, hah," Mr. Gregory said, but without rancor. "I'm pretty sure I don't have any nose hairs left, that's your inconvenience."

Scott grimaced, but ducked into the manager's office, on the other side of the ugly red mesas from the break room. Fran impulsively said, "Is it that bad?"

"Bad enough I don't want to go back until it's fixed." Mr. Gregory crossed to the coffeemaker, discovered there was no coffee, and took a seat as far from the tree as he could get.

The door opened again, less forcefully, and Lily Sinclair entered. She had her white faux-fur trimmed parka wrapped closely around her body, and her matching white boots shed almost no snow on the mat. She quickly shut the door behind her and pushed back her hood, revealing blonde hair barely mussed and a lovely face lightly accented with makeup. "I think there's something wrong with my toilet," she said in a warm, throaty voice.

"You, too?" Mr. Gregory said. "A stink like a thousand yards of roadkill on a sunny day?"

Ms. Sinclair chuckled. "Such a poetic turn of phrase, Mr....?"

"Emmett Gregory," Mr. Gregory said, extending a hand. "Why don't you sit? The manager is making some calls."

Ms. Sinclair sat opposite Mr. Gregory and unzipped her parka, revealing a low-cut red sweater over tight black jeans. Fran left them to get acquainted and let herself into the manager's office.

"I need someone to look at it—no, I understand, but we have guests who can't sleep in the lobby," Scott said. He was seated at his desk, which was barely big enough for a laptop and mousepad, and he was spinning slowly back and forth in his rolling chair the way he did when he was frustrated. "Yes. That's great. Thank you." He hung up the office phone and gazed up at Fran. "Someone's coming to check the toilet."

"They'd better look at room 3 too," Fran said. "Ms. Sinclair reported the same smell."

Scott groaned and rubbed his hands over his face. "I'd better check the other units. If the right wing is leaking, and the left wing has some plumbing trouble—"

"At least no one's going to show up looking for a room tonight, right? On Christmas Eve?" Fran said.

She returned to her seat and watched Scott hurry across the parking lot and out of sight to the left. The snow still fell heavily, blowing in gusts against the window and turning the yellow star with its red tail into shapeless smears of color. Ms. Sinclair leaned close to Mr. Gregory's chair, listening to him say something in a low voice Fran couldn't quite make out. Maybe Ms. Sinclair didn't take holidays off, after all.

In minutes, Scott was back, looking more windblown and cold than before. "It's all the rooms on that side," he told Fran quietly. "The plumber should be here soon. Let's hope it's an easy fix—oh, that's him now. That was fast." Headlights shone through the window as a large truck pulled up outside, its engine throbbing over the howl of the wind. Scott opened the door and then stood in the opening as the snow blew around him, not moving.

"Scott!" Fran exclaimed as the chill air pushed aside all the warmth in the room.

"Sorry," Scott said. "It's—" He left the lobby without closing the door, but when Fran rushed to shut it, he was suddenly back, at the head of a group of bundled-up people of various sizes. "Let's just get everyone inside," he was saying to the tallest of the figures.

"I need to call a garage," the man said. "A repair shop. You have one of those around here, right?"

"It's Christmas Eve," the woman next to him said, in a worried tone of voice that suggested what the man wanted was impossible, but she didn't want to come right out and say it.

"People work Christmas Eve, Donna," the man said irritably.

One of the children clinging to Donna's legs said, "I'm cold, Mommy. Can we get in the car yet?"

"The car is broken, Emily," Donna said in a sweet, tense voice. "Let's let Daddy figure it out, all right?"

"There are two mechanics in town, sir," Scott said, "and I have their numbers, but they normally close at seven, and it's 7:05 now. And on Christmas Eve—"

"Just give me the numbers," the man snapped.

The smaller of the children unwrapped a scarf from his neck and, trailing it behind him, toddled over to the tree and stared at it. Fran felt unexpectedly embarrassed, like the little kid was judging her lack of Christmas spirit. His older sister joined him. "There's no ornaments," she said, and Fran's embarrassment doubled.

"The lights are pretty, though, don't you think?" Donna said. "Why don't you sit here, sweetheart? Daddy will find someone, and we'll be on our way soon."

The boy looked up at his mother. "Need to pee," he said in a clear, carrying voice that stopped Mr. Gregory and Ms. Sinclair's conversation.

Donna looked at Fran in mute appeal. "Is there...?"

"It's back here," Fran said. Technically the employee bathroom was just for employees, but this probably counted as an emergency.

When she got back from showing Donna and her son to the restroom, Donna's husband was pacing rapidly with his phone held to his ear, muttering under his breath, Mr. Gregory was telling Ms. Sinclair a story in the same low tones, and another stranger had entered, this one wearing a worn jacket open over stained coveralls and a knit cap covering most of his graying light brown hair. "I don't know what to tell you," the stranger was saying to Scott. "It's a problem at the mains, and there ain't much I can do about that."

"We can't expect guests to sleep with that kind of smell, and they certainly won't be able to use the toilets," Scott said. He sounded unexpectedly calm, but that might just have been by comparison to Donna's husband, who looked to Fran like he was ready to explode.

"Don't know what to tell you," the plumber repeated. "You got a bunch of rooms that don't stink, maybe you can move people there."

"Those rooms are leaking from the ceiling. Isn't there anything? Some kind of temporary fix?" Scott continued to sound as calm as if this wasn't a horrible crisis.

"I—" The plumber squinched up his face in thought. "Lemme take another look. I got an idea." His phone beeped, and he read the incoming text, then muttered something under his breath before dropping the phone into the breast pocket of his coveralls. He nodded politely at Fran and went out into the storm.

"Fine," Donna's husband shouted, and swung his arm as if he intended to throw his phone at the wall. He stopped mid-motion and shoved the phone into his pocket instead. "They're all closed," he said to no one. "Everyone who can fix a car in this crummy town has gone home for Christmas. We're stuck."

Scott and Fran exchanged glances. Fran didn't want to approach the still-angry man to offer him a room, not when all the available rooms smelled like sewage. Scott gave her a little shake of the head and took a few steps, putting himself in front of her. He was taller than Donna's husband, but thinner, and the man looked like he might be strong enough to snap Scott in half. Fran felt an unexpected rush of pleasure at Scott's protective gesture.

"I'm sorry for your misfortune," Scott said. "It's a good thing the towing service is 24/7, so you weren't stuck on the side of the highway. Can I help you bring anything inside from your car? Anything for your kids?"

To Fran's surprise, Donna's husband sagged. "I guess we need a room," he said. "So much for Christmas with the in-laws."

"We're having a temporary problem with the rooms, but we can make your kids comfortable in here for a few minutes," Scott said.

"Thanks." The man stuck out his hand. "I'm Arlen."

"Scott," Scott said, shaking hands.

Donna returned, carrying the little boy. He struggled to get down once he was within sight of the tree again. Donna watched Arlen warily, but the man sighed and put his arms around her, saying, "I'm sorry. We're not going to make it to your parents' house."

Donna relaxed. "Are you secretly grateful?" she said with a smile.

"Hey, I like your mom. Your dad still thinks you should have married Bob Cassaday, so—"

"He just thinks it's funny to tease you," Donna said, hugging him back. "Did you get us a room?"

"It will be just a little while," Fran said. "Something wrong with the plumbing. But the plumber is working on it."

"Honestly, I could just use a place to sit," Donna said. She took the chair opposite Mr. Gregory. "Emily, Connor, don't touch the tree."

"It needs ornaments," Emily said.

"It's not our tree, sweetie—Connor, no!"

Connor had been eyeing the tree speculatively since leaving the restroom. He held a large plastic Transformers figure in robot form by one arm that he now took in both hands. Fran wondered if he would turn it into a car—she didn't have brothers, and her parents were big on girls being girls, which to them meant dolls and pretend kitchens, but she'd always secretly liked Transformers even now she was twenty-two and presumably past that age. Instead, Connor nestled the figure into the branches. "Ornament," he said with satisfaction.

"Oh, Connor—"

"It's all right," Scott said. "It looks better that way."

Scott was right, the tree looked good with even that one makeshift ornament. An unexpected tingle coursed down Fran's chest and grounded itself warmly in her stomach. She caught Donna's eye and smiled, and Donna smiled back, a natural and unforced expression.

The door swung open again, and the plumber entered. "I got good news and bad news," he told Scott. "The good news is I can fix it—" The plumber's phone beeped, and he held up a hand indicating Scott should wait while he read the text, which he did with no emotional reaction. Then he said, "The bad news is it's going to take an hour or more, and then you'll have to air out the rooms for a good half hour after that."

"I'll take it," Scott said. "Everyone, I'm sorry about the inconvenience, but we'll have you settled before ten. Why don't you…" His gaze fell on Fran, and his eyes widened in panic. Fran guessed he'd been about to offer something to eat or drink, but all they had was the hot water in the coffeemaker, a couple of Diet Dr. Peppers, the remains of Fran's dinner (spaghetti and meatballs, mediocre even when it was hot), and a fruit basket the motel owners had sent as a Christmas present.

"There's hot water, right?" Ms. Sinclair asked. "I have hot chocolate mix in my room. We could share that."

"Thanks, Ms. Sinclair," Fran said.

"It's all right to enter the room, isn't it?" Ms. Sinclair asked Scott. "The smell isn't a sign of something dangerous?"

"No, just a sign of something backed up," Scott said. "Thanks for your generosity."

Ms. Sinclair waved that away. "It's no trouble." She zipped up her parka and headed out into the storm.

The room fell silent, one of those weird pauses where everyone runs out of things to say at the same time. Fran listened to the wind's voice. It was louder than before, and the sign with its yellow and red star wasn't more than a dim outline thanks to the snow. She hoped Ms. Sinclair would stick close to the building. This was turning into the kind of night where she could easily imagine people needing guide ropes to avoid walking into the empty land surrounding the motel and never coming back.

"You were going to visit family for Christmas?" Mr. Gregory said to Donna.

"My parents," Donna said. "It was going to be quite the party, with my sister and brother and their families." She laughed weakly. "Maybe it's for the best. There's always a lot of arguing when we're all together. Friendly arguing, if you get what I mean, but still loud."

"It sounds nice," Mr. Gregory said. "I don't have much family, and it's been a while since I celebrated Christmas. Too much advantage to being the only sales rep willing to travel over the holidays."

Ms. Sinclair returned with a large cardboard box tucked under her arm. "It's really coming down out there," she said. "Do you have cups?"

Fran found an unopened plastic sleeve of insulated cups and set them out as Ms. Sinclair opened the box, revealing a second box filled with envelopes of hot chocolate mix and a scattering of clear plastic spoons. Donna began filling cups with hot water and handing them around, while Mr. Gregory gave out spoons and packets. Fran helped the children, which meant mixing up a cup for Connor. The little boy was quieter than Fran expected from a child his age, not that she knew much about children except from seeing them at the grocery store, and those kids usually screamed or cried or whined endlessly for treats.

The door flew open, letting in a gust of flakes and a well-bundled figure. "Sorry," the woman said, and grabbed the door and shoved it closed against the wind. "Looks like I need a room for the night. It's a real blizzard—too dangerous to drive farther." Her voice was creaky but forceful, and when she took off her hat and scarf and enveloping padded coat, she turned out to be an elderly woman whose lined face and weather-tanned skin said she'd spent a lifetime outdoors.

Scott set his cup on the front desk and walked forward to greet her. "We have rooms, but they're under maintenance for a few hours. Would you like some hot chocolate while you wait?"

The old woman gave him a look that said she thought he was pulling her leg. "*All* the rooms?"

"The half that don't have leaky roofs," Scott said, perfectly straight-faced.

She cast a glance over the room, and her wrinkles deepened in a smile. "Sure, why not," she said. "Sophie Banner. Is that chair taken?"

Fran retreated to her stool again and sipped her drink. Scott leaned against the wall near her. "They're all so cheerful," he whispered. "Must be the holiday spirit." His phone rang, and he frowned at the screen before answering. "Yes? You did? Well, that's —oh. Oh, I see. Can't you do anything about that?"

There was a long pause in which Fran heard the distant voice of whoever had called. Scott's face grew still. "All right," he finally said. "Do what you have to. We'll figure it out." He disconnected and stared at the phone for a while before shoving it into his pocket. Fran hesitated. Scott didn't look happy, and she didn't want to pry in case it was personal.

Scott cleared his throat. "Everyone, I've just talked to the plumber, and he says he's opened up the system and found the problem is worse than he thought. He'll be able to fix it, but we have to turn off the heat to all the affected rooms. That means that even after the system is repaired and the rooms have been aired out, they're going to be cold for a few hours after that."

Groans and a few muttered profanities filled the air. Fran, watching Scott from behind, saw him close the hand he held behind his back into a fist. But his voice was calm when he spoke again. "I'm really sorry, and if these were any other conditions, I'd refund your money and suggest you go to a different motel. But Mrs. Banner—"

"Sophie," Sophie Banner said.

"Sophie says it's dangerous to drive, and that means this is what we have. So I think we should make the best of it. If anyone has any suggestions for how to pass the time, we'd all love to hear them."

No one spoke at first. Then Mr. Gregory rose. "I'll be right back," he said, and went outside. Fran could barely see the outline of his body as he passed the window. She remembered what she'd thought about guide ropes and hoped he would be okay.

"We could bring in the Bluetooth speaker, play some Christmas music," Donna said to her husband. "It's in my travel bag—in fact, I should get the whole bag."

"I'll do it," Arlen said. He left the room, bracing himself against the wind that threatened to take the door out of his hands.

"Let's see what's in that fruit basket," Scott suggested to Fran. Fran nodded and hurried into the break room. Most of the basket was taken up by a pineapple they had no way of cutting, but there were some oranges and some Red Delicious apples, a couple of pears, and half a dozen fuzzy brown kiwis filling in the gaps. Fran left the pineapple on the counter and carried the rest into the lobby, just in time for Mr. Gregory to blow back in. He had a box the size and shape of a pizza box wrapped in festive paper under his arm, but when he set it down atop the magazines and tore off the wrapping, it turned out to be one of those cheese and meat samplers people give as gifts the way the owners had the fruit basket.

"It was meant to be for the man I'm meeting day after Christmas," Mr. Gregory said, almost apologetically as if he was embarrassed at picking such a banal gift, "but he'll never know."

"It's practically a feast!" Donna exclaimed.

Fran refilled the coffeemaker so they could have more hot water, then watched as Donna and Ms. Sinclair portioned out the fruit and Mr. Gregory used a small pocketknife to cut slices of summer sausage and cheddar cheese. While they were doing that, Arlen returned with a cylindrical speaker he set upright on the counter next to Scott's forgotten bottle of Diet Dr. Pepper. After he fiddled with his phone for a few seconds, the opening notes of Mariah Carey's "All I Want for Christmas Is You" filled the room, too loud until Arlen turned the volume down. Fran expected someone to comment on the cliché holiday song, but it only made the laughter and cheerfulness increase.

Why everyone was being so cheerful, she didn't know. It was just as reasonable for them to yell and stomp around and refuse to speak to each other. Her gaze slid over the Christmas tree and paused there. The Transformer had been joined by a pink ribbon tied around a nearby branch, a ribbon Fran had last seen tying up Emily's hair.

She didn't know why the sight made her smile. It was still pathetic, the little tree with its makeshift decorations, and yet the idea of Emily and Connor contributing what they could warmed her heart.

"You kids come look at this," Sophie said, beckoning to Emily and Connor to sit on the floor beside the tree. Sophie sat beside them cross-legged, though Fran thought she looked too old for that to be comfortable. Sophie had rescued one of the empty hot chocolate packets and torn it so it made two rough squares. Inside, the packet was shiny foil dusted with chocolate powder. With a few deft folds, Sophie turned one of the squares into a silver origami star.

"Cool!" Emily said. "Can I try?"

"Sure. Go find more of these," Sophie said.

The door opened abruptly, blown out of the plumber's hands. "Sorry," he said. "I need someone to make sure the heat's turned off in all the rooms before I can go on."

"Okay," Scott said.

He looked like he was nerving himself up to do something awful, and out of nowhere Fran said, "I'll go."

"It's too cold," Scott said.

"Then it's too cold for you, too, but someone has to do it." Fran had no idea where this was coming from. Maybe it was remembering how Scott had put himself between her and what they'd thought was danger; maybe it was feeling like he'd already gone out into the storm too many times. Or maybe it was the influence of all the cheerful people that made her want to do something nice for someone. It certainly couldn't be Christmas spirit.

"We'll both go," Scott said. "It will be faster."

The plumber's phone beeped, and Fran hesitated, though she didn't know why his texts mattered to her. But the man just shook his head over the text's contents and turned away.

Fran got her coat and hat from the break room, and she and

Scott hurried out into the blizzard. Scott immediately grabbed hold of her hand. "Stick close to the wall," he shouted. Fran nodded, though she doubted he could see the movement.

The wind was strong enough that it buffeted them and held them up by turns, sometimes feeling as solid as an air-filled cushion Fran had to press past. Between the wind and the driving snow, her only connection to reality was Scott's hand. Neither of them were wearing gloves, and Scott's skin was warmer than hers and slightly rough, but his grip was firm and Fran welcomed it.

They reached the door to room 1 and Scott pulled her closer. "You do the first three, I'll do the last three," he said, and was gone before she could argue.

The door was unlocked, and Fran gratefully shut herself inside, away from the snow. Then she gagged and opened the door again. The stench was worse than she'd imagined even from Mr. Gregory's thousand yards of roadkill imagery. She breathed in snowy air deeply, then, leaving the door open, she rushed inside and worked the override that would shut down the heating system. After a moment's thought, she wrestled the window open as well. Its screen shuddered in the wind, but held firm.

She repeated the process in the next two rooms. Room 3, in the brief moments she was inside, looked perfectly ordinary. She hadn't expected to see a laptop on the little table by the room's one window. Well, odor and cold couldn't hurt it, and it wasn't as if this was weather for thieves.

When she'd completed her task, Fran leaned against the outside wall next to room 3's door and breathed in deeply a couple of times. She was sure the stink clung to her clothes and as much of her hair as was exposed. The third deep breath was too much, and she shivered and huddled into her coat as she ran for the lobby, one hand trailing along the wall to keep her oriented.

She saw the window as a smear of light and slowed, drawn by

its unexpected beauty despite the cold. The panes were foggy in places, but when she was close enough, she could see the limbs of the Christmas tree, now dotted with stars, and Sophie guiding Emily and Connor in placing more of them.

A memory she hadn't thought of in years stabbed her heart, her Aunt Violet helping her hang ornaments with her chubby little-girl hands and lifting her to put the angel atop the tree. Aunt Violet—Fran closed her eyes against tears. Mom's younger sister, who'd fought with the family and left town years ago and who'd never returned. Memory was stupid, if all it brought was heartache.

She trudged the last few paces to the lobby entrance. Scott wasn't back yet. The speaker was playing "Merry Christmas Baby," a song she remembered from a movie soundtrack. No one so much as looked up when she entered—they were all too busy chatting or folding origami stars using the colored printer paper from beneath the counter. A flash of anger shot through Fran that these strangers had taken from her without asking. "You shouldn't —" she began.

"We borrowed some paper," Donna said cheerfully. "We didn't think you'd mind. The tree looks really good, don't you think?"

Fran got a clearer look at it, covered in silver and pale green and light blue stars, some of them inexpertly folded, and her angry response died. "I guess," she said.

Scott came in just then, blowing on his fingers to warm them. "Just a matter of time now," he said. "This is good. Better than I hoped, anyway."

Fran pushed past him into the break room, shutting the door behind her with a force not quite a slam. She shoved back a chair from the table and dropped into it. Staring at nothing, she suppressed the urge to yell at all of them. Nothing about this night was good. Being cheerful over gross odors and freezing cold rooms and folded paper stars made no sense. Sure, it was good that they weren't all sniping at each other, like they would any ordinary night, but why should Christmas Eve be such an influence on their behavior?

The door opened and shut again, quietly. "Something wrong?" Scott asked.

Fran shook her head. Staring at the tabletop, she said, "I don't see why people have to wait for a holiday to behave well to each other. You know if this was the middle of February all of them would treat each other like crap because they would be caught up in being miserable."

Scott pulled out the other chair with a scrape against the linoleum and sat. "Isn't it enough to be grateful they aren't doing that?"

"Are you saying I'm wrong?"

"No." Scott leaned back in his chair. "I don't know the answer. Maybe it's just that this time of year, when it's dark and cold and the world feels like it's trying to kill us, we get the urge to band together and fight back. And it feels good to help. At least, it does to me."

"My family doesn't really do Christmas. I mean, we're Methodists, it's not like we're celebrating something else instead, just..." Fran shrugged. "It's been a long time since I cared about the holiday."

"I was grateful you were willing to work tonight. The other two clerks wanted to spend time with family."

"What about you?" Fran asked, not caring if it was too personal.

"My family lives far away. I'll call them tomorrow, but...well, you might have noticed I'm not the best at understanding how to celebrate. Thanks for not laughing at the wreath." Scott chuckled, and to her surprise, Fran joined in.

"At least you tried," she said. "It was...nice."

"I hoped," Scott said, then fell silent.

"What?"

"Nothing. Just, I didn't want both of us having no Christmas at all, even if it meant a crappy wreath and burnt-out twinkle lights." Scott stood. "Did you get anything to eat? The cheese is really good."

Fran looked up at him. He was smiling, and that funny tingle shot through her again. She rose from her seat and smiled back.

In the lobby, the origami star brigade had run out of materials, the song was "Silent Night," and the tree looked like a real Christmas tree finally. Fran sat on her stool with Scott leaning against the wall beside her and let the music and the conversation wash over her, picking out fragments here and there.

"...should get a couple of presents out of the car so the kids can have Christmas Eve..." That was Arlen talking to Donna.

"...my kids were little like you, I taught them how to fold stars..." Sophie said to Emily and Connor.

"You're really old," Connor said, and Sophie laughed and hugged him.

"...last interview of the year, so I can settle in for a few weeks of writing," Ms. Sinclair was telling Mr. Gregory.

"Such an interesting job, writer," Mr. Gregory replied.

Fran shot upright. "You're a writer?" she exclaimed, cutting across all the other noise. Her face flamed scarlet as everyone stared at her.

Ms. Sinclair nodded, her brow furrowed in puzzlement. "You sound like you expected something else," she said. "Yes, I'm a writer. I come here when I'm on a deadline because no one knows to find me here."

"But—all those men," Fran said, feeling stupid.

Ms. Sinclair's perfectly plucked and shaded eyebrows rose in an astonished arc. "Those—" She burst out laughing. "Oh," she gasped when she got herself under control, "*oh*, I never thought— oh, no, those are my sources. Some of them want to remain anonymous—I write nonfiction exposes of corporate malfeasance, among other things, and they insist on meeting me privately."

Fran's head was going to pop, it was so swollen with embarrassment. "I'm sorry, it's none of my business."

"Well, thank you for not calling the cops on me," Ms. Sinclair said. "Really, it's perfectly understandable that you'd draw that conclusion. Please don't be embarrassed."

"Children, how about you get in your pajamas, and you can each unwrap one present," Donna said tactfully.

Fran sat back and wished she could disappear. "Did you know?" she murmured to Scott.

"I thought what you did, remember?" Scott replied. "Now I'm really glad we didn't interfere."

Emily and Connor, both wearing footie pajamas now, opened presents—a Barbie doll for Emily, another Transformer for Connor—and then Donna said, "They really ought to be asleep, but I don't know where—"

"We'll figure something out," Scott said.

"Can Santa find us?" Connor asked his father.

"Sure thing, but you have to go to sleep first," Arlen replied.

There was a bustle as chairs and tables were moved and blankets provided so the children could make a nest next to the tree on the side away from the window. Scott turned off the lobby lights, but left the doors to the break room and the office open with those lights on. With the dim lighting and the warm colorful glow of the tree, the blizzard felt less real, less a threat and more a backdrop to some sappy holiday movie. Fran propped her elbows on the front counter and let her eyes go unfocused. She felt unexpectedly relaxed.

Arlen had turned off the music so the kids could sleep. The sound of the wind against the glass whistled and howled by turns, sounding almost musical, though it was an atonal music that wouldn't suit any night but this one.

Then Mr. Gregory shifted in his chair and began to sing.

His voice was a magnificent baritone that in the small lobby resonated as beautifully as if it were a concert hall. Fran didn't recognize the song or even the language he was singing, but it felt sad and hopeful at the same time, and it struck her to the heart in a way no Christmas carol ever had.

When the last notes died away, Ms. Sinclair said, "I've never heard that in Latin before. It sounds even more like a plea for deliverance in that language."

"What's it called?" Arlen asked in a hushed voice.

"It's 'Veni, Veni, Emmanuel,'" Mr. Gregory said. "In English, 'O Come, O Come, Emmanuel.' Emmanuel being Christ, or the longed-for Savior. The song is about the desire to be rescued from the captivity of sin and fear." He chuckled. "I suppose it's overly dramatic, if I say it out loud. I just like the sound of the carol, and this time of year I feel a desire to be more religious than I am the rest of it."

"It was beautiful," Fran said, and hoped her voice wasn't as obviously hoarse as it felt. She wasn't a churchgoer, didn't really feel religion defined her life, and yet for the first time she felt there was something to the idea that this night was different.

The door opened, for the first time without slamming against the wall, and the plumber entered. "Good—" he began, and stopped as everyone else shushed him. "Sorry. I just wanted you all to know the problem with the sewage is fixed, and you can turn the heat back on and let that start warming up while the rooms air out. Plenty of time for a merry Christmas, right?"

"Thanks," Scott said, shaking the man's hand. As he did, the plumber's phone beeped. "You sure are popular," Scott said with a laugh.

The plumber was already reading the text. An enormous smile creased his worn face. "It's happening," he exclaimed, ignoring the shushing. "My daughter's in labor. Gonna have her first baby soon —no, tomorrow, it's later than I thought. Good timing, right? I gotta go."

"You can't go anywhere in this weather," Arlen said.

"Sure I can. Storm's letting up. Not much, but enough to see my way down three miles of road to the hospital." He grinned. "What a Christmas present, eh?"

"Does she know if it's a boy or a girl?" Donna asked.

"Girl. My daughter says she'll always hate having a Christmas birthday, but I say, it worked out all right two thousand years ago." He laughed. "Merry Christmas, all!"

The rest of them rushed to the door after he left, with Fran trailing behind. Sure enough, although the wind was still blowing as strong as ever, the snow had died down, and the Stella Nova's sign was visible again. After a few moments, Scott said, "Fran and I will go turn on the heat again, and in about an hour, you can return to your rooms. I guess you'll want to be moving on?" he asked Sophie.

Sophie shook her head. "There's no saying this storm might not get worse again, and I've got a lot farther to go than three miles. I'll let my family know I'll be there tomorrow."

This time, Fran and Scott didn't need to hold hands to find their way to the rooms. Fran felt unexpectedly bereft. She swiftly turned the heaters back on, relieved that the smell was already fainter, and met Scott on the way back. Not much snow had accu-

mulated thanks to the driving winds, and Fran didn't regret not
having boots.

Restless, she moved around the lobby collecting cups and
napkins and gathering up the uneaten fruit into the basket.
Donna had fallen asleep in her chair near her children, and Arlen
was reading something on a tablet whose dim glow cast strange
shadows across his face. Ms. Sinclair and Mr. Gregory sat side by
side, not speaking, gazing at the tree in silent reverie. Fran dumped
the trash in the break room garbage can and returned to her stool.
After a while, Scott joined her.

"Merry Christmas," he said.

Fran checked her watch. "It's not midnight yet."

"I know, but it feels like we've already had more Christmas
than we deserve." Scott shifted his weight, nudging the ugly photo
and grabbing it to keep it from falling. "Arlen and Donna want to
put the rest of the presents under the tree for the morning."

Again, that strange, happy tingle flooded through Fran.
"That's sweet," she said.

"I thought so. Look, it's getting late, and the storm really has
died down. If you want to go home—"

"No," Fran said, and was surprised at how forcefully she
spoke.

Scott said nothing. Fran blushed. She couldn't explain to him
why going home would ruin everything she'd felt that night, not
without getting far too personal. "I mean, I don't want to
abandon you," she said.

"Thanks," Scott said. "I don't want to be abandoned."

They fell silent again. Fran wished she understood better this
feeling that had taken hold of her. She wasn't sentimental, and she
knew whatever spell this night had cast would end in a day, maybe
two. But she also knew better than to dismiss this beautiful
evening just because it wouldn't last.

Scott shifted his weight again and cursed as the photo fell. He caught it and lowered it to the floor. "I hate this thing. It's the ugliest photo I've ever seen. I bet those mesas are embarrassed they were caught like that."

Fran giggled. "Let's get rid of it."

"Agreed." He cleared his throat. "Hey. I was wondering. Would you, um, like to get coffee sometime? You and me, I mean."

The thought flashed through Fran's mind that he was nominally her boss, and she dismissed it. "Yeah, I'd like that," she said.

Scott's face brightened. "You would? I mean, only if you want."

"I do." Daring, she took his hand and squeezed it lightly, releasing him before he could react. "I'd like that a lot."

Scott nodded. Then, hesitating, he clasped her hand and held it, and the two of them watched the tree with all its lights and stars and its dim reflection in the window. Soon enough, it would be Christmas Day, and Sophie would leave, and Mr. Gregory would move on, and Ms. Sinclair would pack up her laptop and go back to her writing, and Arlen and Donna and their family would celebrate the holiday while their car was being fixed and they'd be gone too. Soon enough, the holiday would be over, and this feeling would leave with the rest of them.

Or maybe, Fran thought, feeling Scott's hand in hers, it was a feeling she didn't have to lose.

Charade in Three-Quarter Time

T*he Crown of Tremontane series is my longest series, with ten novels, a novella, and a very large companion volume of ancillary writings. Despite this, there are stories I never had a chance to tell, and at the top of that list was the story of Julia North's romance. Julia, the Crown Princess in the book* Agent of the Crown, *had a marriage that ended unhappily, and all I knew was that she was alone for ten years before love found her again—and that the story of that romance was too short for its own novel.*

When I decided I was going to publish a holiday collection, I decided I would have to write another three stories in addition to the ones I already had to make it long enough. Brainstorming ideas led to the possibility of a Tremontane story set during that country's solstice holiday, Wintersmeet. And immediately I seized on this as my opportunity to tell Julia's story. It ended up being longer than I expected, but that's not uncommon for me.

1

Julia North stood in front of the portrait of James d'Arden, her who-knew-how-many-times great-grandfather, and pretended to examine his unlined face and aquiline nose. In fact, she was looking at her reflection in the glass, not much more than an outline, but clearly overlaying the image of her ancestor. She didn't actually spend a lot of time, in general, gazing into mirrors; most of Tremontane considered her the most beautiful woman in the country, and she felt admiring herself turned that from a compliment into shameless pandering. How much of that beauty came from her rank and title, she wasn't sure, but she could objectively admit she wasn't hideous.

But she liked seeing imperfect reflections, whether in portrait glass or windows or even glossy, highly-polished wood. It was how ghostlike those reflections were, how glass and lacquer stripped away color and solidity and left only lines and shadows. If Julia focused just the right way, those lines and shadows seemed more real than the world outside the glass. It was an interesting, compelling illusion.

In the reflection, she saw someone approaching, and she put on a smile she knew looked genuine. "Elizabeth, it's been too long," she said, offering her hostess her hand.

"Yes, why don't we see each other more often?" Elizabeth d'Arden trilled. Julia had never been able to tell whether Elizabeth's enthusiasm was real or faked. She didn't think anyone could be that relentlessly cheerful without snapping. Julia's cousin Telaine might know, but Telaine was on the far side of the salon, chatting with two people Julia vaguely remembered. The sound of the string quartet in the corner surged briefly and then subsided into the background again.

"I'm afraid I'm always so busy," Julia said with another practiced smile. "Telaine has made it her goal to drag me into the light, as she put it. And there are so many Wintersmeet parties and concerts she wants to attend."

Elizabeth's smile faded briefly. "Yes, she's certainly the social butterfly. One would hardly know she doesn't spend every day of her life paying calls and attending parties, but—oh, never mind."

Julia knew what Elizabeth hadn't said—that Telaine, once a Princess of the royal house of North, had thrown it all away to marry a blacksmith and live as a commoner on the eastern frontier of Tremontane. *Now* Julia remembered why she didn't have much social contact with Elizabeth. "Indeed," she said coldly. "I'm so grateful she and her family chose to spend Wintersmeet with us."

"Isn't it a lovely time of year?" Elizabeth said, rallying. "My husband and I are looking forward to the grand ball at the palace. I imagine you enjoy it very much. All those handsome men..." She giggled, a sound that would have suited a much younger woman. "I imagine I know who *you* will single out!"

An icy hand closed over Julia's heart. "Do you? I don't," she said lightly. "Excuse me, I should speak to Lady Annadale." She smiled and walked away before Elizabeth could react.

In the moments before she joined Lady Annadale, an elderly woman who mumbled so much conversation was nearly impossible, Julia ran over the list of men she'd had contact with in the last month, wondering who Elizabeth had meant. It didn't even have to be extended contact or even intimate contact. All that mattered, to the kingdom, was believing that Crown Princess Julia North was on the verge of remarriage finally. The speculation drove her mad. It wasn't just Elizabeth; everyone in the kingdom seemed to believe they were entitled to tease her about her supposed matrimonial prospects.

She pretended to understand Lady Annadale's conversation for about a minute, then moved on, drifting from group to group until she was near the exit without having obviously aimed for it. In the next lull in conversation, she excused herself and fled.

The hall was well lit, with lights shaped like flickering candles casting a glow over the pale green walls. They were Devices, magical creations rather than actual candles, but only the lack of the smells of hot wax and burning wicks made the difference obvious. Each light bore a small fir wreath trimmed with silver ribbons and white berries that were no doubt poisonous. It would fit Elizabeth's character.

Julia stopped and squeezed her eyes shut. That was cruel and unfair. Elizabeth d'Arden was shallow and self-centered, but she wasn't evil. Even her attitude toward Telaine could be explained by her complete inability to imagine why anyone would want to be anything but noble, not a personal dislike of Julia's cousin. But Julia couldn't stop seeing that arch, knowing expression, that sly look as if she and Julia were sharing confidences. There was no sense in Julia protesting that she had no intention of remarrying. That was something even her parents, the King and Consort, didn't understand.

Followed by the faint sounds of violin and cello, she walked on down the long corridor lined with more portraits of d'Arden ancestors, some of whom were likely related to Julia as well thanks to James d'Arden, who had married Queen Genevieve North and been her Consort. Julia wondered what he'd been like. Whether he'd felt uncomfortable being Consort to a powerful woman, whether he'd felt overshadowed. Lucas—

She walked faster, trying to leave memories behind. She never thought of Lucas these days, husband, ex-husband, dead ex-husband, unless their daughter was shouting defiance at her, and then it seemed she could think of nothing else. What horrible twist of fate had given her a child who looked and sounded so much like the man she wanted to forget?

She knew, deep down, she was being foolish. One bad experience didn't mean every man was awful. And she didn't hate all men for what Lucas had done to her. But her memories of how she'd loved Lucas made her feel stupid and small and humiliated, and when you combined that with how any courtship would be conducted under millions of prying eyes, all thoughts of romance shriveled and died.

In her hurry to get away from the thoughts that trailed her, she'd taken turn after turn without paying attention to where she was going, and now she found herself in the foyer, with a couple of servants watching her curiously. She glanced past them at the cloakroom. She could leave. No one was going to criticize the Crown Princess for having another engagement. But she and Telaine had come together, and Telaine would certainly want to know why Julia had left without her.

She smiled politely at the servants and retreated, slowly this time, following the sound of the music, which had become oddly discordant with distance. No. She stopped at an intersection of two corridors. Not discordant; there were two melodies, one strings, the other a pianoforte. Curious, she turned until she could hear the pianoforte music clearly. It was—well, of course—coming from the music room.

The narrow hall that led to the music room wasn't as well lit as the rest of the house, and Julia suspected that meant Elizabeth didn't want her guests wandering this way. The thought of defying Elizabeth, even in this small way, gave Julia a fierce pleasure and nearly made up for the woman's snideness about Telaine.

Her pace slowed as she approached. Whoever was playing the instrument was very good. Julia loved music, though she'd never had the patience to learn to play anything, and pianoforte concerts were among her favorite entertainments. This music surged over her, an unfamiliar piece that evoked memories of dark, starlit nights and the wind across the plains and tugged at her heart in a way she hadn't felt for a long time.

The door to the music room stood ajar, and no light emerged through the crack. She would have thought the room empty but for the marvelous music. Gently, hoping not to disturb the pianist, she pushed the door open and stood in the gap, listening, watching.

No lights burned within, but the drapes were open, and cold blue moonlight poured through the floor-to-ceiling windows, illuminating the pianoforte and casting the player, whose back was to the windows, into shadow. He seemed not to notice Julia, since he went on playing without stopping. Like a professional, he put his whole body into his music, bearing down on the keys for a forceful measure and then drawing back for the high, sweet notes that sang at the limits of Julia's hearing. Julia's heart beat faster, and she closed her eyes and let the music pour through her.

With a few delicate, deep-voiced chords, the music came to an end, and Julia opened her eyes to find the musician watching her. She blushed. That had felt unexpectedly intimate, though they were at opposite ends of the music room and it wasn't small.

"I didn't realize I had an audience," the man said. His voice was as deep as those final chords, but rough where they had been sweet.

"I apologize for intruding," Julia said, embarrassment ratcheting her response up a few social notches as if formality could make her less embarrassed. "It was beautiful."

She could barely see his smile in the dimness and, she realized belatedly, against his short, dark beard. Most Tremontanan men were clean-shaven and wore their hair short, but in addition to the beard, this man's hair was pulled back from his face in a long tail. She added, "You play in the dark."

"Only the pieces I know by heart," the man said, rising from the bench. "I promise I'm not a musical savant."

"Maybe not, but I've heard many pianoforte players, and your skill is remarkable. Thank you for the concert you didn't know you were giving."

The man chuckled. "Thank you. Are you one of my sister's guests?"

"Your sister?" Julia blurted out, startled. Elizabeth d'Arden only had two brothers, and Julia knew both of them. This man was a total stranger.

"How refreshing," the man said, taking a few steps toward Julia but not closing the distance between them entirely. "I guess Elizabeth was right about the scandal being forgotten."

Scandal. Elizabeth's brother. Julia reached back twenty years in memory and said, "*Oh*. You must be Eric d'Arden. Excuse me, Lord d'Arden."

"So, not entirely forgotten," Eric d'Arden said with a wry smile. "And it's Lord Eric. Lord d'Arden is my brother-in-law. May I have the pleasure of your name?"

For half a breath, Julia considered lying. She couldn't remember the last time someone hadn't immediately recognized her. But the lie wouldn't last more than a few minutes. "Julia North," she said, walking forward and extending her hand.

Lord Eric's eyebrows rose. "Your Highness," he said, bowing over her hand. His fingers were long and agile, a musician's fingers, and they closed on hers firmly but without crushing them. "I beg your pardon for my ignorance."

"You've been gone a long time," Julia said. "I wouldn't expect you to recognize me."

"You're very generous." Lord Eric released her. "Is it impertinent to ask why you've wandered away from the party?"

"Not if you tell me why you did the same," Julia replied.

Lord Eric smiled again. She liked his smile; it was open and cheerful and totally unlike his sister's. "I'm a novelty, and novelties get whispered about. I stayed for about five minutes at the beginning, and then I made my escape."

"I suppose—" Julia began, then bit her lip in more embarrassment.

"Then you do remember the scandal," Lord Eric said. He wasn't smiling anymore.

"Only some of it," Julia lied. She'd been fourteen at the time, but it was all anyone could talk about: old Lord d'Arden's oldest son, shot a man during an argument, fled to Eskandel ahead of the law. Later testimony had exonerated Lord Eric, proved he hadn't done the shooting, but his supposed victim had been popular, public sentiment was against the young lord, and even after the scandal had been replaced by something else, he hadn't returned home. "What brings you back to Tremontane now?"

"I wanted a change." His voice sounded too airy, but Julia didn't challenge him. "And now you, your Highness. Why aren't you socializing?"

Now he sounded mocking, and it tore at Julia's heart, made vulnerable by his music and her memories. "You think you're a novelty?" she shot back. "Try having your every move, your every contact with a man aged fifteen to fifty, scrutinized and challenged and analyzed by a million amateur matchmakers."

"Oh."

Julia reddened again. "I'm sorry. It's not—you're not at fault."

"No, but I do understand being in the public eye. I didn't realize you're not married."

"I was once. Now I'm the most marriageable catch in all of Tremontane." She hoped she didn't sound as bitter as she felt.

"No wonder you fled. Did Elizabeth try to make a match for you? It seems to be her favorite pastime. The one good thing about having a scandal-ridden past is that it's put me beyond the pale so far as marrying an innocent flower of Tremontanan young womanhood goes."

It startled a laugh out of Julia. "I suppose that's true. And no, she hasn't. Not tonight, anyway." She sighed. "Wintersmeet used to be my favorite holiday, but it's the time of year people start thinking of romance. You know, because it's supposed to be good luck to get betrothed on Wintersmeet Day? Now it's the time of year everyone wants to introduce their brother or cousin or nephew or landlord's son to me. I am positively overwhelmed for choice, but—I'm sorry. You don't need to hear this."

"It certainly sounds like you need to say it," Lord Eric said. "I daresay you haven't told this to anyone."

"Not even my cousin, though that's because this is the first Wintersmeet in years she and her family have been in Aurilien for the holiday." Lord Eric's presence was calming, and between that and the dim light and the solitude, she found herself wanting to open up to him. "I'm always aware that every man I meet, the ones who want a dance or an outing or an evening alone, is thinking 'am I the one she'll choose?' They're so focused on the idea of being the future Consort they don't really care about me. I realize that sounds hopelessly arrogant, but it's still true."

"You're the heir to the Crown. I imagine most people think of you as an object rather than a person." Lord Eric glanced past Julia as the clock in the distant foyer began to strike ten. "I suppose I should return. I promised Elizabeth I'd join them for supper." He offered Julia his arm. "May I escort you, or did you plan to escape entirely?"

Julia looked at his arm, crooked invitingly. Escape. "Actually," she said, an idea forming at the back of her mind, "suppose..." The idea was so audacious, so unlike her, it made her heart beat faster.

"Lord Eric," she said, "you and I are near-total strangers, I know, and you probably will think this is the most ridiculous notion, and maybe you'll believe me mad, but I think we may be the solution to one another's problems."

"I didn't realize I had a problem," Lord Eric said. "You intrigue me."

Julia took a deep breath. "I would like to have one Wintersmeet season where no one is foisting potential husbands on me. You want not to be seen as the black sheep of the d'Ardens. It occurs to me that if we were courting, neither of those things would happen."

Lord Eric lowered his arm. "Courting?" he exclaimed.

Julia's face must surely be redder than a late-season apple, but she forged ahead. "Not really courting, obviously. We'd pretend to be attached—not betrothed, but seeing one another exclusively—and the matchmakers and the gossips would have their teeth pulled, so to speak."

Lord Eric was silent. Julia's eyes had adjusted to the low light enough that she could see clearly his furrowed brow and his frown. "I promise," she began.

"Your Highness," Lord Eric said. "I see the principle. But I'm not sure you want to attach yourself to me, even in pretense."

"Why not? You're of my social class, you're unmarried, and if I can be honest, I like what I know of you."

"I was serious about my lack of eligibility, your Highness. I am no one a well-bred woman should choose for a partner." His voice was harsher than it had been, and though Julia thought he meant to dissuade her, she could hear the pain beneath his words, and sympathy welled up unexpectedly in her.

"Because you were accused of murder? You were exonerated, my lord. If people continue to blame you for a crime you didn't commit, that is their problem, not yours."

"I thought you said you didn't remember."

Julia shrugged. "I suppose it's all coming back to me." She closed her hand on his sleeve. "Please, Lord Eric. I can't express to you how agonizing it is to face all those well-meaning people. It will only be for two weeks, until Wintersmeet Day. And I promise no one will whisper about your scandal when they can have so much more fun whispering about how you caught the Crown Princess."

To her surprise, he laughed. "Like you were a fish?"

"Exactly so. They'll probably want to know what bait you used."

Lord Eric laughed harder. "Very well, your Highness, I accept." He once more held out his arm to her, and this time, she took it. "Shall we agree on the story of how I swept you off your feet?"

"I was thinking more about the story of how I pursued you until you gave in to inevitability, but we can negotiate." Julia smiled. It had just occurred to her that Elizabeth d'Arden was likely to faint when she learned the news. Julia hoped she was in a position to see it.

2

It was past midnight when Julia stepped into the carriage to return home. She settled herself in a corner as Telaine and her husband Ben climbed in after her. Ben looked as relieved as he always did after one of these social functions. He never acted anxious or uncomfortable during a concert or party or supper, and Julia knew there were many high-society men and women who didn't realize he wasn't noble, but he preferred the quiet life.

The carriage lurched into motion. Telaine leaned forward to face Julia. "Talk."

"About what?" Julia said lightly.

"You know what. Since when are you courting with Eric d'Arden? He's only been back in the country for four days, and I know everywhere you've gone during that time. You couldn't have met before tonight. So I want to know what you're plotting."

"Do I have to be plotting something?"

Telaine raised one eyebrow. She'd used that expression to devastating effect in the years she had been a socialite and secret spy, and now she turned it on anyone she judged in need of a set-down. Since she also had the magical ability to hear lies when they were spoken to her, Julia didn't bother trying.

She told Telaine and Ben everything, from hearing Lord Eric play to their agreement. When she finished, her cousin's expression was so neutral it had to be concealing dismay. Ben was frowning. "I don't know, Julia," he said. "Isn't that dishonest?"

"It's completely dishonest," Julia retorted. "And I don't care. It's like a game, or a play, you see? Lord Eric and I are going to put on a show for the country, and it hurts no one except maybe those who are making book on my marriage prospects."

"I understand," Telaine said, still so neutrally it made Julia feel guilty. She hurried on to anger to stop the guilty feeling from growing.

"But you don't approve," she said.

"Dear coz, my approval shouldn't rule your life. I just...Julia, I don't know how to put this without insulting you. I'm not going to tell you you're incomplete without a man in your life, because I don't believe that's true. But if that *is* something you want, doesn't this ruse make it impossible to find real love?"

Telaine's voice was filled with such compassion Julia's anger slipped away, no matter how she tried to hold on to it. "It's not forever," she said. "Just two weeks. Just this season. I don't—I can't bear it this year. I don't know why this time is different. And no, I don't know if I want love again, or a husband. I just want to go a few weeks without everyone believing I ought to marry whatever man I've spent time with the most recently."

Telaine took Ben's hand absently. "I didn't know you felt that way."

"Neither did I," Julia said. "Will you keep the secret? Please?"

"If it means so much to you, of course," Telaine said, but she still didn't look happy. Julia ignored this. Then she had to ignore the guilt she felt over disregarding her cousin's objections. It was a harmless ruse, and in two weeks, it would all be over.

3

The next day, Julia sent a message to Lord Eric, requesting the pleasure of his company on a drive through the Park. It wasn't legally required for the Crown Princess to be the one who made the overtures, not like it would be if she were Queen, but she was determined to make this ruse work, and it had occurred to her that Lord Eric, in the cold light of day, might start to have misgivings. Her resolve, contrarily, had hardened overnight into conviction. She would make everyone believe she and Lord Eric were courting, whatever it took.

But she received a response in half an hour, thanking her for the invitation and agreeing to meet her at the palace stables with his carriage. That boded well. She didn't enjoy driving and hadn't liked the idea of meeting him at Elizabeth's mansion, as if he were her subordinate. Julia changed her clothes and strolled down to the stables.

Lord Eric was waiting for her, as agreed. She climbed onto the seat beside him without help and said, "I hope you didn't think I was being forward."

"We haven't established what kind of relationship we have yet, your Highness." Lord Eric snapped the reins, and the pair of horses stepped out smartly. "Aside from our mutual attraction, as we revealed at last night's supper. Am I to be forceful and manly, or do you prefer a man who admires your take-charge attitude?"

He said this with such dry humor Julia laughed. "I had no idea plotting a pretend courtship would be such fun."

"Well, as long as we're putting on a show, it should be a good one, don't you agree?"

"Indeed, my lord." Julia considered. "I couldn't respect a man who let me order him around and was meek and humble. I think you should be forthright and possessed of your own opinions, but respectful of mine as well. I admire strength paired with kindness."

"I'll do my best." Lord Eric nodded to a man driving a passing carriage, who stared at them with his mouth hanging open. Julia smiled brilliantly, making the man look even more stunned and then pull up sharply to avoid driving into someone else.

"It's already working," Julia said. "Did you know him?"

"I know almost no one in Aurilien, but I've found a surprising number of people recognize me." Lord Eric guided the carriage through the gates of the Park. "I think it's because everyone in the upper-class set knows each other, and it's not hard to guess who the stranger is, given that Elizabeth has freely let it be known that her scoundrel brother is back from exile."

He still sounded amused, but Julia said, "Surely you're not a scoundrel."

Lord Eric shrugged. "Whatever you call it. The black sheep of the family. It doesn't bother me."

Curious, Julia asked, "Why did you come back, then? It's been twenty years—has something changed?"

"Me, I suppose. I realized I was tired of living abroad. Eskandel is beautiful, but I'm obviously not native, and that's wearying over time. And I had the opportunity to study in a well-known musical conservatory here. So I wrote to Elizabeth, who was unexpectedly happy about the prospect of receiving me, and..." He shrugged again.

"I wouldn't have thought you needed more study in music, not after what I heard last night."

"You flatter me, your Highness. There's always something more to learn, some greater understanding of music. It's something I love, playing and composing."

Julia raised her eyebrows. "You write music, too? Are you also a singer?"

Lord Eric laughed. "With this voice? Definitely not. I told you I wasn't a savant."

"Still, that's remarkable. What else do you do? How did you make a living in Eskandel, all those years?"

He shot her a narrow-eyed glance before returning his attention to the road. "I don't recall our agreement signing me up to be interrogated, your Highness. Shouldn't you answer some questions as well?"

He was teasing, so she didn't take offense. "You're quite right. We should know things about one another. Ask away."

"What does a Crown Princess do all day? Is it all social calls and traditionally womanly pursuits, or do you have other employment?"

The carriage bounced on a rough patch on the path, and Julia instinctively took Lord Eric's arm to steady herself. "I have a position in the Foreign Affairs department. It's meant to prepare me for the rigors of ruling a country. I used to be in Finance, and before that in Transportation—it's how my father was taught by my grandfather. And I sit in on Council meetings, which are held weekly. Aside from that, I visit with friends and attend social events, and I spend time with my family."

"That's a busy schedule."

"Well, you're now a part of it. For many of those events, it's appropriate for me to have an escort."

"With pleasure, your Highness."

They fell silent for a while, observing the beauties of the Park. At this season, there weren't many beauties: the trees' bare branches looked like skeletal arms reaching for heaven, and most of the bushes and shrubberies, the few that kept their leaves year round, looked dull, faded as if cast in perpetual shade. But red berries crowded the glossy dark green leaves of the holly bushes, and vines blossoming with white and gold flowers twined through the iron hoops arching over the path, enough color to keep the Park from feeling dead.

They came around the curve that revealed the small ornamental lake and the waterfall. There were no swans swimming in it at this season, but Julia liked the sound of the water flowing and crashing down the short drop.

"For several years, I was a clerk for a trading business in Eskandel," Lord Eric said abruptly. "I gradually made a name for myself as a musician, and for the last five years I've supported myself that way. I had a position with the Eskandel Opera House for a while, but mostly I gave concerts."

"That must be so satisfying," Julia said. "I can't imagine doing anything creative, myself. I'm good at needlework thanks to my mother's teaching, but it's not something the Crown Princess can make a living at."

"And you have a daughter, I've heard. Did you pass on your needlework skills to her?"

For a moment, discomfort kept Julia from answering, though she didn't know why Lord Eric shouldn't ask about Emma Telaine. "No," she finally said. "Emma Telaine is too restless for needlework. My mother says it's the influence of her namesake, who is also terrible at sewing."

"I was surprised to learn Princess Telaine had adopted out of the royal family. And she was an agent of the Crown?"

"For many years. It was a surprise to everyone. But she's happy with her life."

"How fortunate," Lord Eric said.

Julia didn't know what to make of that. He didn't sound critical or disparaging, but his words sounded as if they meant more than what they did on the surface. Finally, she said, "Emma Telaine plays the pianoforte as well. I thought she should try many things, not just needlework, to see what activities appealed to her. She complains about her lessons, but she practices without being forced to, so I think she enjoys it. I would love for her to become as skilled as you are."

"I didn't start learning until after I was in Eskandel. It was something to do to pass the time. Then it turned out I loved it. Music takes people that way sometimes." Lord Eric slowed the horses so they could enjoy the waterfall a while longer. Some distance away, on the pedestrian path, men and women slowed as well to stare at them. Instead of embarrassment, Julia felt cheerful. Yes, let those people see she had an escort, and let them tell their friends.

She realized she was still holding her companion's arm. His gloved hands gripped the reins loosely, but in a way that told her he wouldn't let the horses run away with them. She remembered the shape of his fingers, his hand clasping hers, and she shivered for no reason she could imagine.

"Are you cold? There's quite a nip in the air despite the sun," Lord Eric said.

Julia shook her head. "I'm fine. But perhaps we should finish our drive."

"I was thinking we should get dinner together," Lord Eric said as the carriage moved more quickly. "Somewhere public."

Julia laughed. "Now, *that* is the kind of forceful decisiveness I like in a man," she said.

4

Julia hadn't expected, when she proposed the pretend courtship, that she would have so much fun. She and Lord Eric spent their mornings visiting museums or art galleries and their evenings at whatever event the Crown Princess had been invited to. Julia enjoyed watching her peers tie themselves into knots finding discreet ways to pry into Julia's business. She pretended complete and airy ignorance about their prying.

Lord Eric, for his part, was a charming and considerate companion, making her laugh with his tales of life in Eskandel's music community and listening intently to her stories about her work and her family. She began to feel as if she'd known him all her life. How unfortunate that fate had driven him away from Tremontane—except he wouldn't be the man he was if he hadn't fled to Eskandel, and she liked the man he was.

The third night after the beginning of their ruse, they attended a salon held by Lord Colman, an evening reading featuring some of Aurilien's most famous poets. Lord Colman's parties were always exclusive in the most literal sense of excluding anyone he didn't think had the proper sensibilities, irrespective of titles or wealth. Julia was honored by the invitation. She was pleased for other reasons as well; Lord Colman's sister Yvonne was a friend, and the Colman mansion sat nearly at the top of Aurilien's hill and thus had a fabulous view of the lights of the city, sparkling like a dowager's jewelry cabinet.

Devices hidden in the wainscoting of the foyer played recordings of chamber music to welcome the guests, another sign of Lord Colman's proud eccentricity. Most of the wealthy hired actual performers, but Lord Colman was fond of Devisery, and he never let others' opinions dictate his actions. Julia held her head high as she sailed into the foyer on Lord Eric's arm, tilting her chin just so. It was enough to make him say, in a low voice, "You look like a warrior queen making a triumphal entry."

She warmed all over at his words. "My mother was a warrior of the Kirkellan, so that's not too far from the truth."

"Well, I—"

When he didn't immediately continue, Julia said, "What is it?"

"I shouldn't say. You'll think me impertinent."

Julia drew him closer. "Don't force me to have our first fight here in front of all these people."

He let out a laugh he instantly stifled, though not fast enough to keep those nearest them from staring. "Very well," he said. "I was thinking it was my good fortune to escort the most beautiful woman in Tremontane tonight."

She was used to hearing such compliments, but on his lips, so off-handed and at the same time so serious, they sent a tingle of pleasure through her. "I thank you for the compliment," she said lightly, not wanting him to know how he'd affected her.

"It *was* my good fortune," he continued in his low, rough voice. "And then I realized how many men are staring at me as if they'd like to stab me through the heart."

Julia choked back a laugh. "It's not that bad."

"I assure you it is. It's a good thing dueling is out of style."

She glanced at him. He was about the same height as she, maybe an inch or two taller, which made him very tall indeed. "Are you saying," she said in a teasing tone, "you'd fight a duel for me?"

He met her gaze steadily. "We're courting," he said. "It's practically compulsory."

Julia's smile fell away. He'd been joking. Hadn't he? Embarrassed, she searched for a humorous reply, but the sound of the bell signaling the beginning of the performance saved her.

They sat together, not touching, and Julia tried to focus on the readings. Instead, she found herself unexpectedly conscious of Lord Eric's closeness, of how his hands rested loosely on his knees. She should take his hand. That would reinforce the illusion that they were courting. It was natural. But the thought of touching him uninvited made her uncomfortable, like it was an intimacy that went beyond their pretend courtship. Which was ridiculous, because they liked each other, and they were becoming friends, but that was all.

Lord Eric escorted her home and bowed over her hand as he said good night. Julia held his hand a moment too long, and in her embarrassment blurted out, "I think it's going well, don't you? No one's so much as hinted that they know someone I really must meet. What about you?"

"You were right," Lord Eric said. "Nobody whispers about my sordid past. It's all speculation about our courtship. I admit I'm surprised. I didn't think anyone would believe it."

"I suppose we are better actors than we thought," Julia said. "Good night, my lord."

"You should call me Eric," Lord Eric said. "It will make the illusion more realistic."

Again, that unexpected tingle ran through her, as if he'd said something more intimate. "You're right. I hadn't considered that. Will you call me Julia?"

"If you wish, your Highness. Julia." Eric bowed again and walked away.

Julia watched him go. Then she made her way along the old familiar corridors to the east wing, where the royal family lived. Were they friends, now? She hadn't had a male friend she wasn't related to in...well, ever. So maybe she just didn't know how that friendship was supposed to feel. Or maybe she was letting her imagination run away with her. Pretending to court meant doing many of the same things one did in an actual courtship, and that meant it was natural for her to be confused.

And he *was* handsome despite the beard, she thought as she readied herself for bed. Or possibly because of it. Handsome, and tall, and nothing like Lucas— She stopped that line of thought and made herself go mentally over Council business until it bored her to sleep.

5

Julia and Telaine sat together in the great drawing room of the east wing three days later. The drawing room had looked the same throughout all of Julia's life, sofas and chairs upholstered in umber or cream or sage green silk, tables scattered through the room at random, and the enormous half-circle fireplace with its hearth of river stones. The fire was never extinguished even in the heart of summer, and Julia found it comforting. Her mother could have redecorated, since that was the Consort's prerogative, but Imogen North didn't care anything about interior decoration and was satisfied with the way the previous Consort, Julia's grandmama, had left things.

Now Julia cast an eye over the room in general and saw how widely spread the furnishings were. Mother had unbent enough to arrange them into small groupings for intimate discussion, but whenever the whole family was present, the chairs always got rearranged to suit whatever was happening. It still meant the room was far too large for its furniture. Julia couldn't imagine what they might add to make the room seem less about to swallow them all whole.

At the nearest table, Telaine, dressed in plain trousers and a shirt with a grease stain on one sleeve, was fiddling with Julia's pocket watch. Julia stole glances at her between stitches. She was embroidering flowers on the cuffs of one of Emma Telaine's shirts, which was more difficult than embroidering fabric that could be cut and stitched into a shirt, but had the advantage of looking exactly as Julia wanted.

"I realize this will destroy my reputation as a talented Deviser," Telaine said in the distant way she had when she was focused on repairing a Device, "but I think you may need a new watch. This one is going to go on losing time no matter what I do to it."

"That is quite the admission," Julia said. She lowered her embroidery hoop. "I hear children's voices."

Telaine's head came up. "A lot of children's voices. A mob, even. Remember how quiet the east wing was when we were children?"

Distantly, Julia heard the sound of a door banging shut, and the shouting grew louder. In another few seconds, seven children ranging in size from small to nearly adult burst into the drawing room. Emma Telaine was at the head of the pack, her golden hair mussed, her blue eyes gleaming with excitement. She was followed by Telaine's two oldest children, Julia's brother Jeffy's three oldest, and her brother Edward's second daughter.

"Mother," Emma Telaine said, panting, "Mother, may we play in the garden? We're going to build a fort—"

"Two forts," Telaine's son Owen said.

"Two forts," Emma Telaine went on, "and we're going to have a battle with North soldiers and Ruskalder warriors, can we please?"

"Have you finished your lessons?" Julia asked.

Emma Telaine scowled. "We can do lessons anytime. It's almost Wintersmeet!"

"Which is why lessons should be finished early so you'll be

able to enjoy the holiday." Julia felt she sounded reasonable, but the awkwardness she always experienced when she and her daughter were at odds crept over her. Emma Telaine always managed to make her feel as if Julia was wrong in expecting her to behave herself, to do as she was told.

Sure enough, Emma Telaine came back with, "We can do our lessons after Wintersmeet just as easily, Mother."

The other children joined in a chorus echoing Emma Telaine's words. Julia's heart froze. She was a terrible mother, terrible at getting her one child to obey, and everyone knew it, not least of whom was her daughter, who played on Julia's insecurities.

"That's enough," Telaine said. "Children, Aunt Julia is right. I think we can have a compromise. Let's have today be the last day of lessons, and as soon as you finish, you can build your forts."

Now the drawing room echoed with the sounds of disappointment. Julia said, "We're being reasonable, and I think you should be, too."

It was a mistake. Emma Telaine glared at her. "You always say that like I'm a child," she said. "I'm eleven. I know what's reasonable."

"Eleven years old is a little old for building forts," Julia snapped.

The room fell silent. Emma Telaine's glare could have melted iron. "I hate you," she said, and ran away down one of the long, dark halls toward her room.

Julia didn't know where to look, but it didn't seem anyone wanted to meet her eyes. "She'll calm down eventually," she said.

Telaine cleared her throat. "Off to the schoolroom, and Mister Schotton will hear your lessons and report to me."

The children walked away in the direction opposite the one Emma Telaine had taken. Julia waited for her cousin to say something, but Telaine remained silent, flicking a loose coil of wire that protruded from the watch Device. Finally, unable to bear the pressure, Julia said, "I never say the right thing."

"She doesn't hate you," Telaine said.

"I'm not sure about that. We fight all the time, and—well, it's as I said. I never know how to talk to her. I was never like this to my mother. What am I doing wrong?"

"I'm not the one to give parenting advice."

Julia let out a harsh laugh. "Your children are perfectly behaved. I don't know who'd be better at it."

"They're as stubborn as their father. Maybe we don't have the same fights you and Emma Telaine do, but they defy me often enough." Telaine changed seats so she could sit next to Julia and put an arm around her shoulders. "I'm sure this is something she'll grow out of."

Julia blinked and realized her eyes were brimming with tears. "She's been bragging about her father again," she said in a low voice.

Telaine's arm stiffened. "You haven't told her the truth?"

"I have no idea how to go about destroying her illusions. Some of what Lucas did isn't suitable for an eleven-year-old child's ears. And I know she's built him up in her mind as this wonderful hero mainly because it hurts her that she's the only child in this family without a father. I know it's all self-defense. But—" Julia wiped her eyes. "It hurts so much to have her talk about Lucas and how amazing he was, and then turn around and tell me she hates me."

Telaine held her in silence until Julia got herself under control. "She'll know eventually," Telaine whispered. "You're a wonderful mother. That matters even if she doesn't realize it."

Julia nodded and hugged her cousin back. Then she rose and packed her needlework away in its tapestry bag. "I'm engaged to go to a ball with Eric tonight. I should get ready."

"Eric," Telaine said. "You've spent every day with him since Elizabeth's party. Is your ruse successful?"

"It is. I wish I'd thought of this years ago."

"I'm glad you didn't," Telaine said, and wouldn't elaborate.

On the way to the ball, Eric was unusually silent. Finally, Julia asked, "Is something wrong?"

"I shouldn't have agreed to this," Eric said.

His words sent an icy spear through Julia's chest. She managed, "This—what? This pretense?"

"Oh, no," Eric said. "This ball. I don't actually know how to dance."

"You don't know how to dance?" Julia exclaimed.

"You could shout it a little louder," Eric said wryly.

"We're in a carriage. No one can hear us but the driver, and he's not listening. Why didn't you say something?"

Eric shook his head. "Because usually when I attend a ball, I mingle with the crowd and don't ask anyone to dance, and it's not an issue. I don't know why I didn't consider that that won't be an option when I attend with the woman I'm courting with."

"Hmm." Tremontanan dances weren't the sort of thing one could fumble one's way through. They were complex and varied even before one considered the social rules: dancing once with someone was politeness, dancing twice showed an interest, and dancing two or more dances in a row meant love or even betrothal. "I suppose I'll have to teach you."

Eric's eyebrows rose nearly to his hairline. "In the middle of the ball?"

"There are easy dances. And besides, you don't have to learn more than two." Julia rested her hand on his knee briefly. "It will be fun!"

His lips twisted in sardonic amusement. "You have a very strange definition of 'fun.'"

Their hosts' home was one of those built a century ago in the district below the palace, tall and thin but extending far to the rear. It blazed with light at every window, even the upper stories where no guests would be expected to go. No other carriages waited at the gate, indicating that Julia and Eric had arrived late. The dancing would be well underway. Perfect for what Julia intended.

She rushed Eric through the foyer and the ballroom entrance, where she barely stopped long enough to greet her hosts without seeming rude. Like the house, the ballroom was long and narrow and occupied most of the back of the property. The roof was made of glass, long curved panes that with the backdrop of darkness reflected the many dancing couples below, upside-down doppelgangers clinging to the ceiling. Julia had been there often enough she didn't bother looking up.

She dragged Eric after her through the ballroom and onto the wide patio circling it on three sides. The night was chilly, but her exertions made the environment pleasant. The patio lay in a bubble of light from the many windows and quiet music, beyond which the gardens were nearly invisible in the darkness. Julia tucked her hand into Eric's arm, and they strolled, waiting for the next dance to begin. Eric's arm was unexpectedly tense. "You're not afraid of a little dancing?" she said.

"I don't like standing out," Eric said, so curtly she regretted her light tone. Then he sighed, and covered her hand with his. "I apologize. No, I'm not afraid of dancing, just of looking foolish."

"That's how everyone feels, my father tells me. He says, remember everyone else is so worried about how they look they're too busy to worry about other people's mistakes. I think that's a little optimistic, given that—well, anyway." She couldn't believe she'd almost brought up her own ten-year-old scandal. "Here, this is a good musical piece. The dance that goes with it is also danced to four other tunes, so if you remember which ones those are, you should be fine."

She arranged their arms, his left hand low on her waist, her left hand on his shoulder, their right hands clasped and raised high. "Just follow me—you're a musician, you can keep a beat. It's in three-quarter time, a steady *one*-two-three, *one*-two-three..."

Eric was an awkward dancer, but the waltz wasn't a complicated dance, and before long he managed to stop looking at his feet and could watch her. His expression was so comical, part surprise, part terror, that she had to suppress a smile that might have hurt his feelings. She was paying attention only to him, so she was unaware of her surroundings until the music came to an end and someone said, "Well, I have to say I've never seen the waltz danced quite like *that* before," in a drawling, amused way.

Eric's hand closed on hers tightly. Julia looked over his shoulder at Edgar Hussey, standing in the door to the ballroom and smiling his cruel smile. Julia had never liked him, hanger-on and useless society drone that he was, but for once his words struck home. She didn't dare look at Eric, didn't want to see humiliation on his face. "Mister Hussey," she began.

Eric turned, releasing his hold on Julia's waist but keeping a tight grip on her hand. "Hussey, is it?" he said, his voice rougher than usual. "I suppose you were watching us because you couldn't attract a partner of your own. Don't worry, I'm sure there's someone around here willing to overlook your poor fashion sense and personal odor."

Julia suppressed a gasp. Hussey took a step forward. "Why, you—"

"Think before you say anything else." Eric walked forward, bringing Julia with him. "I don't take kindly to anyone insulting her Highness. You're a typical blight on Tremontanan society, quick with a sharp word and quick to pretend you didn't mean anything by it. Leave now, before I forget I was raised a gentleman."

Hussey's gaze flicked to Julia and back to Eric. With a snarl, he backed away and disappeared into the ballroom.

Eric seemed to realized he was crushing Julia's hand and released her. He walked to the patio rail and stood gripping it, his head bowed. Julia slowly moved to join him. "He wasn't insulting me," she said, feeling stupid.

"I know, but I thought he would back down more quickly if he believed his insult had been misconstrued," Eric replied. "I reacted poorly."

"You did not. Edgar Hussey is a terrible person. I don't know how he keeps managing to get invited to social events. Telaine hates him—she'd be your new best friend if she'd seen what you just did."

Eric smiled, but he still didn't look at her. "I don't like being mocked. Never have. I'm afraid it makes me angry, and then I lash out."

"Fine, but this time it was warranted, I assure you."

Finally, he turned. "You are far more generous of spirit than I, your Highness."

"You agreed to call me Julia," Julia said.

"You're right. I'd forgotten." He gazed at her thoughtfully. "How is it," he said, "that—no. Never mind. I don't want to pry."

Julia stared at him. "You know," she said, "I always wonder, when people say 'I don't want to pry,' if they're saying it so they have an excuse to do so? Because it just makes the other person curious about what you meant to say, and then they insist you say it, and if it truly is something awful, you're both hurt."

"I didn't mean that," Eric said. "I forgot myself for a moment, that's all. Pretend I didn't say anything. Let's talk about the weather."

Julia sighed. "I'm going to regret this, but I insist you tell me the horrible thing you wanted to ask that will make me hate both of us forever."

Eric tilted his head back. "Aren't the stars beautiful? I understand we're to have clear weather up until Wintersmeet Eve."

"Eric!"

"I don't want you to hate me," he said, his expression still and his eyes intent on her. Again that icy spear stabbed her heart.

"I won't," she assured him. Why she was pushing so hard, she didn't know, but in the moonlit darkness, with the sounds of distant music and laughter drifting into the cloudless sky, she wanted nothing more than to know what had made him sound so thoughtful.

Eric let out a deep breath and bowed his head again. "Why is it," he said, "that a woman as beautiful and clever and funny and powerful as you hasn't ever been courted the way you deserve? Why *aren't* you married to the man of your dreams?"

All the blood drained from Julia's face. She put a hand on the cold stone of the railing to steady herself. She'd heard variations on that question a million times and it never failed to feel like a rebuke. Like it was a failing in her. And maybe it was.

Eric didn't seem to realize he'd struck her dead. She made herself meet his gaze. He looked curious, not critical, but she wished him gone anyway. Except she couldn't leave without him, and she couldn't go flying through the ballroom to escape him.

"I was, once," she heard herself say. "Lucas Wentworth. I loved him more than anything. And he didn't love me. He wanted a royal title, and he lied and schemed to make me love him. And all the time he was—he had lovers, and eventually a mistress he fathered a child on. When he thought he was safe, that I wouldn't risk scandal by divorcing him, he taunted me with the knowledge of his infidelity and with the most horrible insults you can imagine."

Eric said nothing. Julia drew a shuddering breath. This was more than he'd asked, but it felt like lancing a boil, like draining away the poison that had filled her veins for ten years. "He was wrong about what I was willing to endure. I divorced him, and then he died, and by now everyone's forgotten the scandal except me, and I can't not remember it."

Eric's expression softened. "You're right," he said. "I shouldn't have asked."

Julia shook her head. "You shouldn't. And I shouldn't have made you."

She turned away so he wouldn't see her cry, but no tears came. Maybe ten years was long enough for the pain to fade. Or maybe she was so tired of holding on to her personal tragedy she couldn't summon the energy to cry.

Eric put a hand on her shoulder and turned her to face him. He looked like he was searching for something to say. Then he put his arms around her and held her. His embrace was warm and solid and comforting, and without thinking she hugged him back. She ran her hands lightly over his broad shoulders, felt him rest a hand low on her back as if steadying her against a storm. She didn't know what anyone who saw them would make of it and didn't care.

They stood holding one another in the chilly dark, not speaking, not moving, and Julia closed her eyes and rested her head on his shoulder. She hadn't felt this secure in a long time, and she didn't think she'd ever felt this comforted.

After a time, she stepped away from him and said, "Thank you."

"I'm sorry," Eric said. "I don't want to cause you pain."

"You didn't. It was all me." Julia let out a deep breath. "I'm freezing."

"So am I." He extended an arm to her, and they strolled back into the ballroom, where the ball was in full swing. No one paid them any attention, though cold air must surely be wafting off them in freezing waves. "Should we dance again?"

Julia regarded him closely. "I think we should leave."

"You don't want to make a show of our attachment?" Eric said.

Julia remembered holding him in the moonlight. "I don't think we need to," she said.

6

"Are you sure I shouldn't be blindfolded?" Eric said. "You're being so mysterious about where you're taking me."

Julia squeezed his arm lightly. "It didn't occur to me. Besides, it's not that mysterious."

Eric turned his head to look in every direction. "I've never been in the palace before. That makes it mysterious."

They were walking down one of the wide corridors that radiated out from the palace Rotunda, straight as a wheel spoke, though if the Rotunda was the wheel's hub, it would be an ungainly, impossible wheel with spokes all of different lengths and no rim. The palace had grown up over the course of hundreds of years, with different Kings and Queens of Tremontane adding onto it as their whims dictated. This gave it a patchwork appearance Julia liked. She loved to imagine the rooms and halls spreading out like an inkblot, irregular in shape and décor, reflecting trends in architecture and interior decoration. The confines of the city meant the construction had finally been checked right around the time Julia's ancestor Willow, the first

North Queen, had taken the Crown, but Julia thought 'up' had tremendous possibilities.

This corridor had no carpet, so their footsteps sounded loud in the stillness, Eric's heavier tread matching Julia's softer slipper-clad step on the floorboards. To the left, pedestals bearing white marble busts of famous Tremontanans lined the wall at five-foot intervals. Julia didn't know who most of them were meant to be, but she guessed they must be famous indeed to be immortalized like that. The walls were dressed stone, which didn't match the polished floor or the busts, but that was another thing Julia found appealing, these places in the palace where design elements were mismatched. It kept the place from being intimidating.

Ahead, natural light made a square on the floor at the end of the hall, and Eric's pace quickened until Julia slowed him. "Did you bring me all the way through the palace only to take me out the far side?" he asked.

"No. Be patient. I promise it's worth it."

The hall ended at an open doorway through which brilliant sunlight poured. Julia escorted Eric the last few steps into the warm, slightly humid room and waited for his reaction.

Eric let his arm fall and walked forward into the greenhouse garden. He tilted his head back to look up at the clear glass panes set in the iron framework, then turned on his heel to take in the pots and raised beds filled with richly green-smelling ferns and shrubs and tall, graceful trees. "Extraordinary," he said.

Julia ran a hand over a lilac bush blooming out of season. The sweet scent filled her. "That's not all."

"There's more? I can't imagine what more there could be."

Eric followed Julia through the aisles made by the garden beds and came up short at the sight of the pianoforte. Julia kept going until she could lay her hand on its glossy lid. "This is Queen Vivienne's pianoforte," she said. "She loved to play, and family legend says she hated the instrument in Queen Genevieve's drawing room. It's in a room near the top of the palace that is exposed to every wind you can imagine, and it's usually freezing cold."

"Those aren't the best conditions for a pianoforte," Eric said. He'd walked around until he was standing near the keyboard.

"No, and I don't think these are, either. All this damp air. I don't know much about pianofortes, but this one has a Device regulating the climate's effect on it, and it still has to be tuned frequently. Anyway, Queen Vivienne loved this conservatory, and she arranged for a pianoforte to be installed here so she could play comfortably year round. A play on words, maybe—a conservatory in a conservatory. Or something. I know the thing takes tremendous maintenance, but it has a beautiful sound. I thought...maybe you'd like to try it out."

"Me?" Eric sounded awed rather than surprised. "This is a piece of Tremontanan history."

"I know. Would you?" Julia gestured. She was starting to feel she'd done something foolish and sentimental, something that didn't mean as much as she'd hoped.

Eric ran his fingers down the keys, not pressing down so they made no noise. Then he settled down on the bench and flexed his hands before resting them lightly on the keys again. After a second's pause, he started playing an exercise Julia recognized, a piece Emma Telaine played to warm up. From the exercise, Eric went into something more complicated, a fast and rippling melody called "Snow River Rush." Julia moved to where she could watch his hands. They were elegant and graceful and exquisitely masculine, and she found herself holding her breath as if her breathing might interfere with the song.

Then the music changed. The rhythm slowed, and the melody dropped lower and was joined by powerful bass notes that echoed it. Gradually, the melody rose in pitch and grew louder, so sweet it brought tears to Julia's eyes. It reminded her of sunny, peaceful afternoons and nights spent cuddling her baby and of a nameless emotion that wrenched at her heart with longing.

"That's beautiful," she said. "What is it called?"

Eric didn't look up. "It doesn't have a name," he said. "I wrote it for you."

His words struck her to the heart again, this time with a numb astonishment that froze her to the spot. She opened her mouth, closed it again. The music continued to wash over her, rousing that nameless emotion until she felt she might burst. She'd never heard anything like it.

He'd written it for her.

With a few soft chords and a final high note, the song ended. Eric still didn't look up. His hands rested on the keyboard again. Surprise and joy and heartrending sorrow filled Julia until she didn't know what she felt. She knew he was waiting for a response. She cleared her throat, and said, "Eric—"

The bushes rustled. A page dressed in North colors, dark blue and silver, emerged into the open. "Excuse me, your Highness," she said in her high-pitched child's voice, "the King requests your presence in his office immediately."

Julia had never come so close to ripping into anyone. Without looking at Eric, she said, "Thank you. I'll go right away. Eric, will you...will you...you'll stay, yes?"

"I'll be here," Eric said.

She hurried after the page, cursing herself for being both glad and angry about the interruption. She didn't know what to say. She didn't know what he meant. Maybe he wrote songs for all his friends...songs that felt like a lover's caress, like a kiss in the darkness? But theirs wasn't a real courtship. She was certain of that.

No, that was a lie. She no longer knew what they were to each other, and she certainly didn't know what she wanted from him.

But he was kind, and handsome, and funny, and just the right kind of serious, and she'd never been this close to any man, not even Lucas. So maybe that was a lie, too, and she did know what she wanted.

She ran through the halls to the north wing. Either her father had the worst timing in the world, or he'd saved her from embarrassment, but either way, it was a reprieve.

She knocked on the King's office door and was bade to enter. Father stood at the window behind his enormous claw-footed desk, looking out over the parade grounds off to the side. "I hope I didn't interrupt anything important," he said.

For a mad moment, Julia thought he'd magically seen her with Eric in the conservatory, that he knew what had passed between them. "I don't think so," she managed. "Is it something urgent?"

"Not urgent, but not something I want to put off. Sit." He took one of the seats in front of the roaring fireplace and gestured for Julia to sit opposite him. "I hope you won't see this as prying, but I wanted to ask you about your relationship with Eric d'Arden."

Julia wasn't sure her heart could take any more surprises. "What about it?" she asked, stalling for time, hoping some part of her knew the answer.

"You only just met him a week and a half ago, but you've singled him out for your attention. Is there something you want to tell me?"

She wasn't going to tell him about the charade now, not if she hadn't told him from the beginning. "I like him, and I enjoy his company," she said, and immediately felt guilty, as if she'd lied but didn't know what about.

"I see." Father steepled his fingers in front of him. "Is that what you would tell Telaine?"

Father knew about Telaine's magical ability to hear lies. This was a sideways way of telling Julia he thought she wasn't being honest with him. "Telaine knows all my secrets," she said.

Father frowned. "I don't know how much you know about d'Arden," he said. "That was a nasty business he was mixed up in. Another man, Stephen Bailie, eventually claimed responsibility for the shooting, but the fact that d'Arden fled even though he wasn't guilty meant I had suspicions about what else he might be hiding."

"He was exonerated," Julia said angrily. "Isn't that enough? Or do you think he should have to bear that guilt for the rest of his life?"

"I only want you to be happy, Julia." Father let out a deep breath. "I don't want you to be hurt again."

"Well, you're not the keeper of my happiness," Julia snapped. Instantly, she regretted it. "I'm sorry, Father, I didn't mean—"

"I wish I'd never consented to your marriage to Lucas," Father said. "You don't know how I regret it. I could have forbidden the match, and he wouldn't have been in a position to abuse you."

Julia closed her eyes briefly. "Please, don't," she said. "I was stupidly in love—emphasis on 'stupid'—and if you'd forbidden it, I would have run away with Lucas, and he would have abandoned me, and I might not have felt I could come home and I'd be living a miserable life somewhere else right now. It's not your fault any more than it was mine."

"That doesn't stop the regret, does it?"

"No," Julia said, "but I think...I think I've started leaving it behind."

Father looked at her narrowly. "Because of Eric d'Arden?"

His question cleared away all her uncertainty. "I think so," she said. "Maybe. Yes."

Father rose from his seat. "In that case, I wish you the best, whatever that turns out to be." He hugged her briefly and let her go.

Julia ran back to the conservatory by the long route, not because she wanted to delay—every moment she wasted was agony —but because the long route meant not encountering anyone who might want something from her. She hoped Eric hadn't given up and left. She hoped she understood what it meant that he'd written that song for her. She hoped she was right about her feelings. It might still all be a mistake, but she hoped...

She heard piano music as she approached the door to the conservatory, but this was halting, tentative, someone playing the same eight measures repeatedly as if practicing. She slowed her steps. Surely Eric was more advanced a musician than that?

As she walked between the garden boxes, she began to hear two voices, one low, one high. After another moment, she realized it was Eric, speaking to Emma Telaine. Julia had forgotten her daughter liked to practice in this room, though it was out of her way compared to the other music rooms. Julia stopped to listen.

"...remember to keep your wrists arched and your fingers curved," Eric said.

"That makes my hands ache," Emma Telaine said. Her voice didn't have the whine in it Julia so often heard directed at her.

"That's because your hands aren't strong yet. Keep doing it, and soon it will be habit and you won't feel any pain." Julia heard a couple of trilling arpeggios and then a long, descending scale, and then, to her astonishment, Emma Telaine's giggle.

"Can I show you what I'm learning?" Emma Telaine said.

"Of course. Is this it? I don't think I've ever played that one." There was a rustle of paper.

"I'm not good yet, but I'm getting better, my pianoforte master tells me." Music began, a familiar tune Julia had heard Emma Telaine working on many times. Julia knew just enough about music to tell that her daughter had improved in the last few weeks.

A sour note, and then a few more sour notes, brought the music to a stop. "I always miss those notes," Emma Telaine said.

"May I try?" Eric started playing just before the difficult part and sailed through it with no trouble.

Emma Telaine gasped. "You said you hadn't played it before!"

"I'm good at sight reading. Look, if you change which fingers you use to hit the three notes before, you won't have any more trouble." Julia heard a couple of chords and a trill of notes, then the same thing again. The third time, the notes were the same, but more tentative, and Emma Telaine exclaimed, "I did it!"

"Of course," Eric said. "I can tell you love music because you didn't give up."

"I don't like giving up. Mother gets upset at me."

Julia didn't want that line of conversation to continue. "Eric?" she said, rustling the bushes as she passed to draw attention to herself and make it seem she hadn't heard those last terrible words. "Oh, Emma Telaine. I'm sorry, I didn't know you intended to practice here today."

"Lord Eric showed me how to play that one part," Emma Telaine exclaimed. "It's easy when you know how."

"Well, thank Lord Eric, and he and I have to leave now."

Emma Telaine's face screwed up in a frown Julia knew all too well. "I want him to stay and listen to me more. He's a good teacher."

A familiar despair began creeping over Julia, the knowledge that nothing she said would be right. "Lord Eric has better things to do with his time, sweetheart."

"Well, I—" Eric began.

Emma Telaine overrode him. "You mean I'm not important,

don't you? I think he ought to be able to decide for himself and not be bossed around by you!"

"Do not take that tone with me," Julia said, hating how overbearing she sounded.

"You say that every time I stand up for myself," Emma Telaine shouted. "I'm old enough to know what I want, and you can't tell me what to do! *I hate you!*"

"That's enough," Eric said, rising from his seat. "Apologize to your mother immediately."

Emma Telaine gaped. "What?"

"Your mother cares enough about you to want what's best for you, and you're behaving like a self-centered brat," Eric said. "If you can't treat her with the respect she deserves, what makes you think you deserve any respect yourself?"

"I—you're horrible!" Emma Telaine gathered up her music sheets and ran out of the room, shoving past Julia and sending up a terrible ruckus from the plants as she tore past.

Julia, stunned, said, "Why did you do that?"

"I won't stand for you being treated that way," Eric replied.

Five minutes before, his words would have thrown her into happy confusion. Now, they just made her cold. "Really?" she said, putting that ice into her voice. "I don't see how it's your business to discipline my daughter."

"Well, someone has to," Eric said.

Julia sucked in a breath. "How *dare* you," she snarled. "I am perfectly capable of raising my own child, and I did not invite you to share your opinions on the subject."

"You're behaving as if she's six and you can still control her," Eric said, his voice as cold as hers. "You don't believe she has opinions worth hearing, and she knows it. Why are you surprised when she fights you?"

Julia pointed in the direction of the door. "Get out."

Eric walked wide around her to the exit. She barely heard the bushes rustle. When the room was once more silent, she sat on the piano bench and, remembering how he'd played for her, slammed her fist against the keyboard in a loud, discordant pulse of sound that echoed off the glass-paned roof.

7

She and Eric had been meant to attend a musical evening that night, but three hours before they should have left, Julia received a note from Eric pleading indisposition and asking her to excuse him. She thought about going anyway, realized how it would look, and threw the crumpled note into the fire that burned year round in the east wing drawing room.

She ate supper silently, surrounded by her noisy family. Even when the children didn't join them, five siblings, four spouses, her parents, Ben, and Telaine made for a loud meal. Fortunately, it was loud enough that no one, not even the observant Telaine, realized Julia wasn't as cheerful as usual. The idea of carrying on small talk sickened her.

After the meal, she made a show of having a headache, fended off her mother's ministrations, and hurried to her rooms. They'd been her childhood suite, left behind for about a year while she was with Lucas and returned to with relief, like they'd been waiting for her to come to her senses. Sitting room, bathroom, bedroom, dressing room, just like all the other suites in the east wing. She'd redecorated the year Emma Telaine turned one, and now she stood in the sitting room and contemplated doing it again. Maybe she needed a change.

The sitting room felt stifling all of a sudden, though there wasn't much in the way of furnishings. They were all such old-fashioned furnishings, though, the couches heavy dark wood with velvet upholstery, ornately-carved tables and chairs that might be mistaken for works of art, a marble fireplace so heavy she didn't know how they'd gotten it up three flights of stairs. There weren't any portraits or art on the walls, and the curtains were heavy blue brocade that always looked dusty. Something had to be done, she decided, but not tonight. That headache threatened to become a reality.

She trudged into her bedroom, which was as light and airy as the sitting room was heavy and ponderous. Maybe this was why she put up with the sitting room; she had another, better room to retreat to. She removed her clothes without calling her maid and put on a nightdress, then unpinned her hair and brushed it until it shone. Her nursemaid had always said two hundred strokes a night would make it grow long and lush, but Mother said that was ridiculous. Still, Julia continued the ritual because it calmed her.

Someone knocked on the outer door. Julia pulled on a dressing gown and hoped whoever it was didn't have some dire news for her, though that would suit the day she'd had.

The person at the door was Emma Telaine.

Julia stared at her for a moment. Her daughter stared back. She looked like she'd been crying, but her eyes were dry, her mouth was set in a petulant frown, and she had both hands wound into the fabric of her dress. Finally, when it became clear Emma Telaine wasn't going to say or do anything else, Julia said, "Come in and have a seat."

Julia sat opposite her and watched her look at the walls, the mantel, the furnishings, anything but Julia herself. Julia felt a sudden exhaustion that made her incapable of shouldering the burden of conversation. She waited.

"I'm not a brat," Emma Telaine blurted out.

Julia said nothing. She didn't think it was true, but it wouldn't help matters for her to confirm or deny that statement.

"I'm *not*," Emma Telaine insisted. She swiped an arm across her face. "And I'm not self-centered."

Julia shifted her weight so she was leaning forward slightly. "I think you might be," she said. "But if you are, it's at least partly my fault."

"I—" Emma Telaine shut her mouth. Then she said, "Why?"

"Because I love you, and I thought that meant making you the center of my world," Julia said. "I felt guilty that you didn't have a father, so I tried to make it up to you by being both. But that only taught you the wrong lesson."

"You don't let me do everything I want," her daughter said. "You tell me no all the time."

"But I do it in the wrong way. I tell you no because I think other people are judging me for being too indulgent. And I never listen to what you say. You were right about that."

To her surprise, Emma Telaine began to cry. "I don't hate you," she said. "You're my mother. I want you to love me."

"Of course I love you," Julia exclaimed, and rocked back as Emma Telaine threw herself at her, sobbing. Julia held her and let her own tears fall.

"Lord Eric was right. I'm a brat and I don't respect you," Emma Telaine cried.

"Lord Eric was *not* right, and he was wrong to say those things," Julia said, her heart constricting and freezing over once more.

"Because he's not my father?" Emma Telaine asked.

"That's right." But even as she spoke, Julia's doubts crept up on her again. Maybe Eric hadn't had the right to discipline Julia's daughter, but he *hadn't* been wrong. He'd realized what Julia hadn't seen—that she didn't accept that Emma Telaine was old enough to be treated differently than a child, and that Julia didn't respect her daughter any more than Emma Telaine respected her when she had those tantrums. It was embarrassment and anger that had kept Julia from acknowledging that Eric had a point.

"So will he be my father?" Emma Telaine asked.

Julia froze. "Where did that come from?"

Emma Telaine sat back. "Everyone's saying it. That you're courting with him. Will you marry him?"

Julia didn't know why she couldn't give her daughter a simple "no" answer. "How would you feel about it if I did?"

"I don't know. He's good at pianoforte, and he seems nice, even though he said those horrid things. But I don't know if I want another father."

"Don't worry about it, then. I don't know that he wants to see me again, after we fought today." The memory of that fight loomed, dark and bitter.

"It's all right. I already had a wonderful father."

"You—" Almost Julia stayed silent. But she reflected on Eric's words, how he'd accused her of not treating Emma Telaine like a young woman whose opinions mattered, and said instead, "Let's talk about your father, all right? You're not going to like what you hear, but I think—I think it's time you knew the truth."

8

Julia sat still while her maid Lucy pinned her waist-length black tresses high on her head while letting a few shorter locks dangle free around her face. She made herself examine her face dispassionately. She was thirty-four, no longer in the first bloom of youth, but she thought—again, dispassionately—she was prettier than she had been as a teen and young woman. Her skin had always been clear, but now it glowed, her cheeks pink without artifice, her lips rosy red. She'd never been slim, and she'd put on weight since

Emma Telaine's birth, but that weight gave her curves and rounded her face in a way that suited her.

Lucy wound each remaining lock of hair around the heated iron, turning them into loose corkscrew curls. "Did you want the silver necklace, my lady?"

"No, my mother gave me Grandmama's diamonds as a Wintersmeet gift." Mother hadn't said why, either, just pressed the box into Julia's hand with a smile and a "I hope you have a marvelous evening, sweetheart."

She clasped the antique necklace around her throat and ran her fingers over the row of brilliant-cut diamonds, beautiful without being gaudy. It was fun to imagine her late grandmother attending the Wintersmeet Ball, dressed in one of those corsets that had been in style sixty-plus years ago. Father always said she and Grandpapa had loved dancing. The necklace made Julia feel connected to her family, though she wasn't sure she loved dancing as much as that. Or maybe she'd just never had the right partner.

The thought made her heart ache. She hadn't seen Eric, hadn't received any messages from him, since that disastrous day in the conservatory three days before. She'd written at least a dozen messages she hadn't had the courage to send. Torn between wanting to make things right and the feeling that the Crown Princess shouldn't be a supplicant even if she'd been wrong, she'd burned every one of those messages. And now she had no idea what to expect.

It didn't matter if Eric didn't come to the ball. The season was over after tonight, after all, and their pretend courtship would have been at an end even if they hadn't fought. But letting it end this way couldn't be right. Unless they weren't friends, after all. Maybe they weren't. Maybe this had all been Julia's imagination, spurred by loneliness and the first feelings of attraction she'd experienced in ten years.

Tradition said the royal family left the palace by a side door to be conveyed by white and silver carriages to the front door for a grand entrance. Julia decided tradition could go hang. She walked slowly, admiring the palace she loved, through the halls to the sloping one that led up to the ballroom entrance. The herald didn't indicate that he thought she'd done something strange in arriving alone, just announced her. Julia was used to the hush that fell over a crowd when she entered a room and no longer felt embarrassed or excited over it. She lifted her white silk skirt overlaid with silver lace and descended the stairs to the ballroom floor.

She'd walked through the palace more slowly than she realized, because she was late, and with the ballroom as full as it was of dancers, her entrance was more dramatic than she'd planned. She pretended calm and sailed through the crowd in search of a cool drink. If she moved quickly enough and didn't stand still for more than a few seconds at a time, no one would have the opportunity to ask her to dance. She felt a strange guilt at not wanting to dance, as if she was letting the diamonds down, but the room was hot and loud and crowded, and all at once the idea of making small talk with men, even men she knew, made her wish she hadn't come.

She secured a tall glass of sparkling wine and sipped it as she made her way around the dance floor. It was a beautiful sight, she had to admit, all those men and women in silver and white and black like a midnight snowstorm, with the music leading them in their hopping, gliding paths. She realized she'd stopped to admire for too long and walked more rapidly to compensate, ending up near the musicians. The noise there was overpowering, but that meant fewer people to potentially accost her.

Someone said, "Julia."

Her heart lurched. She turned to face Eric, who'd pitched his voice to carry over the music. He looked wonderful in a dark suit that showed off his broad shoulders, with a silver-edged white cravat pinned with a diamond that might have come off her necklace, it was so closely matched. His face was still, his gaze intent on her. Julia couldn't think of anything to say. It was a face that defied ordinary conversation.

The music came to an end, and the crowd applauded. Eric glanced past Julia at the musicians, then returned his gaze to her. "I hoped to speak to you," he said, not as loudly as before. "Will you walk with me?"

Julia set her half-empty glass on a nearby table and took his arm. She expected to feel a thrill at his touch, but her heart was racing and she didn't feel anything but ill, as if the glass had contained acid and not fine wine.

They walked, not speaking, as couples formed up for the next dance. No one paid the two of them any attention, which suited Julia. She'd decided to let him be the first to speak, since he'd made such an effort to reach her.

When they had nearly reached the base of the stairs, Eric said, "I want to apologize. I had no right to interfere in your family matters and none at all to criticize you. I spoke out of turn, and for that, I beg your forgiveness."

A dozen possible responses flooded to Julia's lips, tangling her tongue. "You shouldn't have interfered," she finally said. "But if you hadn't, I don't think my daughter and I would have finally reconciled. Thank you."

"I don't think I deserve thanks for my rude behavior."

"I'm the one you offended, so it's my prerogative to choose how to react." Julia squeezed his arm lightly. "And you did say you were moved by a desire to protect me. I appreciate that."

Eric stopped and faced her. "Do you?" he said.

She couldn't look away from his eyes. "More than you know."

Applause sounded, and for a heart-stopping moment, Julia

imagined the attendees of the Wintersmeet Ball were applauding the two of them. She smiled, and a second later, Eric smiled back, that brilliant, cheerful smile she remembered from the night they'd met.

The musicians struck up a series of chords indicating what song they'd play next, what dance it would be. A waltz. "Shall we dance?" she said.

"Are you sure you want everyone to see me tread on your toes?" Eric replied.

"You're better than you realize. We don't have to if you'd rather not."

Eric bowed over her hand. "It will be a fitting conclusion to our courtship, your Highness."

She was over-warm and probably red in the face, but his words made her pale. Their courtship. Their false courtship. She'd thought—but no, she'd been a fool. Of course he hadn't meant anything by it. This was where it had always been going. She didn't know why she'd let herself expect anything else.

She put on a practiced smile and let him lead her onto the dance floor. She could at least give the world the impression that she'd meant it to end this way. And she certainly wasn't going to hint to Eric that— She made herself stop thinking about it and focused on the steps.

He was so much improved from their last dance she wondered if he'd been practicing. They sailed around the ballroom, with its walls shrouded in silver tulle and the chandeliers lowered to cast a more intimate light across the dancers. Julia almost looked up at the ceiling, which was painted with a starry sky the exact replica of the positions of the stars on this most magical of nights, but she was afraid of distracting Eric, in case he wasn't as confident as he appeared. He'd regained his still, unsmiling expression, and it made her heart ache with longing.

They were near the center of the ballroom when the music came to a final flourish. All around them, men and women bowed or curtsied. Eric gracefully raised her gloved hand to his lips. It felt like farewell, and in that moment, she knew she couldn't let him go.

"Dance with me again," she said. "Right here. The next dance."

His eyes widened. "We don't need to play this charade out any longer. It's almost midnight."

"Not a charade," Julia said. "I want the world to see us dance. I want you to—" She swallowed. "I want you."

Eric stared at her. His cheeks were as flushed as hers were pale. Gently, he tugged his hand out of her grip. "No, your Highness," he said, and turned his back on her and walked away.

If anyone had seen that, Julia couldn't hear their whispers over the roaring of her pulse in her ears. The sick, poisoned feeling had grown until her body felt numb. Then the great clock over the musicians began to strike the hour, and in the next moment, she felt the tugging sensation that was the lines of power, the magical lines that bound every Tremontanan to earth and to one another, shifting their alignment in response to the changing year. For three seconds, she felt her bonds to her family, a beautiful, warm sensation that countered the numbness. Then it was over, and she became aware of those around her murmuring in pleasure at the shared feeling.

Distantly, she heard music playing, and she made herself leave the dance floor, one leaden step at a time. She could still see Eric in the distance, his head bowed as if from a great weight. Her steps sped up, and then she was running, pushing past those crowding the edge of the ballroom. In the next moment she had Eric by the arm and was towing him toward one of the little doors around the circumference of the ballroom that led to rooms where lovers had trysts. She'd never used them herself—couldn't imagine having the nerve to carry on an affair with hundreds of people hovering just outside—but she'd never been more grateful for their existence than now.

She pushed him through the door and closed it behind them so rapidly she was sure almost no one had noticed their exit. The room was dimly lit and furnished only with a pair of over-long sofas facing one another. It smelled musty, as if it hadn't been cleaned in a while, but Julia barely noticed.

Eric opened his mouth to speak, and she held up a hand and demanded, "Why not?"

"We put on a show for the kingdom," Eric said. "It wasn't real. We both know that."

It would have been a slap to the face if Julia hadn't been able to see his eyes. "Don't," she said. "Don't pretend that's all it was. I don't think it ever was just a charade, even at the beginning."

Eric's shoulders sagged. "It doesn't matter. I can't be what you need."

"You've never been anything else," Julia said. "I love you. I can't believe I ever thought I was in love before, now that I have you. Don't leave. I want to show the world—"

"I *can't*," Eric shouted. He turned his head away slightly, pinching his lips tight as if trying to contain the outburst that had already escaped. "I'm not fit to be yours, not for real."

Anger filled her, and she shouted, "Why are you so determined to make yourself unworthy? I don't care who you were, and I'm not sure anyone else does either, not after twenty years."

"You don't know the truth." Eric turned his back on her again. She grabbed his shoulder and dragged him around to face her.

"I do know the truth," she said. "Your friend, Stephen Bailie, shot a man accidentally and made it seem you'd done it. Father told me. Bailie was dying of lung fever and he confessed the truth on his deathbed. Why do you insist on carrying this guilt that isn't yours?"

"Because it is mine," Eric said. "Stephen Bailie lied."

Julia let go of Eric's shoulder. "What?"

Eric was breathing heavily. "I was the one who shot that man," he said. "We were arguing, and he was brandishing a pistol—I thought he would shoot me, but when I tried to take the gun away, it went off and killed him. I was already known for being wild, and everyone knew we were enemies. I didn't think anyone would believe it was an accident, so I fled. And when Stephen was dying, he told everyone that he'd done the shooting and I'd taken the blame to protect him. He wanted to help me. But it was a lie. I am guilty of murder."

Julia's head throbbed. She blinked several times to dispel the dizzy spots before her eyes. "But—"

"Shut up!" Eric roared. "Stop trying to make this about what you want! Didn't it occur to you that maybe I don't feel the same? That I was playing a game all along? That's what you wanted, isn't it? A convincing charade? Well, it's what I gave you, your Highness." He strode to the door and put his hand on the latch, gripping it tightly. "I'm going back to Eskandel. Tell your father the truth if you feel you're obligated to bring a murderer to justice. I'll disappear more thoroughly than before." He flung the door open and was gone before she could take more than two steps toward him.

Julia found her legs were shaking too much to support her. She sank onto one of the sofas and made herself breathe until the spots went away. What she wanted. Playing a game. A convincing charade. His words tangled with her memories, every coarse and hurtful thing Lucas had ever said, until she wrapped her arms around her chest to keep her heart from breaking in two. Then she wept, curling up on the sofa and crushing her dress, with the diamond necklace tugging at her skin and her careful coiffure coming down around her face.

She didn't know how long she lay there, but at some point, she ran out of tears and made herself sit up. She had to look like a wreck, like the victim of an attack, and she'd never been so grateful she didn't need cosmetics, because a smeared face was all this tragedy needed. She pushed her hair back from her face, then gave up and removed all the pins so it dangled loose to her waist. She could say she was setting a new trend.

She closed her eyes and sat with her head tilted back, and thought back over every moment of her and Eric's false courtship. She remembered the way he'd looked at her, his gentleness and understanding, his protectiveness. And she remembered the song he'd written for her. That hadn't been public, and she was the only one who knew about it. He hadn't faked that. Which meant everything he'd told her before slamming out of the room had been intended to push her away. And she wasn't going to let him have the last word.

Julia straightened her gown and ran her fingers through her hair, smoothing it as best she could. Then she left the little room and went in search of her father. She didn't have much time.

9

By the time Julia reached Elizabeth d'Arden's house, it was nearly three a.m. and her eyes were scratchy and dry from tiredness and crying, but she pounded on the front door anyway. She waited impatiently until it became clear no one would answer. Then she circled the house to the rear and climbed to where she could see over the wall to the stables. She had taken a precious ten minutes to change out of her gown and put away the diamonds, ten minutes that had felt like an eternity, all the while imagining Eric on a fast horse disappearing south. Now she wore rough trousers and a heavy coat and a knit cap pulled over her loose hair and felt anonymous. Whether anonymity mattered, she'd find out soon enough.

The stables were well-lit even at this hour, and a few people moved in and out of the stalls. The carriage house doors were flung open, revealing the building was empty, which meant Elizabeth and her husband weren't back from the ball yet. Julia whistled, a piercing sound she'd learned how to make from her brother Mark. Two stable hands turned, startled, and one of them approached her.

"Miss, what are you doing?" he asked, looking as if he couldn't believe a thief would be so careless as to make her presence known *and* try to steal from the stable yard.

"Did Lord Eric d'Arden leave a little while ago?" Julia asked.

That pushed the stable hand from surprise into downright confusion. "Lord Eric, miss?"

"Yes, Lord Eric. I need to stop him from doing something stupid. Where is he?"

The stable hand hesitated. Behind him, two other men approached, one young, one middle-aged. "Miss, I think you should go," the first stable hand said. "Lady d'Arden won't be gentle with you if you try to rob her house."

"Do I look like I'm trying to rob the house?" Julia exclaimed, thinking Elizabeth needed to employ smarter help. "Please, just tell me if Lord Eric left here sometime after midnight."

"Who are you, miss?" the middle-aged man asked.

Julia swiftly considered her options. "Someone who cares about Lord Eric very much and doesn't want him to ruin his life twice."

The man's eyes widened. "Your—I mean, miss," he said.

"Lord Eric took one of the horses and asked us to convey his apologies to his sister. That was at just after one o'clock."

A two-hour start. Julia refused to give in to despair. "Did he say where he was going?"

"The d'Ardens maintain horses all along the post route south through County Cullinan," the man said. "The first stop is the King's Arms, in Perelton. I doubt he'll try to ride through the night. Lord Eric isn't one to ruin a horse."

"Thank you," Julia gasped.

"Good luck to you, your—miss," the man said, sweeping her a bow that was inappropriate to direct at a young woman climbing other people's walls. Julia slid down and ran for her own horse, tethered outside the d'Ardens' gate.

The stable hand's warning applied to more than Eric, she realized. The streets of Aurilien were lit brightly all night long, every night of the year, and she and her horse couldn't come to grief there, but Perelton was south of the forest that cradled the southern wall of the city, and riding at speed through the darkened woods might kill both of them. On the other hand, the helpful stable hand was likely right that Eric would put up at the King's Arms until morning, but once the sun rose, he would put himself beyond her reach. Which meant Julia didn't have a choice.

She rode as fast as she dared through the city and pounded along the southern road for the few miles it took to reach the forest. Then she slowed her horse to a walk. With the trees denuded by winter, it wasn't as dark beneath the branches as usual, and the path was straight, so she wasn't worried about getting lost or falling. But clouds were massing overhead, obscuring the moon, and she could smell snow on the air. Even if the weather had been clear, there were a lot of possible obstructions, roots and holes and things, and when she took that into account she and the horse moved so slowly she wanted to scream.

She reminded herself that Eric had had to travel slowly himself, but her mind persisted in throwing up visions of him cantering through the woods, pausing to change mounts at the King's Arms, and riding on without stopping again. It was ridiculous, especially if it did snow, but her aching heart seemed to have settled on those visions as a way of torturing her.

What she would say to him, she didn't know. She couldn't help remembering what he'd said about her wanting to make this all about what she wanted, and she wasn't totally sure he was wrong. It had been so long since she'd wanted anything this badly, she couldn't tell if she was being selfish. She decided she didn't care. She couldn't make him love her, but she could tell him how much she loved him, and then...maybe she'd ride back to Aurilien alone, and maybe not, but at least she'd have her honor.

She didn't think honor was nearly as satisfying as everyone said.

Her new watch, an early Wintersmeet gift from Telaine, had a soft light illuminating the dial, and Julia started checking it every fifty steps. It gave her something to do so she wouldn't go mad. Four o'clock. Four-thirty. Twelve minutes to five. Julia didn't know what time exactly the sun rose, but she was sure Eric wouldn't wait for full daylight.

Snow began falling at exactly five o'clock, partly blocked by the branches arching overhead. She couldn't help imagining a raging blizzard, and leaving the forest to lose herself on the great southern plains of County Cullinan, passing Perelton by accident... She stopped once and screamed, a sound that the clouds caught and swallowed, and then trudged onward. Nothing for it but to keep going.

When she emerged from the forest, it was twenty-five minutes past six, and the snow was falling more heavily, but not so heavily she couldn't see the lights of Perelton not a mile to the south. She gasped in relief and nudged her horse faster—not much faster—and rode for the town.

As she rode, she indulged in a moment's despair. She didn't know Perelton at all and had no idea where the King's Arms was. Then she remembered her time in the Transportation department and felt stupid. The inn was on the post route, which meant it would be along the main road, either as one entered Perelton or as one left it. She wished now she'd given more attention to memorizing the post routes, but nobody did that, so she shouldn't feel guilty about it now.

The falling flakes had become a white curtain by the time she found the sign with the stylized crown over the door of the King's Arms. Her heart pounding, she rode into the stable yard and surveyed the stalls, not knowing what she was looking for. Her eyes and back ached, her mind was fuzzy, and she kept touching the saddlebag out of fear that she'd either forgotten its precious contents or they'd leaped from it and gone running off to hide in the forest.

A woman exited the inn's side door and approached Julia. "Take your horse, miss?"

"Is Lord Eric d'Arden here?" Julia asked.

"Don't know anyone by that name," the woman said. "Were you expecting to meet his lordship here, miss?" She sounded curious but not judgmental, not as if she thought Julia intended a scandalous liaison.

"Wait. No." Julia wished she could think straight. "He would have arrived here a few hours ago. Sometime after three-thirty, maybe. He might not have given his name, but he was riding one of the d'Arden post horses."

The woman's face cleared. "Oh, *him*," she said. "I should have realized. He's in the private dining room, eating breakfast. I was just readying his new mount. He must be in a hurry to need to ride in this mess, and on Wintersmeet Day."

Julia felt faint. She'd come so close to losing him. "May I—will you care for my horse? I need—" She slid down, staggered, and dug the scroll case out of the saddlebag. "Thank you," she added, and ran for the side door.

The door opened on a long hallway that smelled of ham and roasted potatoes and fresh cream and coffee. Julia brushed snow off her shoulders and cap and ran down the hall, pushing through a couple of doors, until she came to the tap room. It was empty except for a maidservant wiping down tables. "Where's the private dining room?" Julia demanded.

The maid jumped. "Um...through there?" she said, pointing at a door on the far side.

Julia nodded and hurried past. She paused at the door to gather her courage, then pushed it open.

The room was small, with only one table and a handful of chairs surrounding it, but the fire burning in the hearth made it cheerful, and the room smelled the same as the inn's back hallway. The heavily falling snow shrouded the windows in gray-white curtains, and occasionally the wind's voice howled mournfully across the panes. Julia stopped on the rag rug someone had probably thought gave the room a down-home look.

Eric sat alone at the table, a half-finished meal before him. He stared at her, astonished, and said, "Julia."

"Eric," Julia replied, and groped for something else to say.

He pushed back from the table, but didn't rise. "How did you find me?"

"That's not important," Julia said. Seeing him again, she was stunned that she hadn't realized sooner what he meant to her. That feeling propelled her forward. She slapped the scroll case on the table and said, "Happy Wintersmeet."

Eric glanced at the scroll case and then back at her. "Excuse me?"

"Your gift," Julia said. "I wanted to make sure you didn't leave the country before I could give it to you."

At any other time, his expression of utter confusion would have amused her. Now she felt so tense she was afraid she might snap if she lost her forward momentum. Eric fumbled with the scroll case, removing the cap with his long, agile fingers, and shook its contents out into his other hand. He unrolled the paper and began to read it. About halfway down the page, he stilled so completely she almost thought he'd been paralyzed. His eyes shifted back to the top, and he read it again.

"What is this?" he finally said, in a voice so quiet she had to strain to hear him over the fire.

"What it looks like," Julia said. "It's a royal pardon."

Eric's gaze shifted back to her. She could tell he was struggling for words, and fear and impatience made her say, "It was an accident, Eric. You've more than paid for what happened."

He swallowed. "The King doesn't know that. How did you get this?"

Her heart was beating so fast she feared it would leap from her chest. "I told him it would look very bad for him to send his future son-in-law to prison, whatever the reason."

Eric's hand closed convulsively on the paper, crushing it on one side. "Julia—"

"Just listen," Julia said desperately, "and I promise I'll never say this again. I know this all started as a game. Something to fool the country. And maybe I'm wrong, and for you it's never been anything else. But somewhere in the last two weeks, I lost my heart to you. You're kind and caring, and you're bold in my defense, and when I look at you, I see the man I love with all my heart. If there's even the smallest chance you might learn to love me, I want to take it. And I'm sorry if that's selfish, but I didn't—"

Eric stood so rapidly he knocked the chair over. In his next swift movement, he took her in his arms and pulled her close enough she could feel his heart beating in time with hers. "Enough," he said, his rough voice hoarse, and kissed her.

His lips on hers were hard and fierce, and she returned his kiss with a passion she hadn't known she had in her. She touched his shoulders tentatively, then, growing bolder, embraced him as he drew her closer. His hands settled on her waist, steadying her, and she twined her fingers through his hair and then ran them down his spine, making him shiver. She smiled against his mouth, enjoying the feel of his beard against her skin, and then gasped as he kissed her until she forgot to breathe.

He paused for a moment and murmured in her ear, "Forgive me for saying such cruel things?"

"What? Oh, you mean in the palace. Yes, that was terrible. I think you should kiss me again to make up for it."

Eric's eyes gleamed with amusement. "If that's the price I have to pay," he said, and kissed her again, long and slow, caressing her cheek with his agile fingers. "I love you. I've loved you almost since the beginning."

"So have I loved you." Julia laughed. "A pretend courtship. Do you suppose we were the only ones fooled?"

"Elizabeth has been giving me suspicious looks ever since the day I came back from our ride in the Park. I thought I was simply a much better actor than I imagined, but—" He kissed her again, gently this time, and pushed back a stray lock of hair that had escaped confinement under her cap. "It doesn't matter. Did I hear you propose marriage to me?"

Julia blushed. "It was more a presumption of your acceptance."

"Then—marry me, Julia. I want you to be mine, sworn and sealed to me forever."

"I will, if you'll agree to take my name."

Eric smiled. "I can't imagine anything better. No, I can. Marrying you this instant would be the best thing I can imagine."

"Eric, my parents will kill me if I marry when they're not there. And Telaine will do something dire I don't dare imagine."

"My love," Eric said, running his fingers along the curve of her cheek again, "this snowstorm is going to go on for hours, and you and I are going to be trapped here. Just think of the possibilities if we were husband and wife."

"Oh." Julia shivered with pleasure. "Hmm. Maybe—"

Eric laughed and drew her close again, this time to hold her tight. "We can wait. And there's a pianoforte in the tap room. Shall we see if I can play for our supper, so to speak?"

10

Julia sat in the east wing, on one of the chairs that had been pushed out of the way, and listened to Eric tune Queen Vivienne's great pianoforte. From her position, she could see her dim reflection in its glossy black lid. Her image was wavery but distinct despite the marks of the many hands that had guided it from the conservatory up three flights of stairs to the drawing room. If not for the Devices that countered its weight, she didn't think it would have been possible.

She turned her head and watched her reflection do the same until she had to look out the corner of her eye to observe her profile. From that angle, her face was nothing but lines and shadows, ghostly and unreal. It was an interesting perspective, but she far preferred the real world and the people in it.

"All right, try A above middle C," Eric told Emma Telaine,

who was seated on the bench in front of the keyboard. Emma Telaine pressed the key, which gave out a lovely clear tone. To Julia, it sounded just the same as it had the last three times, but she had come to terms with the fact that she was going to spend her life being one of nature's appreciators of music, and would leave the performing to her family.

"I think that's it," Eric said, straightening. "Why don't you play something?"

"Don't you want to?" Emma Telaine said.

"Queen Vivienne was your ancestor. I think it's fitting that you be first." Eric wiped his hands on a handkerchief. "Do you know 'Late in Spring'?"

The girl nodded. "I can sing it, too." She shifted her position on the bench and settled her hands on the keys. Julia observed how she held her wrists high and her fingers curved before Emma Telaine began to play the introduction to the popular music-hall song. She missed a few notes, but didn't stop playing as she moved into the first verse and started to sing. She had a nice, clear voice, maybe a little thin and certainly nowhere near the quality of Telaine's husband Ben's, but pretty and sweet and well-suited to this song.

Eric walked around the piano to stand behind Julia. He rested his hand gently on her shoulder. "She'll be great someday," he murmured, "if she keeps at it."

"I didn't think—this may be terrible for a mother to say, but I didn't think she was extraordinarily talented," Julia replied in the same low voice.

"Talent isn't nearly so important as hard work," Eric said. "She's willing to work at a piece a hundred times if it means she gets it right the hundred and first. That's a remarkable skill."

The song came to an end, and Emma Telaine swiveled around

to face them, her eyes alight with pleasure. "It sounds even better in here."

"Yes, the conservatory wasn't bad, but this is an improvement," Eric said. "That was well done."

Emma Telaine eyed him speculatively. "Should I call you Father?" she said abruptly. "Now that you've married Mother?"

Julia held her breath. Eric took a few steps forward and squatted to put himself at her eye level. "What do you want to call me?" he asked.

She paused, biting her lower lip in thought. "I don't feel like you're my father. Not yet."

"Then you should call me Eric," Eric said, "and if you ever feel like our relationship has changed, you can change that as well. But I think you should know I'll be proud to be the father of someone like you."

Emma Telaine nodded and rose from the bench. "I do like you," she said, and ran from the room.

Julia let out the breath she'd been holding. "You have a knack for saying the right thing," she said.

"I also have a knack for saying the wrong thing, if you'll recall," Eric said with a wry smile. "I'm glad you don't hold that against me."

"We have many years ahead of us to say the wrong thing, and to make amends, and say the right things instead." Julia embraced him and thrilled at his kiss.

They held each other for a few moments, and then Eric said, "Shall we see what I can do with this instrument?"

"And then we can rearrange the furniture to suit its presence," Julia said. "There's never been a pianoforte in the drawing room before, but it feels like this enormous room has just been waiting for us to remedy that lack."

Eric seated himself on the bench and flexed his fingers. "Do you have any requests, my lady wife?"

Julia dragged her chair closer. "I think you know."

He smiled, and ran through a few exploratory chords before going into something low and melodic, with bass notes echoing the melody as his hands moved up the keyboard. The music rose, and Julia's heart rose with it, aching at its beauty. Her song.

"This is when I knew I loved you," she said. "The first time you played this for me."

"I put everything I felt for you into the music," he replied. The tune changed, became something brighter but no less beautiful. "And this is my hope for our future."

Julia wiped away tears. She watched Eric's elegant, agile hands move over the keyboard, and her eye was drawn to their reflection in the glossy wood behind the keys, what Eric called the fallboard. They danced and wavered like ghosts. Her eyes shifted back and forth, from one to the other, and finally settled on his real hands. So dramatic, those ghostly reflections, but nothing could compare to reality.

The music came to an end, and they sat together in silence for a while, until Julia said, "Thank you."

"It's my pleasure," Eric replied. He rose from the bench, taking her hands and bringing her with him. "Do we move furniture now?"

Julia's whole body sang with happiness. "Someone else can do it," she said. "I have something better in mind."

Eric's gaze shifted to look beyond her, in the direction of their rooms. "I should write songs for you more often."

She slipped her arms around his waist and drew him closer. "One time is all it took," she said, and leaned into his kiss.

Gift of the Oracle

This story takes place after The Book of Destiny, *in which the story of* The Last Oracle *comes to a conclusion, and before the beginning of the new series* The Living Oracle, *which opens ten years later with the main character Helena happily married with three wonderful children. There are therefore spoilers for* The Last Oracle *series in this story. (And in this paragraph. Sorry.)*

Watch for Helena's new series, beginning with the book Hidden Realm, *in 2023.*

Trivia: My favorite Christmas song is "It's the Most Wonderful Time of the Year" as performed by Andy Williams. Accept no substitutes.

T he Christmas tree took up most of the wall of windows that looked out from our great room across the wide sweep of our back lawn. It was pre-lit, something I secretly liked despite being vocal about losing the joy of spreading out long lines of lights and figuring out which bulbs had burned out this year, and just tall enough I only needed a stepstool to place the star at its top. It even smelled fresh despite not being a live tree. It should have filled me with Christmas spirit. Instead, it only made me feel tired.

I sat on the sofa facing the tree and surveyed the great room, which was cluttered with plastic boxes containing ornaments and other Christmas decorations. In a minute, I would turn on the speaker system and start my Christmas playlist. In a minute, I would figure out which of the boxes held the tiny Nativity set I always put on the mantel first so the Holy Family could watch me decorate. In a minute, I would find the switch to turn the tree lights on to make decorating easier and more fun. That seemed like a lot of minutes, and I wasn't sure I could find even one.

The timer chimed the hour, ending quiet time, and soon I heard the thumping of small feet on the stairs and my son Duncan shouting, "You didn't decorate without us, right? I want to put my ornaments on!"

"Duncan, please don't shout," I said, rubbing my temples where a headache was starting to form.

"I think they're in this box," my older son Alastair said, tugging at the lid of a plastic storage box and failing to get it off with his seven-year-old's fingers. "Mommy, help?"

A scream from upstairs jolted me out of my fugue. "Wait, and don't touch anything," I ordered the boys, and pelted up the stairs and into little Jenny's room. Jenny sat up in her bed, sobbing, occasionally letting out a shriek. I picked her up and held her close, whispering, "It's all right. It's just pictures. Don't cry."

Jenny's sobs gradually diminished. "Saw a man with a stick," she carefully enunciated. She was eighteen months old and hadn't begun speaking until just two months ago, at which point she'd startled all of us by using complete and articulate sentences. "He hit a dog and the dog tried to run, but his leg didn't work."

My heart sank. Another one. "It's all right, Jenny. Try not to think about it."

I carried her downstairs, my feet plodding as heavily as if I wore cast-iron shoes. Motherhood was hard enough with three children under the age of seven. It was even harder when all of those children had the ability to see the future. They were oracles, and so was I, but on days like this, when Jenny once more saw a terrible vision she could do nothing about, I couldn't see the oracular gift as anything but a burden.

I reached the great room and stopped, aghast. "Alastair! Duncan! Didn't I tell you not to open that box?" Brightly colored ornaments, some delicate, were scattered across the floor in a sea of what had been protective wrappings when I'd put the ornaments into the box last January.

"We were careful," Alastair said, but he looked furtive.

"One broke even though we didn't do it," Duncan said.

I sank onto the sofa and set Jenny down. "Jenny, don't," I said, but without much force, and Jenny ignored me and toddled over to the box, where she began snatching up paper wrappings and tossing them in the air, giggling.

I closed my eyes for a moment, reaching for calm. It had been a rough six weeks. My husband Malcolm's private security company had become unexpectedly busy, and Malcolm had been needed in the office six days a week, all day, sometimes into the night, which meant I was now entirely responsible for household duties, cooking, and childcare where before Malcolm and I had shared those burdens. Jenny woke screaming from frightening visions at least twice a week, so I was sleep-deprived as well as exhausted. Add to that taking the boys to school, helping out occasionally in their classes, and handling business relating to my own oracular gift, and I was at the end of my rope and not at all in a Christmas spirit or any other kind of happy mood.

"*Stop,*" I said forcefully. It was sharp enough to make all three children stop dancing around the open box and stare at me. "We can decorate the tree, but only if all of you cooperate. Now, I'm going to turn on the music, and then I will give each of you your ornaments, and I will see if I can fix the one you broke. *Do not move* until I return."

We decorated the tree in glum silence, with even the bright sounds of Andy Williams belting out "It's the Most Wonderful Time of the Year" unable to penetrate the gloom. I felt guilty at having infected the children with my mood, but it was a distant guilt that wasn't enough to change my attitude. Each child had a set of ornaments that belonged to them, some handcrafted by my mother, others given them by friends, and they hung those on the lower branches while I put the more breakable ones up higher. Usually, I'd reflect on each as I hung it, but my brain was so foggy and tired I didn't have the energy for memory.

When the tree was decorated, I had the kids collect the wrappings and dump them back in the ornament box, and then I stacked the other boxes beside the tree. More decorations would have to wait for later. I was just too tired.

When I sat on the sofa again, Jenny crawled into my lap and Alastair, to my surprise, sat next to me and leaned against my side. They were such tender, trusting gestures my bad mood melted. I put an arm around Alastair and said, "Duncan, do you want to come up here?"

Duncan sat facing the Christmas tree with his back to me, his shoulders slightly hunched. He didn't respond at first. Then he leaped to his feet and shouted, "Underwear for Christmas? I want a Tonka truck!"

Surprised and still a little foggy, I just gaped. Then I realized what he'd done. "Duncan, what did we discuss about you prophesying what you're getting for Christmas? You know what happened at your birthday."

Duncan scowled. "It wasn't fun because I knew what I was getting and it wasn't a surprise. But I like knowing!"

"*I* don't," Alastair said.

"Alastair, don't be smug. Duncan, you're the one who chooses whether to ask for prophecies about your gifts. It's completely up to you."

Duncan sat on the end of the sofa. "Christmas is boring."

"Christmas is supposed to be a time for thinking of others," I reminded him. "That's why we give presents. We show how we love our friends and family by giving them things they will really appreciate." Though at the moment, the idea of shopping for gifts made me want to lie down and sleep for a thousand years. Whether going to the store or shopping online, either way I had to make an effort, and I didn't have the energy.

"What are you giving Lucia?" Jenny asked.

"I don't know. She's hard to shop for." Lucia Pontarelli, custodian of the magical nexus the Gunther Node, tough-as-nails administrator, judo champion, and relentlessly unsentimental defender of magery, was a complete marshmallow when it came to Jenny. Lucia had no interest in any other children, not even Jenny's brothers, and I didn't dare tease her about her attachment for fear she'd tear my head off and use it as a basketball.

"Lucia needs a present," Jenny persisted. "And Aunt Viv, and Aunt Judy, and Gramma and Papa Keller—"

The recitation felt like being pelted by gravel-filled snowballs. I groaned. "What do *you* think we should give Lucia, then?"

Jenny looked up at me, her small round face solemn. Then her eyes, brown-blue like mine and her brothers', flashed bright silver for a moment. "What's a spa day?" she asked.

Stunned, I didn't at first answer her. Jenny's visions, at her age, were erratic, and while not all of them terrified her, mostly they didn't mean anything. And they all occurred spontaneously. I hadn't thought she had the understanding to deliberately ask for a prophecy. "Jenny," I said, concealing my surprise, "did you have a vision?"

Jenny nodded. "I thought about what to give Lucia, and I saw a pool and someone said spa day. Is that like swimming?"

"No, it's like you go to a place where they give you rubs and you sit in mud," Duncan said. "It makes you get younger."

I boggled. "Duncan, where did you hear that?"

Duncan shrugged. "Sophia said Aunt Judy has spa days every month. She told me."

Sophia was my best friend Judy's daughter, born within weeks of Duncan. "Well, that's...more or less true. It's supposed to help you relax. But, sweetie, I'm not sure spas are Lucia's thing."

Jenny frowned. "You said visions are true."

"I did, but—" My unease increased, but I recognized it as discomfort at doing something potentially stupid. I could buy a gift certificate for a spa day for Lucia easily enough, but I could just as easily hear her laughter at the gift. Unless she accepted politely and went away to laugh about it in private. Still, Jenny had seen it in vision, and in all the more than eight years I'd had the oracular gift, I had yet to have a prophecy that didn't come true unless I took steps to prevent it happening.

I looked at Alastair, who was watching Jenny, and then at Duncan, who was watching me. "Hmm," I said. "Boys, what do you think? What should we give Lucia for Christmas?"

Both boys stilled, and Duncan's eyes flashed silver, with Alastair's doing the same half a second later. "I saw a sign that said Essence, and it felt warm," Alastair said. "And there were people in bathrobes walking around."

"I saw a place with lots of plants, and bathtubs full of mud," Duncan said. "How come I can't have mud in the bathtub?"

"Because you don't want to get any younger," I said. "Well, that seems fairly conclusive. It seems like a very weird gift to give Lucia of all people, but I can at least find out if there's a spa called Essence anywhere around here."

Duncan bounced excitedly. "This is fun!"

"Yeah, I like this!" Alastair exclaimed. "Who should we do next?"

"I don't," I began. Then I took in their bright, enthusiastic faces. "Prophesying for Christmas," I said, slowly, considering the possibilities. It wasn't something that had ever occurred to me to do before, but the idea caught hold of my imagination, lifting my spirits in a way decorating and music hadn't. And if it taught the children something about the joy of giving...

I stood. "Get your shoes and coats on. Let's go."

T parked my enormous Tahoe, which I referred to as my land yacht, in the small lot behind the record store called Tracks and helped everyone out, hoisting Jenny to perch on my left hip. "Remember not to touch in here," I told the boys. "Most of what's here are vinyl records, and some of those are old and all of them are breakable. Tell me what you see in vision and I'll pick it up."

"We know not to touch, Mommy," Alastair said impatiently. His tone was maybe justified, since I'd given them this warning at least three times already. So I didn't chastise him, just led my little gift-finding squad around the corner to the front door.

The glass door and the two large windows flanking it were rimmed with multicolored twinkling lights behind that fake snow spray I didn't see much anymore. Someone had painted MERRY CHRISTMAS across the right-hand window in fancy curly letters and HAPPY HANUKKAH on the left-hand window. When I pushed the door open, cheerful little bells tinkled, barely audible over the sound of the music, a jazzy rendition of "It's Beginning to Look a Lot Like Christmas." A whiff of cinnamon passed my nose, cinnamon mingled with the musty smell of dusty wood and paper. The combination took me back in time eight years, to a store filled with bookcases standing at weird angles to each other and books crammed in any old way. My eyes filled with unexpected tears I blinked away.

The store's bright lighting illuminated rows of low cabinets filled with albums in cardboard sleeves. Neatly lettered signs indicated musical genres, or whatever it was you called different types of music: *Classical, Alt Rock, '80s Pop Classics, Songs Your Dad Listens To*. Two men and a woman glanced up when we entered the way people do in stores, not really interested but reacting to something new. Fake fir branches circled the ceiling, with fake-snow-crusted pinecones attached here and there. I couldn't imagine how hard it would be to keep the records clean if real evergreen needles kept falling into the cabinets.

A man with a large belly and a heavy beard, someone who might be angling to play Santa in another thirty years, sat up from behind the old-fashioned cash register. Again I was reminded of my days in Abernathy's Bookstore, with its antique register with the Victorian lace doily appliqued to its top. "Can I help you find something?" He eyed my children in obvious concern.

"It's all right, I don't have something specific in mind. And I've warned the children not to touch anything."

He settled back. "All right. There's a section in the back for discounted titles, and prices are marked on the back of each album. You're sure you don't need help?"

Rather than annoying me with the implication that a mother of three couldn't possibly know anything about music, his tone amused me. "It's fine. I'll know it when I see it. Thanks." After all, I *didn't* know anything about music. I was depending on a different guide.

Alastair had taken a few steps away from me and was scanning the section titles. He'd been reading since before he was three, and I was used to him being independent when it came to reading books, magazines, newspapers, signs, and nutritional information on the sides of cereal boxes. "I saw Punk Folk in the vision," he told me, "but it's not here."

"Let's keep walking," I told him in a low voice.

Duncan, for once, stuck close beside me and gripped my coat with one hand like he wanted to keep it from exploring without permission. Normally my five-year-old terror had to be physically contained when we went shopping as he tore through the aisles like a small blond tornado. "There was a wreath like Greek gods wear, and it had a heart. But a real heart."

"Okay, that will help." I finally saw the sign for Punk Folk and led the children that way, passing the woman, who was browsing the albums in the Emo Ballads section and didn't look up as we walked past. At the Punk Folk section, I set Jenny down and then flipped slowly through the records, two-handed, making sure Alastair and Duncan saw each one. Jenny clung to my legs, which was uncomfortable, but at least I knew where she was. The covers were interesting, but the artists' names were mostly unfamiliar. Well, I already knew Viv had a quirky taste in music.

"That one," Alastair and Duncan said in unison.

I'd stopped on an album with a tan cover and an illustration of a heart—a real heart with valves, as Duncan had said—with a cassette tape embedded in it, surrounded by a laurel leaf. *Tape Deck Heart*, a ribbon across the heart said, and below that, the artist's name, Frank Turner.

"Are you sure?" I was positive I'd seen this one before at Viv's house. The ridiculousness of buying an album for someone who had an extensive collection suddenly struck me—"Coals to Newcastle," as Cary Grant said in *The Philadelphia Story*. Despite my confidence in the oracle, I couldn't help remembering that the oracle didn't solve problems any of us could solve ourselves.

Jenny grabbed the edge of the cabinet and stood on tiptoe to look at the album. "Aunt Viv," she said, like it was the most obvious thing in the world.

I suppressed a sigh and picked up Jenny again, then took the album out of the cabinet and carried it to the cash register. The bearded man took it from me and flipped it over to check the price. He glanced at me again, and now I was annoyed, because it was the look of someone extremely dubious about my coolness being sufficient for an album like this.

"You a fan of Frank Turner?" he asked.

"It's a gift for a friend," I said automatically, without thinking how that would sound.

"Ah." He made that one syllable sound like the answer to a dozen mysteries. I smiled and paid, all the while increasingly convinced that, oracle or no, we'd picked a really dumb gift. But I wasn't about to say that and ruin my children's fun.

Back in the car, the boys burst into excited chatter about how Aunt Viv would love her present. They were so excited my misgivings evaporated. Viv would understand the thought and caring that had gone into choosing it, and that was more important than any small details like how she had a dozen copies already.

"All right, settle down. We need to move quickly if we're going to do this before dinner," I told them. "Where next?"

"Aunt Judy!" Jenny exclaimed.

Alastair's eyes flashed silver. He frowned. "I don't know where they put lots of pictures you can buy on the walls. It looks like a museum, but you can't buy things in museums, right?"

"An art gallery," I said.

As if my words were a trigger, Duncan's eyes flashed. "I saw big windows made of lots of black squares," he said, "and a gold square next to the door, except I can't read the words."

"Hmmm." I used my phone to search for *art galleries in Portland OR* and then switched the results to show pictures instead of a list. I showed the pictures to Duncan, slowly scrolling down until he shouted, "That one!" and pointed.

"Don't shout, Duncan." I tapped the picture. "Wolford's Fine Art. It's not too far from here."

Christmas music playing, I drove to the gallery. Though the sun was dropping lower in the sky, there was still plenty of light, but the interior of the gallery, visible through the black-latticed windows, blazed with the glow of dozens of bulbs. I could barely see the walls with their unframed canvases through the lattices.

I parked the car and said, "You remember what I said about not touching? That is even more important here. The people who run this place will ask us to leave if you get close to the paintings.

This is where you have to show everyone that you are not—what are you not?"

"We're not wild hoodlums," chorused Alastair and Duncan, with Jenny a step behind.

"Right. Let's go."

We hurried from the warm bubble of the land yacht through the evening chill and into the comfortable warmth of the gallery. The faint scent of lemongrass filled the air, subtle enough that my awareness of it immediately faded after one strong whiff. White walls made a maze that took advantage of the full interior space, with exactly one painting on each wall. We appeared to be the only ones there.

"Let's—" I said, and a woman wearing a little black dress that instantly made the gallery look more upscale came around the corner. She stopped abruptly and pursed her lips. "I'm sorry, children aren't allowed," she said. Her voice was thin and whiny and smug and put me on edge.

"They won't touch anything," I said, staying calm.

"It's our policy. Sorry." She sounded even more prim and smug than before.

I considered my appearance, how I was wearing jeans and a sweater under last year's coat and hadn't put on makeup today. Compared to Miss Little Black Dress, I looked like a homeless person who'd come to the gallery for a free art show, though I wasn't sure how often homeless people sought out cultural appreciation. I certainly didn't look like someone whose fortune could buy every art piece in the gallery and not even blink. Which I was, and could.

I made a decision. "I'm sorry, I didn't realize. We were out shopping and I was struck with the desire to buy one of your pieces as a gift for a friend. Why don't the children stand here by the door, and then they won't interfere—they're very well behaved." I silently prayed, as I occasionally did, that none of them would do anything to give me the lie.

"We're not babysitters," the woman said.

I chose not to point out that there was only one of her. "I assure you you won't need to be." I hitched Jenny higher on my hip and strode away. Arguing only meant increasing the possibility that she would kick us out, and I was following prophecy.

I strolled around, looking at the art. I wasn't as knowledgeable as Judy, but I was past the "I know what I like" stage, and what I saw on the walls was good without being great. They were small to medium sized, so getting my purchase home wouldn't be hard. Oils and watercolors, a couple of mixed media pieces, all of them reasonably priced, which only mattered because I knew Judy would kill me if I spent a hundred thousand dollars on her gift.

At every stop, I glanced at the children. They were watching me with interest, but never reacted as if I'd found The One. I stayed a while at one of the mixed media pieces, admiring the sheen of color, blues and greens with slashes of yellow, combined with the flat nickel-plated washers that made a shower of silver coins. I might buy that one for myself.

I continued on, feeling the pressure of Miss Little Black Dress's gaze. She clearly believed I was wasting her time, and her attitude was starting to grate on me. I walked a little faster to round a corner and put myself out of her sight.

Then I heard Alastair and Duncan calling out, "That one, that one!"

"Aunt Judy will put it on her wall," Jenny said.

I stared at the painting in dismay. Everything else in the gallery was in a modern style, abstract, the kind of art people liked to say their kindergartener could do. But the one I was looking at was representational, more or less. It showed a stark, leafless tree super-imposed on a sun, with the sun at the center of a set of rings that went from yellow to blue in color. The artist had laid the oils on heavily, and while I liked the texture, it seemed so plain and, well, banal I couldn't imagine Judy liking it.

"Boys, come here," I said, pretending not to hear the woman's squawk of dismay. "Are you sure this is the one?"

"Yes," Alastair said. "It's like winter."

"It's definitely that," I replied. It did give the feeling of how the bright sun in a winter sky failed to beat off the cold. "All right."

"I'll take this one," I told Miss Little Black Dress. "And the one over there."

The woman's eyes widened. She flicked a glance at the card beside the painting, with the title and the price. "We don't offer a payment plan," she said.

That nearly pushed me over the edge. Then I saw the children watching me closely and decided to be the bigger person. "I don't need one, but thank you for the information. Please box them up, and if you have a supervisor, perhaps that person can take payment?"

The supervisor was another woman in a little black dress, but she smiled pleasantly and said nothing about the children's presence. She accepted my card with no comment, nothing snide about whether my bank had an upper limit on purchase amounts, but I overheard her whispered reproof to her colleague, at least in part: "...*Mrs. Campbell, haven't you heard of...philanthropist, worth more than this entire gallery...better not insult her.*" Too late for that. I hadn't expected to be recognized, but the supervisor's reaction satisfied me.

Miss Little Black Dress carried the boxes to the land yacht

herself. I said nothing to her as she loaded them into the back, and then I smiled and said, "Merry Christmas. I hope you enjoy your commission."

Her mouth fell open. I settled the kids into their seats and drove away, humming along to "Jingle Bells."

The gallery had taken longer than I'd realized, and long shadows pointed the way east toward the Willamette River. "Maybe we should finish this tomorrow," I said.

A chorus of disappointed "no's" greeted this statement. "This is fun, picking gifts," Alastair said. "We can't stop now."

"Besides, Daddy won't be home until late," Duncan said, with the assurance of someone who'd seen the future.

I glanced in the rearview mirror at Jenny, sitting alertly in her car seat. "All right. One more," I agreed. "For Gramma and Papa Keller." The Kellers were friends, not the children's actual relatives, but they were close enough to us it was like having a third set of grandparents.

"Oh!" Duncan exclaimed. "I know where it is! The thrift store!"

"The—you mean ValuMart?"

"That's the right one," Alastair said.

My uncomfortable feeling returned. I liked thrift store shopping despite not needing to save money by buying used. It was a good, cheap way to get enough books to satisfy Alastair's reading addiction, and I sometimes went with Viv and Judy in search of unusual treasures. But I couldn't give Harry and Harriet Keller, who were extremely well-to-do and had an exquisitely decorated home, a tchotchke purchased at ValuMart for five dollars. "Kids," I began.

"Mommy, you said we could prophesy," Alastair said, his words and tone a reproof. "We didn't make anything up."

Now I felt guilty. "You're right. I'm sorry. Let's see what we can find at ValuMart."

At least at the thrift store, no employees gave me the stink-eye for bringing children inside. I got a shopping cart mainly so I'd have a place to put Jenny, who'd gotten heavy over time, and then called out, "Boys! Stay with me!"

They ignored me, racing ahead to the Housewares section. I sighed and pushed the cart after them. Bright fluorescent bulbs dispelled all possibility of shadows and made my eyes ache. I reflected that every store we'd been to had been brightly lit, and yet the light had been different in each place, clear and white at the record store, warm and inviting at the gallery. At ValuMart, the light gave a hard edge to the shelves and the racks of clothes, making them seem more solid than they would in daylight. I glanced over the racks idly, assuming the children's prophecies wouldn't choose used clothing or shoes. Prophecy or no, there were things I wouldn't do, and wrapping a secondhand shirt for a gift was one of them.

Housewares had aisles and aisles of dishes, glasses, table linens, and silverware. Those aisles were adjacent to the row of purses, which was next to the toy aisle, which was where I found Duncan. "You're supposed to be choosing something for the Kellers," I said.

"I forgot. Can I have this?" He held up a yellow dump truck with chipped paint and scuffed wheels.

"We're not here for you, Duncan. Aren't you hungry? We should be getting home for dinner." Though I'd already decided on takeout, after the day I'd had.

Duncan scowled and put the truck back. "I want—" His eyes flashed silver, and he fell silent, staring at nothing. Then he shook himself like a dog shaking off a flea and said, "It's a sheep."

"A sheep?" I glanced around, but saw no sheep figure or painting or even a photograph. "The gift is a sheep?"

Duncan wandered away. I followed him and came upon Alastair, standing in the middle of the glasswares aisle with his hands clasped behind his back. "You said no touching stuff that breaks," he said. "It's on this shelf somewhere."

The shelf was full of glass and ceramic figurines, the kind of figurines no one ever admitted to having despite there being ample evidence that people did, if only to donate them to the thrift store. I scanned the rows for sheep and found a whole cluster of them, as if some helpful employee had grouped the figurines according to type. As I looked closer, I realized that was literally true; there was a collection of chicks and hens, and one of shepherdesses, and another of china dogs with sappy faces.

"Which one?" I asked Duncan, who'd returned to my side and was hanging off the side of the cart.

"I dunno," he said, sounding completely uninterested.

Jenny reached out a chubby toddler hand. "That one," she said, making a grab for a china sheep at the middle of the irregular flock.

I rescued it and turned it over in my hand, examining it. It was actually quite pretty, a black-faced ewe with curly china wool, lying with her legs tucked under her round body. The price sticker said seventy-five cents. "Kids," I said, "are you sure? This is...I mean, what are Gramma and Papa Keller going to do with it?"

"They'll like it," Alastair asserted. "Can we eat now?"

I sighed. Harry and Harriet would be happy with anything the children chose for them, but...and now I was being ridiculous. Hadn't I told them just an hour before that Christmas was about showing our love for others? It didn't have to be about expensive gifts, it just had to be the right gifts, chosen with care and a desire to make someone else happy. I needed to trust the oracle and stop fretting about whether the gifts made me look stupid or cheap.

ValuMart was a good twenty minutes from home, so I decided to pick up chicken meals from Impeckables, one of the better fast food restaurants in our area, on the way rather than go home and leave again. I tuned out the children's chatter and listened to Bing Crosby sing "Silent Night" and let my mind wander. I felt better than I had in weeks, tiredness aside. Maybe using the oracular gift to choose presents benefited more than just the kids.

I came back to reality with a jerk as all three children started shouting. "Stop, stop!" I exclaimed. "What's wrong?"

"Daddy, that's for Daddy!" Jenny shouted.

"Right there, stop, Mommy," Alastair exclaimed.

"It's the one right there, right there, Mommy," shouted Duncan.

I pulled up to the curb and put the land yacht in park. "What are you—no, stop yelling, please. What are you talking about?"

Duncan and Alastair pointed out the car window. I'd stopped next to the Cineplex, on the outer side where movie posters hung behind Plexiglas sheets, enticing viewers with the movie theater's latest offerings. I followed the pointing fingers with my gaze and said, "*Force Majeure III*. What about it?"

"That's Daddy's present," Alastair said. "He needs to see that movie."

I eyed the poster again. It showed a muscular man and a woman in a low-cut tank top and jeans racing away from an improbably high tidal wave. Both the man and the woman had guns. I almost protested that Malcolm didn't like movies like that when, to my surprise, a spontaneous prophecy overtook me, sweeping me up like being carried away on eagles' wings. I saw the movie poster again, but in motion, the wave arching higher and higher until its crest blocked out the sun. I saw Malcolm and myself in the place of the couple in the poster. Then the vision faded. I let out a breath. "I'm not going to argue anymore," I said. "I'll buy him a ticket."

The sun shone brightly Christmas Eve day, but its brightness was an illusion, because the air was cold and felt like knives against the skin. Malcolm took the kids sledding, but they returned in half an hour, their cheeks red and dry-looking. "Too cold, Mommy," Alastair said. "Can we have hot cocoa?"

"I have everything ready for hot cocoa," I said.

With the boys settled at the kitchen nook table with their mugs and Jenny seated in her high chair with a sippy cup filled with barely-warm cocoa, I poured hot water for Malcolm and me, but I hadn't begun to scoop cocoa mix into our mugs when my husband took me in his arms and kissed me, a long, satisfying kiss made more endearing by the tip of his still-cold nose rubbing against my cheek. "Merry Christmas," Malcolm murmured.

"It's not Christmas Day yet," I pointed out with a smile.

"I like to think the holiday starts today." He kissed me again, and I responded eagerly. It felt like years since we'd kissed.

"I know these last few weeks have been difficult," he continued when we came up for air, "and you've had a lot to manage, between the kids and oracle business and the house. I hope you know I appreciate your sacrifice."

"I've missed you," I said, "but I understand about work sometimes taking precedence."

"I don't think it should. Campbell Security has been around for four generations. Our children will only be young for a few years. So I've done what I can to keep this overwork from happening again." Malcolm drew me closer. "It's not just sharing the burden here at home, love. I don't want to miss out on our family."

My heart swelled. "I love you," I said. "Also, you're never sexier than when you're playing with the kids."

Malcolm laughed. "I'll remember that. Is there anything I can do for you? Any last-minute preparations? I realize it's probably too late for that."

I shook my head. "Everything's done. We just have to enjoy ourselves. There's the Christmas Eve party, and then Christmas Day at my parents' house, and—oh, but that's a secret." The children had insisted Malcolm's movie ticket Christmas present be purchased for 5:40 p.m. on Christmas Day, which had nearly broken my resolve to obey the oracle. I'd compromised by buying two tickets. If Malcolm's present was a dud, at least I'd share it with him.

"A secret, huh?" Malcolm gave me an amused, knowing look. "I can't believe how much you've accomplished this month. You must be exhausted."

"Less so than I imagined, honestly." Our oracle-inspired gift giving had eased my heart, and I'd found that focusing on helping other people made it easier to bear my burdens. I'd even resorted to prophecy a few times to guide me in solving personal problems. It wasn't my usual approach, since I felt the oracle shouldn't be used for selfish reasons, but every time the oracle directed me in helping with the boys' classes or taking a treat to a neighbor, I felt at peace.

My phone, which I'd left in the great room, rang with the

trilling bell sound I'd selected as fitting to the Christmas season. I hugged Malcolm one last time and hurried to answer it.

It was Lucia. "Did you know this was going to happen?" she demanded.

"I, um, did something happen?"

Lucia snorted. "Then it wasn't the oracle that told you to give me that spa gift certificate, which by the way gave me a good laugh. You've got more of a sense of humor than I realized."

I blushed. "It wasn't me, it was the children. They prophesied that it was the right gift." I realized halfway through that sentence that I sounded like I was making excuses for myself and forged on. "Was it not good?"

There was silence on the other end for long enough that I said, "Lucia? Are you there?"

"So it was a prophecy," Lucia said. She no longer sounded amused.

"Lucia, what happened?"

Lucia cleared her throat. "I opened all my gifts early because Dave and I are going out of town for a week, leaving tonight. And yes, I did laugh myself sick over that gift certificate. But then I figured, I've never been to a spa, so why not?"

"I'm glad. I was worried—"

"Just wait, Davies. I made an appointment for yesterday, figured it would be a relaxing start to my vacation. Essence is out of my way, but then everything is by comparison to the Gunther Node—"

I nodded, though she couldn't see me. The Gunther Node access point was far north of Portland, almost to the Columbia River.

"So I go there, late afternoon, and I admit I liked it. Very soothing, and the massage was great. But then I'm leaving the place, and I hear shouts, and someone's running toward me at top speed, acting like he's being chased. So I took him down."

I winced. Lucia looked like a slightly overweight middle-aged woman, but I'd seen her clothesline someone who didn't get up again for nearly a minute. "Was he a robber or something?"

"Worse. He'd assaulted a woman, beat her and stole her purse. The people chasing him...let's just say they had the look of men who didn't want to be the next ones beaten, but they had to chase him so they didn't look like jerks." Lucia let out a short, mirthless laugh. "I kept him subdued until the cops arrived. I learned this morning that law enforcement has been looking for this guy for a long time. Seems he's wanted in several assaults and possibly two homicides."

I realized I'd been holding my breath. "Lucia!"

"The point is, Davies, that I wouldn't have been there if someone hadn't given me that gift certificate," Lucia said. "I don't know what prompted you to ask the oracle for guidance, but it was inspired."

"It was the children who saw it," I said, still breathless. "That is, they didn't know about the attacker, just that this was the right gift for you."

"Then thank them for me," Lucia said. "And Merry Christmas." She hung up as abruptly as she always did.

I lowered my phone and gazed at Malcolm, who was watching me with the curiosity of someone who'd only heard my half of the conversation. "I don't believe it," I said, and repeated what Lucia had told me. "I thought it was a stupid gift."

"If you didn't already know the oracle works in unexpected ways, that would be revelatory," Malcolm said. "Double meaning intended."

I glanced back at the kitchen table, where the children were still drinking cocoa peacefully. "I don't know what to tell them."

"The truth," Malcolm said. "They should know how their gifts benefit others."

T he day proceeded as peacefully as I could have hoped. We read the Christmas story from the Bible—we weren't terribly religious, but I felt it was good for the kids to know there was more to Christmas than gifts and trees and colored lights. Then Alastair read some other stories, Christmas picture books, aloud to all of us. We hung stockings handmade by my mother on the mantel, beautiful creations of felt and sequins and sparkling beads.

Five o'clock came, and with it came our friends for our annual Christmas Eve party: Judy and her husband Mike and their daughter Sophia, and my other best friend Viv and her partner Jeremiah. When I was growing up, Christmas Eve dinner was cold cuts and vegetables, crackers and cheese, clam chowder with tiny oyster crackers, and a shrimp ring, and I carried on that tradition with my friends, who added touches of their own: Viv's famous spinach dip and bread rounds, Judy's chocolate cake whose recipe was a carefully-guarded secret.

The adults ate, and talked, and laughed. The children nibbled on whatever tidbits caught their eye, too excited for what came next to have much appetite. Because for them, the real point of Christmas Eve was getting to open one present. My secret policy was to wait until they'd asked three times, politely, if it was present time yet.

Finally, I said, "All right, just one present," the way I did every year. The three older children shouted excitedly and dove for the tree. Last year, we'd let them bring the presents for the adults to open, and they'd loved the new idea so much they'd made it tradition.

But when I saw Duncan and Alastair carrying Viv's record carefully between them, all my misgivings returned. Suppose she disliked it? She wouldn't be rude, but Alastair and Duncan and Jenny had been so excited...

Judy accepted her wrapped gift from Jenny, who could barely carry it in her chubby arms. "You're getting so big," she exclaimed.

"It's a secret," Jenny said. "For your wall."

"Jenny, I thought we talked about this," I said before she could elaborate.

"For my wall, eh?" Judy gave me a suspicious look. "This had better not be something hugely expensive."

I decided not to answer. It hadn't been *hugely* expensive.

When everyone had a gift to open, we started with the youngest and took turns going around the circle, one at a time. The children all got new pajamas, another tradition of my childhood, with a small toy tucked inside so they wouldn't feel cheated. I was used to them ignoring the adults' presents in favor of playing with said toys. But to my surprise, Alastair and Duncan sat staring at Viv, and Jenny was bouncing beside them, almost vibrating with excitement.

Viv eyed them curiously. "You sure this present is for me? Because you're looking at me like you're going to ask for it back."

"Open, open, open," Jenny chanted.

"It's really cool," Alastair said.

Viv tore off the wrapping paper the way she always did, like she was a Vegas magician whipping away a tablecloth to reveal an empty cage. Her hands stilled. "Oh," she said, and my heart sank, because it sounded like the "oh" of someone disappointed and trying not to show it. "I love Frank Turner. Thanks."

"Look at it!" Duncan demanded.

Viv glanced at him, then slid the vinyl record out of the sleeve. She froze again. "Holy sh—crap," she said. "It's signed. You got me a signed Frank Turner album."

"What?" I exclaimed.

Viv held up the record. A spidery glyph that looked like really loose Japanese characters splayed across the label at the center of the album, bright silver overlaying what was printed there. "How did you manage this? Did you find it online?"

"Um, no, it was at the record store," I said, still feeling stunned. "Did you kids know?"

"I told you we saw it was the right present," Alastair said.

"This is amazing," Viv breathed. She carefully slid the record back into its sleeve. "Now I wish I'd gotten you something big."

"It's not about the present, it's about showing that you care," Duncan said.

"Aunt Judy!" Jenny shouted, flinging herself forward to hug Judy's knees. "For your wall!"

I covered my face with both hands. "Jenny doesn't understand secrets yet."

"It's all right. I can feel it's a mounted canvas." Judy removed the wrapping paper more tidily than Viv had and rotated the canvas so it was right side up. Then she sat looking at it, not speaking, while the rest of us watched. My anxieties reared up again, making me squirm inside with mingled embarrassment and self-consciousness.

Finally, I said, "If you don't like it—I know it's not your usual thing—"

"It isn't," Judy said. "But it's exactly what I need."

"Wall!" Jenny said, giggling.

"That's right, Jenny," Judy said. "But not a wall in my house. I plan to redecorate my store after the first of the year, in a four seasons theme—you know, a different season in each corner. But I haven't found anything good for Winter yet, nothing that will tie it all together. This is perfect." She turned her gaze on me. "How did you know?"

"Well," I said.

"We prophesied!" Duncan exclaimed. "This is way better than a Tonka truck!"

All the adults laughed, and Malcolm quickly assured Duncan we weren't laughing at him. "You used the oracle to choose presents?" he asked me.

"I didn't. The children did. I thought—" Except I didn't know how much of that had been me, given that I'd resisted every prophecy the children had had. "I wanted them to feel joy in giving, and this was how they did it," I finished.

"Well, I approve," Viv said. She was cradling her album like a flat cardboard baby.

Judy's eyes narrowed. "You're not going to tell me how expensive this was, are you?"

"Let's just say we gave the salesperson a very merry commission," I said.

We had a hard and fast rule that the children couldn't go downstairs Christmas morning without their parents, and they weren't allowed to wake us until eight o'clock. I usually slept until then, but this Christmas, I woke around 7:40 and lay in bed listening to them running from one bedroom to another and talking and giggling in low voices.

Malcolm stirred, then rolled onto his side to face me. "Merry Christmas," he said.

"Merry Christmas," I replied, and kissed him.

We cuddled in each other's arms in silence until the knock on the door and Duncan's voice saying, "We waited, and we were quiet!" announced the arrival of the chosen time, at which point we rolled out of bed to play out the rest of the ritual. This started with Malcolm asking if the kids were sure they wanted presents, and when they finished jumping up and down and saying they did, he lined them up at the top of the stairs while I went down to turn on the speakers and set the Christmas playlist to the traditional song whose music would officially start Christmas, "Santa Claus is Coming to Town."

I loved hearing their running feet on the steps and how they rushed into the great room only to come up short and stare at the presents under the tree. Malcolm followed more slowly and put his arm around my shoulders. We watched them explore the contents of their stockings—Duncan made a face at the package of underwear—and then Alastair read labels while Duncan passed gifts out to their recipients.

In the middle of this, my phone rang. I considered not getting it, then realized anyone calling at this hour on Christmas morning probably had a good reason. I settled on the couch and answered. "Harriet, how are you?"

"Very well, dear," Harriet Keller said. "We just opened your gift, and I simply couldn't believe it. I didn't think you knew we were missing one. Such a wonderful surprise!"

"I—just a minute." I covered the phone with my hand and said, "Hush a moment, it's Gramma Keller calling to thank us for the sheep." I was confused enough that when I returned to the phone, all I could think to say was, "You liked it?"

"We *loved* it," Harriet said, and to my surprise she sounded near tears. "The set hasn't been complete for twenty-five years, not since Danny broke the original. I've tried so hard to find a replacement, but those were never sold individually. Even eBay was a dead end. And then you found—"

"Hold on, Harriet." Normally I wouldn't go into detail about where I'd found a particular gift, and I certainly didn't want Harriet to know we'd gotten it at ValuMart, but things were starting to fall together. "I don't want to take more credit than we deserve. We found that at a thrift store, and...actually, the kids prophesied about what to get you, and that's why we picked it. I didn't know it had any value, or that you had been looking for one."

There was a long pause. Then Harriet laughed so hard it startled a smile out of me. "A thrift store," she finally said, gasping for breath. "Helena, it's a Mariche sculpture. Part of the artist's Nativity set. The odds of you finding it lying around at a thrift store—well, guided by the oracle, I suppose the odds would actually be very good."

I knew the name Mariche. I also knew how much her sculptures went for. Our seventy-five cents had netted us something tremendously valuable. Though in truth it was Harriet's reaction that was priceless. "I'm so glad it was a good gift."

"It's a *wonderful* gift. Thank the children for us, will you?"

I said I would and hung up to find everyone watching me. "Sorry," I said.

"Can I go first?" Duncan said.

"Jenny goes first," Malcolm said. "But you can be next. What did Harriet want, Helena?"

"I'll tell you all later," I said. One after another, the oracle's gifts had turned out to be exactly what was needed. The kids needed to know that, but it could wait until after presents.

After Harriet's call, though, Christmas felt a little anticlimactic. I oohed and aahed over the things the children gave me and admired my remaining presents from friends, but it wasn't until we were on our way to my parents' house for round two of the gift-giving orgy that I realized Malcolm hadn't given me anything. I was sure he would have gotten me something, but I felt weird about asking, like I was seven years old and greedy for presents. Maybe he was waiting until we opened gifts at Grandma and Grandpa's.

But when all the presents were opened, I still didn't have one from Malcolm. Now I wondered if I was wrong, and in all the work hustle he'd forgotten. There was no way to ask him gracefully over my mother's famous barbecue turkey, not if the answer might be a shamefaced "I forgot," and no way to ask after dinner when the children were tearing through the house playing with their new toys.

By the time we had to leave to go to the movie, I'd decided, somewhat sulkily, that it didn't matter if Malcolm got me anything. It wasn't like I didn't have everything I ever wanted, so what would be the point? Besides, I had felt the joy of the season, and seen the happiness of my friends over the gifts the oracle had chosen, and that was pretty amazing.

"So, why this movie?" Malcolm asked as he parked the car and we got out.

"I don't know. It was the children, and the oracle, who picked it." I caught sight of the *Force Majeure III* poster again and winced. It looked even dumber in full darkness with white lights surrounding it. Probably it couldn't be as bad as it looked.

I was wrong. It was as bad as I'd suspected. I tried to tell myself that at least it wasn't *worse* than the poster, but my consciousness of Malcolm sitting motionless beside me made me want to cringe, and then leave the theater. But the oracle had been right all the other times, so I didn't suggest walking out. Five times I thought about leaving; five times I made myself stay.

When the credits finally rolled, I said meekly, "I'm sorry."

"It's not your fault," Malcolm said. He took my hand and twined his fingers with mine. "Though I admit I was expecting something spectacular, after the things everyone else got."

"Maybe I made a mistake and thought the kids were pointing at this poster when they really meant something else." I stood up when Malcolm did and walked with him out of the theater. The halls were crowded with moviegoers, proving that Christmas really was a big theater day. Malcolm ended up walking a little ahead of me, breaking the crowds so I didn't have to dodge.

He pushed the big glass door open, and a blast of frigid air struck us. I shivered. "Let's get the kids and go home and watch a real Christmas movie in bed, all right? Maybe *The Bishop's Wife*? Cary Grant?"

"That idea just made the last 147 minutes vanish," Malcolm said, smiling. He scanned the parking lot, looking for our car. Then his hand in mine stiffened, and he froze in place.

"Malcolm? Is something wrong?" I asked, looking around for what had caught his attention.

Malcolm ignored me. He let go of my hand and took a few steps along the sidewalk. "Christian Everett? *Chris?*"

A man a few paces away stopped and turned to face us. He was shorter than Malcolm, blond and beefy like an athlete just starting to go to seed. His eyes widened, and he took a hesitant step in Malcolm's direction, as if he needed to get close enough to see him clearly. "Mal," he said. "I don't believe this. Malcolm Campbell!"

I trailed behind as Malcolm strode toward the stranger and the two men embraced, pounding each other heartily on the back. "This is amazing," Malcolm said. "It's been almost twenty years—"

"Nineteen and a half," Christian Everett said, grinning. "I thought you joined the Navy."

"I did, and then I left to run the family business." Malcolm sounded like he'd been hit by a steel girder and knocked for a loop. "You dropped out of school to travel the world."

"Yeah, and—well, this is my wife. Ashwathy, meet my friend Malcolm." Christian held out a hand to a beautiful dark-skinned woman who smiled at Malcolm and then at me. "We met in Mumbai."

"Oh." Malcolm turned as if he'd lost me temporarily, which would have annoyed me if he hadn't looked so thrilled. "My wife, Helena. Helena, this is Christian Everett. We played high school football together, and Chris went on to play for the Ducks before —" He ran a hand through his hair. "I can't believe this. I didn't think I'd ever see you again. Are you living in Portland now?"

"Just visiting my parents. Then it's back to Bengaluru where we live now. What are the odds of both of us leaving the theater at the same time, on the same night?"

Malcolm's head jerked around so he stared at me. "What are the odds," he whispered. Then he took me in his arms and kissed me. "Best Christmas present ever," he said in my ear. To Christian, "Do you have some time? I'd love to get drinks and hear what you've been up to, if you can spare a minute."

"I was just thinking the same thing," Christian said.

wo hours later, Malcolm and I were headed back to my parents' house. "They were surprisingly accommodating of our extended absence," I said.

"Yes, I suppose they were," Malcolm said. "Thank you for your patience. It was wonderful seeing Chris again."

"I didn't mind. He and Ashwathy were a lot of fun. Too bad they live in India and we can't see them more often." I ran my fingers along the rubber seal where the door met the window. It was almost as chilly as the glass.

"Even so, I know it wasn't what you planned for your evening." Malcolm glanced at me. "Are you ever going to ask?"

"Ask what?"

"About your present. From me."

I blushed. "It's not important."

"Helena, you can't seriously believe I'd forget to buy you a gift. I don't know how you managed to go all day without saying anything."

"I figured you would tell me when you were ready," I lied.

Malcolm gripped my left hand briefly so my wedding band pressed into my finger. "The truth is," he said, "you weren't the only one who had some help. I asked the children to use their oracular gifts to pick the perfect present for you."

I gasped. "And they didn't say anything!"

"Yes. Amazing, isn't it? I'm not sure Jenny really understands the concept of secrets yet, but none of them said a word." Malcolm reached inside his coat and handed me a long white envelope. "I hope it's as meaningful as I believe."

The envelope wasn't sealed, and inside was a single sheet of paper folded three times. I removed it and clicked on the light above my seat to read it. There were just a few lines, written in Malcolm's elegant handwriting:

You chose generosity over selfishness,
Kindness over spite,
And charity over greed.
You earned peace, satisfaction, and joy.
No one will ever be able to take the memory of this season from you.

My eyes narrowed. "But I—" I began, and everything I'd done with the help of the oracle came rushing back, paired with the reactions of everyone who'd received gifts and how wonderful I'd felt. "Oh. I suppose...Malcolm, I was so tired and angry at the beginning of the month, but teaching the children how to give, and finding that spirit in my heart—I feel like what the oracle gave me was myself again. Thank you."

"I know it's not a typical present."

"It's lovely. Besides, what else do I not have that you could give me? I don't wear a lot of jewelry, and—Malcolm, why are we home?" Malcolm had just pulled into, not my parents' driveway, but our own.

Malcolm smiled, a mischievous expression. "I'm afraid I don't have as much faith in the oracle as you do," he said, and removed another long white envelope from inside his coat. This one was also unsealed, and it was a lot fatter.

I took out the wodge of papers and unfolded it. My mouth fell open. "Malcolm," I said, "are we going to Hawaii?"

"I can't believe you didn't see me sneak the kids' suitcases into the back of the land yacht," Malcolm said, "and then into your parents' house. Didn't you think it was odd that your mother didn't resist at all when you said we'd be back late? Or that they had the port-a-crib set up in your parents' room?"

I gaped again. "I didn't even notice."

Malcolm drove into the garage and turned off the car. "We fly out tomorrow morning for six days on Kauai. Unless you don't like this present and want to take it back."

"Don't you dare, Malcolm Campbell." I flung my arms around his neck and hugged him tightly. "I would have been satisfied with the other, you know."

"Well, I wouldn't. It feels like we haven't seen each other in months, and I intend to change that." Malcolm kissed me lightly on the lips. "Now, let's go watch that movie, and sleep peacefully, and—"

I kissed him passionately, stopping his words. "Forget the movie," I said. "I have something better in mind."

Malcolm arched one dark eyebrow. "You do? Is there something better than a classic movie on Christmas?"

"It really *has* been too long, love," I said, and pulled him close for another kiss.

About the Author

Melissa McShane is the author of many other fantasy novels, including the novels of Tremontane, the first of which is *Servant of the Crown; Burning Bright,* first in The Extraordinaries series; and *The Book of Secrets,* first book in The Last Oracle series.

She lives in the shelter of the mountains out West with her family, including two very needy cats. She wrote reviews and critical essays for many years before turning to fiction, which is much more fun than anyone ought to be allowed to have. You can visit her at her website **www.melissamcshanewrites.com** for more information on other books and upcoming releases.

For news on upcoming releases, bonus material, and other fun stuff, sign up for Melissa's newsletter **here**.

Also by Melissa McShane

THE EXTRAORDINARIES

Burning Bright

Wondering Sight

Abounding Might

Whispering Twilight

Liberating Fight

Beguiling Birthright

Soaring Flight

Discerning Insight

THE LIVING ORACLE

Hidden Realm (forthcoming)

THE BOOKS OF THE DARK GODDESS

Silver and Shadow (forthcoming)

THE LAST ORACLE

The Book of Secrets

The Book of Peril

The Book of Mayhem

The Book of Lies

The Book of Betrayal

The Book of Havoc

www.ingramcontent.com/pod-product-compliance
Lightning Source LLC
Chambersburg PA
CBHW070820180626
46818CB00001B/342